DESERT FEUD

Center Point
Large Print

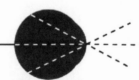

**This Large Print Book carries the
Seal of Approval of N.A.V.H.**

DESERT FEUD

William MacLeod Raine

CENTER POINT LARGE PRINT
THORNDIKE, MAINE

This Center Point Large Print edition
is published in the year 2013 by arrangement with
Golden West Literary Agency.

This title was previously published as
The Desert's Price.

The text of this Large Print edition is unabridged.
In other aspects, this book may vary
from the original edition.
Printed in the United States of America
on permanent paper.
Set in 16-point Times New Roman type.

ISBN: 978-1-61173-639-7

Library of Congress Cataloging-in-Publication Data

Raine, William MacLeod, 1871–1954.
[Desert's price]
  Desert feud / William MacLeod Raine. — Center Point Large Print
edition.
  pages cm
  "This title was previously published as The Desert's Price."
  ISBN 978-1-61173-639-7 (library binding : alk. paper)
  1. Large type books. I. Title.
PS3535.A385D47 2013
813'.52—dc23
                                                    2012038093

TO
EUGENE MANLOVE RHODES
Generous friend, indignant foe,
champion of lost causes

A son of the frontier whose stories
bring back to us the smoke of
vanished camp fires

DESERT FEUD

CHAPTER I

The Jornado de la Muerte

FROM THE bench where Wilson McCann had drawn up his horse he looked across the shimmering desert. Ribbons of heat, reflected from the burning sand, danced in an opalescent atmosphere. The plain was a mirage of shifting colour undulating like the Sargasso Sea in summer.

Beyond the level waste were sun-drenched lomas in the draws of which patches of shadow rested, welcome to the spirit in a landscape so flooded with light. Up one of these arroyos he would ride to the Frio River country where his father Peter McCann was lord of the Middle justice, the High, and the Low. Against the horizon were the sharp-notched peaks of the Sierra Mal País, harsh and dry in the unsparing light of this rarefied air.

The young man regarding the panorama sat at loose ease in the saddle. He had shifted his seat so that one foot was lifted from the stirrup and the other supported part of his weight. The dark brown face was hard, with lean jaw set tight. Nothing of the thoughts behind were mirrored in the inscrutable gray eyes.

Unmoving, he sat for many minutes. The desert

held for him fascination. All his years he had lived on the edge of it and he still found there an unsolvable riddle. It was the dominating influence not only of his own life but of that of all living near. At times he hated everything it stood for— drought, starvation, and bleaching bones, fierce struggle, temporary victory, certain and final defeat. None the less it was a magnet to his thoughts. What was the mystery of its enticement? How could he find the key to its hidden meaning? He wanted to read what was written in a language beyond his ken.

Jornada de la Muerte had come down from early days as the name of the desert. Those who lived on its border rarely used the Spanish designation for it. To call this sand stretch the Journey of Death would have been a concession to sentiment and to dread that few cared to make. Painted Desert was the word these grim taciturn men preferred.

But the Spanish name was well chosen. For everything within reach of its dry winds fought for existence. Vegetation was tough, saw-toothed, stinging. Each moving creature had developed highly its means of attack and defence, its barbs and poisons and chameleon-like deceptions.

The desert set the conditions for men too, young McCann thought bitterly. To survive he must have in him something of the tough skin of the cholla, of the poison of the sidewinder, of the pouncing lust to kill of the wild cat. He must endure heat and thirst and hunger or he must perish. He must conquer nature and his fellow man or succumb.

A lean coyote slipped through the mesquite. His eyes followed the animal's slinking purposeful stealth. It seemed to him the perfect desert type. Unless man could meet the test as that gaunt wolf did he would have to go under or back to an easier civilization.

Through the stillness of the drowsy land a shot rang out sharply. McCann listened, intent and crouched. In this wilderness of desolation the explosion might mean one of many things: a man in a hill pocket, his back to a rock wall, flinging defiance at a circle of enemies; a bullet flung from ambush and a sprawled figure huddled on the dry sand; a pilgrim lost and panic-stricken; or the mere wanton exuberance of a vaquero.

A second and a third shot followed, at intervals evenly spaced. It was a distress signal, a call for help.

McCann drew his revolver and fired into the air to let the one in need know that help was on the way. Then, swiftly but without panicky haste, he turned and rode along the bench. He guided his horse through the chaparral with the skill acquired by long practice, avoiding the catclaw and the prickly pear adroitly.

Presently another shot echoed down the ravine up which he was moving. This was meant to direct him, McCann guessed, and he fired once more for reassurance to the one in distress.

"Go to it, Jim-Dandy," he urged, and put his horse at the steep incline leading up from the arroyo.

The cowpony climbed like a cat, starting small avalanches of rubble each time a hoof dug into the loose ground. The muscles of Jim-Dandy's shoulders stood out like ropes as the animal plunged up the bank.

A gentle slope led from the edge of the arroyo to the base of a hogback which rose knobbily like emaciated vertebrae of Mother Earth's spine. The quick eye of the rider searched for and found a way up. With a rush the horse went at the ascent, sure-footed as a mountain goat. It clambered up the last twenty feet of rock-rim on the run.

From the summit McCann looked down on a small grassy park. This was old Jim Yerby's place. In what seemed to this young fellow pre-historic days he had settled here because of a spring that not even in the most arid years dried entirely. On the opposite slope of the valley a cluster of live oaks had taken root and become great trees. Among these nestled a low adobe cabin.

In front of the hut a woman was standing. She had in her hands a rifle.

The side of the hogback fell precipitously to the edge of the valley. Jim-Dandy took the decline by zigzag diagonals, slithering down on all four feet and on his haunches.

On safer ground, the rider looked across the little park and discovered that the woman was young, almost a girl, slender and graceful of figure. As he came closer the impression of youth and dark good looks became more definite. He wondered who she could be.

"Jim Yerby's hurt," she said, waiting for no introductions. "He's broken his leg. Horse fell on him."

While she elaborated the facts the young man's train of thought still clung to her. What was she doing here? Where had she come from? How did it happen he did not know her, since residents were few in this end of the county and he was acquainted with them all?

McCann followed her into the cabin. It was a one-room shack, rectangular, with two small four-pane windows. A man lay on a home-made bed in one corner of the room. He was a little wrinkled fellow in blue overalls, gray-haired, with small quick beady eyes. The blue smoke of a cigarette curled up from his fingers.

" 'S matter, Jim?" the newcomer asked.

"Done bust my laig," the oldtimer answered nonchalantly. "My damned broomtail fell on me. Got scared at a diamond back."

"When?"

"Yest'day evenin'. About two, I reckon. In Dry

Cañon. I seen a bunch of wild hill cattle an' was trailin' 'em when the bronc piled me."

"Couldn't get on yore hoss?"

"It lit out for home. I'd kinda liked to 'a' gone too, but I didn't get to go. No, sir. I laid right there on them rocks three years till Miss Julia come along an' seen me."

"It must have been awf'ly hot," the girl said gently.

"Tur'ble hot, an' me dry as a cork laig. I sure got good an' gaunted. It et into my patience consid'rable, but I hadn't no engagements that wouldn't keep. That country up there is ce'tainly filled with absentees. My prospects looked bilious when Miss Julia drapped round this mo'ning an' said 'Howdy?' to me. I disremember ever spendin' a night an' a day so dawggoned long. Hotter 'n hell with the lid on up on that ledge after Mr. Sun got to goin' good. Looked like it was gonna be fried gent for supper."

"No water bag, Jim? Wasn't that kinda careless?" McCann asked.

"All of that, Wils. An' that ain't but half of it. I'd run outa the makin's. Might as well have been a '*No se permite fumar*' sign painted on one of them rocks."

He was a garrulous old fellow and the reaction of relief from the long hours of helpless waiting —hours during which he had not known whether life or death was in store for him—loosened his tongue and lifted him to a mood akin to gayety. He had broken his leg of course, but he had not come to the end of the passage. Yerby was inclined to be jubilant about his escape. There would be plenty of time in the weeks when he was tied to a bed to "cuss" about the leg.

CHAPTER II

"Who Is She?"

WILSON MCCANN was no spendthrift of words or of time when action was the order of the day. He stepped outside the cabin, took some water from the olla, and washed his hands.

This done, he examined the broken leg and made preparations to set it temporarily until a doctor could be brought. Life in the saddle carries with it obligations that make every rider a potential surgeon. McCann found some boards from the top of an old box and whittled them down for splints while the girl was rummaging in Yerby's war bag for a clean cotton shirt. This she tore into strips to serve as bandages.

"Ready, Jim?" the young man asked.

"Sure, Wils. Right damned now."

Yerby endured without a groan a few minutes of intense pain. The perspiration stood out on his forehead in tiny glistening beads, but no sound came from between his clenched teeth. He had the primal virtue of the frontier—courage to endure quietly torture that would have set many a city man screaming. This is the common heritage of all living creatures that dwell in the barren lands. The rough hard life toughens and gives stamina.

When the amateur surgeon had finished Yerby

relaxed with a sigh. "I reckon the lid woulda come off'n my private can of cuss words if you hadn't been here," he told the girl, grinning cheerfully.

She had suffered with him during the ordeal, but the hands that had helped McCann had not trembled. "I know it hurt a lot," she replied. "Now I'm going to wash your face with cold water. You'll feel better then."

As soon as she had gone out of the cabin to get water from the olla the younger man fired a question at Yerby. "Who is she?"

Into the black beady eyes of the oldtimer a gleam of humour flickered. "Boy, ride yore own range. Ain't this young lady done saved me when I had a through ticket for Kingdom Come? You go read yore story books an' see how it always comes out after that."

"You durned old alkali, you knocked the bark off the first live oaks ever grew in this country. Methusaleh would be a good name for you. Come clean. Who is she?"

"Nothin' to that. Nothin' to it a-tall," Yerby sputtered. "I'm a well-preserved middle-aged gent, as them matrimonial papers say. Sensible young ladies like her don't aim for to rob the cradle to get a husband. You go 'way off an' grow up."

"Well, who is she?"

The oldtimer slowly blew smoke rings toward the ceiling. "My, this li'l boy's a regular parrot.

17

Don't know but one sentence, looks like. Course I don't blame him none. She's ce'tainly a mighty easy young lady to look at. But no use him lookin'. He's clear outa the runnin' before he ever starts."

"Why am I? She isn't married?"

"Not fur's I know."

"Or going to be?"

Yerby looked at him reproachfully. "Sure, she's going to be. Ever know one like her that wasn't when she got good an' ready? All the footloose men this end of the county are going to find business up her way sure as you're an inch high."

"You haven't told me yet who she is."

The old man looked at him and grinned with friendly malice. "She's Miss Julia Stark, daughter of old Matt Stark, who's such a close friend of you and yourn."

Over the eyes of young McCann a curious film of blankness passed. His face set to harsher lines. There was a slight narrowing of the lids. Of course. He might have known it. Who else could she be except the daughter of the arch enemy of his house, that daughter who had been away to school in Los Angeles half a dozen years? During that time he had not seen her. The last glimpse of her had been a characteristic one. Astride a bareback horse she had flashed past him, a stringy thirteen-year-old girl, all long legs and flying black hair and big dark eyes. It was hard to believe that wild little hoyden had grown up into a beauty. He remembered her a pert and saucy minx, brought up wholly among men except for an old Mexican cook. Once, in a gust of temper, he had heard her swear like a sergeant. She had been used to having her own way, and when she did not get it there was a breeze in her neighbourhood. On that particular occasion he had been the disturbing cause of her anger. Even then there had been war between the McCanns and the Starks, and it had pleased him to score one against the enemy.

His instinct now was not to let her know just yet who he was. He did not search for the reason of it. The feeling was enough. It was clear she did not recognize him. Five years had transformed him from a gangling boy to a man. No wonder she did not know him.

"Unless you want a rookus in the house better not tell her who I am, Jim," young McCann suggested. "She's a sure enough pepper box when she gets to going good."

Yerby chuckled. He too had his memories of her. "Tha's right, Wils. I dunno as there's any use startin' anything. She'll find out soon enough anyhow."

The girl returned with a basin of water, a towel, and a piece of torn rag for a wash cloth.

The oldtimer protested. "Now looky here, ma'am, I'm a heap obliged to you, but I can wash my own face an' not trouble you."

"No, you lie there and rest. I want to get your fever down."

"It won't gimme a fever to wash my face, will it?" He was embarrassed at this superfluous attention, especially in the presence of another man. "I been doing it a right smart time without a valley."

"Off an' on—for a hundred an' how many years, Jim?" murmured the young man.

"Hmp! I'm fifty-seven, if you want to know. An' I never was sick a day in my life. You young sprouts think—" Jim became sputteringly inarticulate.

"I like mature men myself," Miss Stark announced and sat down on the edge of the bed prepared for business.

Before Yerby could muster effective opposition a soapy rag was travelling over his face. It filled his mouth when he opened that orifice to reject this kindness.

"Wash him good behind the ears, ma'am," advised McCann solicitously.

"You go to—Yuma!" retorted the indignant homesteader.

His nurse took charge imperiously. "Better go out and take the saddle off Mr. Yerby's horse. I put it in the corral."

McCann went. The horse was a square-built short-backed bay with a barrel body. Out of the corner of an eye it watched the man in shiny leather chaps who was approaching. Nothing can look so innocent as a cowpony before or after a spree of misbehaviour. This one drooped languidly on three feet and the edge of a fourth upturned hoof.

"You pink-eyed cayuse, do you know what you've done? Broke yore master's leg! If I was sure you knew what it was for I'd whale you good. Here, stand still, can't you? Whoa, there! I'm only takin' off the saddle."

The bay jerked up its head, tried to pull away, and otherwise manifested evidences of wholly unnecessary fear. When saddle and bridle were at last off it flung up its heels and went flying round the corral.

Meanwhile Miss Julia Stark was asking her host a question.

"Who is he?"

"Fellow from over the Frio way. I get them young riders all mixed up," he answered evasively.

"One of McCann's' riders?" she asked quickly.

"Well now, he might be at that. *Quien sabe*?"

"I don't remember him."

"They're always driftin' in an' out. Mostly their homes are under their hats."

"Yes," she agreed, not wholly satisfied with this explanation. She had an impression that she had seen him before and ought to remember who he was.

McCann appeared in the doorway. "Expect I'd

better go for Doc Sanders now," he said to the girl. "Unless you'd rather ride home and have one of yore boys go for him. Maybe that would be better."

"No, I'll stay. But I wish you'd stop at the Circle Cross and tell my father I won't be home till late. He'll get to worrying. Tell him not to send for me. I'll come back with the doctor."

On the brown face of the young man was a faint sardonic grin. In not letting her know who he was he had built a trap for himself. He reflected that he would be as welcome at the Circle Cross as a June hail storm in a grain-raising country. But he had to go through now or drag his tail.

"I'll stop on my way," he promised.

CHAPTER III

"Meet Mr. Wilson McCann"

THE sun's rays streamed down the arroyo through which McCann and Doctor Sanders rode. By the time they came to a sight of the desert long shadows were stretching across from the lomas. The porphyry sierras were less starkly bare. Soon now the ball of fire behind the riders would be disappearing in a hill crotch of the horizon.

McCann drew up. "I reckon here's where we part, Doc. See you later."

Doctor Sanders, a small plump man in a land of lank giants, gave him the valedictory of the plains. "So long."

The McCann country was well to the south, that of the Starks straight through the hill gash ahead of the horsemen. The doctor deflected, to follow a trail leading sharply to the right. His companion pushed into a small gorge in front of him.

The Flying V Y and the Circle Cross ranches were twenty miles apart, but distance could not obliterate the hatred of the owners. They had been close friends once, Peter McCann and Matthew Stark. In their youth they had side by side chased Texas brush-splitters over the salt grass bumps. Together they had followed the westward tide of migration to Arizona. In their hours off duty they had frolicked as side partners at the round-up camps and at the small tendejons of the border towns. On the Chisholm trail they had night-herded the sleeping or the browsing cattle, hearing each other's voices as they crooned lullabies to the restless beasts. Their comradeship had been a byword in the country where they were known.

Into their lives a girl had come, Jessie Farwell, daughter of the cattleman for whom they both worked. This in itself might not have driven them apart, though they were heady youngsters. But the campfire raillery of companions and the whisper of a ubiquitous friend had sown seeds of distrust. They quarrelled.

Stark won Jessie for his bride. The years passed, and each left both men more prosperous, more powerful in the community. Their enmity was known of all men even before their political ambitions and their financial interests collided. On opposing tickets they ran for sheriff and McCann was elected. Their wandering herds over-lapped. The punchers of each took up his employer's grievance. They clashed over water holes, over calves wrongly branded by mistake. Charges of rustling were bandied back and forth, at first out of animosity rather than any serious belief in their truth. Trouble followed. There were gunplays and long-distance fusillades meant to intimidate rather than to kill.

Then, dramatically, the curtain rolled up for a

scene of grim tragedy. A Circle Cross rider was found lying face down at the bottom of a cut bank. He had perhaps been dry-gulched, shot from ambush, but this was not sure. Who did it nobody knew, but at the Stark ranch suspicion flew straight to the Flying V Y. This had been less than two weeks before the afternoon when Wilson McCann rode through Tincup Pass to carry word to Matthew Stark that his daughter would not be home till late.

When young McCann reached the summit of the pass the gulch pockets of the mountains were glowing opaline and the peaks above were fire-tipped crags. Even as he rode out of Tincup the fires began to die down. The rainbow-hued sea that flooded the sky became less vivid till the deeper shades predominated, merged into a purple haze, finally lost distinction in dull garnet tones. Soon darkness would fall over the land, wiping out harsh and gaunt detail. The stars would come out, innumerable and close, and moonlight would magically transform plain and mesa.

In the last of the sunlight the windmill and tank of the Circle Cross flashed heliograph signals at the rider. He was descending into a valley. Before him were checkerboards of irrigated grain and pasture meadow centering around the houses of the ranch. Back of these was a wide stretch of unfenced open range running up into the hills.

Cattle were browsing in the valley. Leisurely a

rider was moving across the plain toward them. All was peaceful as old age.

Directly in front of McCann's horse a spurt of sand flew. The crack of a rifle shot echoed back from the walls of the pass.

Instantly McCann's brain registered impressions and moved him to coordinated action. Someone had fired at him. The V-shaped sand spurt told him the attacker was almost dead ahead. With only a revolver against a rifle Wilson McCann was as helpless at this range as a child with a popgun. He swung Jim-Dandy as on a peg and spurred for the shelter of a large boulder beside the trail. Before he reached cover a second explosion boomed.

McCann dismounted and stood beside his horse. The second shot made it plain that the first could have been no chance bullet. Coming out of the pass, his figure had been clearly silhouetted against the skyline. He had been recognized beyond question.

For long minutes he waited, every nerve keyed to tension, eyes and ears alert for any sign of movement in the mesquite. It was a trying business, this crouching inaction, a test of the steely quality of his nerves. The ambusher might be circling round to get at him from the rear. There might be two of them. The only course open to him was to let developments occur.

Out of the painful silence came sounds the trapped man knew at once—the thud of galloping hoofs, of a horse crashing through the brush. He stood a moment, stomach muscles tight, to make sure the man screened in the chaparral was not charging him; then flung himself, foot not touching the stirrup, into the saddle and lifted Jim-Dandy in a stride to swift pursuit.

In the gathering dusk they raced toward the ranch house, Jim-Dandy gaining with every reach of the hoofs. The rider in front looked back, not once but half a dozen times. McCann could see him urging his horse and knew that he was spurring in a panic of fear. Down the valley slope they flew, the pursuing rider hard on the heels of the other's horse.

The ambusher had forgotten that he could use his rifle. He was in terror of the swift Nemesis riding him down. He shouted for help as his horse plunged into the open space in front of the big adobe house. Even as he threw himself from the saddle, men appeared out of the gloom to join him—one, two, three of them.

The third came out of the open hallway of the house to the porch. He was an elderly man, big and rangy, bowlegged and still strong, with hard eyes in a harsh leathery face. This was Matthew Stark.

"What's the rumpus?" he asked in a heavy voice. Then, with a flirt of a brown hand toward the farther rider. "Who is this fellow?"

The pursued man was on the porch, near the

entrance to the "gallery." The rifle was clutched tightly in both hands. He was breathing heavily.

The puncher from the Flying V Y moved forward from behind Jim-Dandy. "Meet Mr. Wilson McCann," he said hardily, and there was a jeer in his voice.

All those present knew him, but in the darkness, screened by his horse, they had not recognized him. His announcement made a little ominous stir. Competent hands moved quietly to be ready for an emergency.

The owner of the Circle Cross looked at him steadily without speaking. The others waited for him to give them their cue.

"What are you doing here?" Stark demanded at last abruptly.

"Why, I came to bring a message—two of 'em in fact, Mr. Stark." The answer was low, unruffled, and carried a suggestion of mocking insolence.

Stark glared down into a face bold and reckless, the cool eyes of which met his unwinkingly.

"Not interested," the old man retorted brusquely.

"Still, I'll deliver 'em now I'm here. First is that yore no-count jayhawkin' son bushwhacked me up there in the pass an' skedaddled to save his hide after he'd sent a coupla blue whistlers at me."

The cattleman turned to his son. "How about that, Jas?"

There were weakness and vice in the face of

young Jasper Stark, slackness in the jaw. He answered sulkily: "I didn't aim to kill him—shot to warn him to turn back."

"That was why you fired at me again while I was makin' for cover, was it?" McCann asked with a little skeptical laugh of scorn.

"Tha's a lie. The second shot was when you plugged at me."

The rider from the Flying V Y unbuckled his belt and handed it to Matthew Stark. "Look at my gun an' see who's a liar. All the chambers are loaded."

The old man broke the revolver, examined it, and returned it to its owner. "Don't prove a thing. Like as not you reloaded it."

"While my hoss was hittin' the high spots tryin' to catch that lobo wolf," the son of Peter McCann suggested with obvious sarcasm.

Stark carried the war into the enemy's country. "You got a nerve to talk about bushwhackin' after what you did to pore Tom McArdle," he burst out angrily.

The young man's answer was instant. "Tom McArdle would be alive to-day if he hadn't died till a Flying V Y rider killed him."

"Don't tell that to me. I know you an' all yore lying breed," Stark flung out bitterly.

"I'm tellin' it to *you,* Matt Stark," the man at the foot of the porch steps steadily replied.

"An' I'm tellin' *you* that I'd as soon put faith in

a yellow coyote as in any McCann ever born. An' I'm sendin' word to Pete McCann that there's a day comin' when I'll settle with interest a-plenty for what he did to McArdle. Now fork that fuzzy an' light out. I don't want you here."

"What about that gunplay up in the pass?"

"It goes as it stands. The boy's story suits me."

"Different here, an' I'm liable to tell him so when we meet again," McCann said boldly.

The old man's eyes blazed. "Like to tell him now maybe?"

The Flying V Y rider looked from Stark to the men waiting tensely for the word or the lift of a hand that would serve as an order to begin hostilities. His lip curled in an ironic smile. "Not now, gentlemen."

"Then hit the dust *pronto*."

"Don't get on the prod, Mr. Stark. I haven't onloaded that second message yet. It's from yore daughter."

"From Jule?"

Wilson could see that the old cattleman had been struck to instant apprehension.

"She sent word by me to tell you that she'd be home late. I saw her up at old Jim Yerby's. He's broke his leg. The doc's on the way there now. You're not to send for her, Miss Stark says; she'll come with Doc Sanders when he leaves Yerby's place."

"Does Yerby need any help?"

"I'll look out for him. I sent word to the Flying V Y to have a pack hoss with my plunder an' some grub sent up. You don't need to worry about Yerby none."

McCann swung without any haste to the saddle, glanced coolly from one to another of the watchful silent men, and headed Jim-Dandy toward Tincup Pass. He jogged away into the gathering darkness, not turning once to make sure that swift impulse would not send a bullet flying after him.

To the men of the Circle Cross, still watching him as he disappeared, there came back the taunting rhythm of a cowboy song:

"Roll yore tail, and roll her high,
We'll all be angels by an' by."

CHAPTER IV

At the Yerby Cabin

HIS message delivered at the Circle Cross, McCann rode through Tincup Pass and dropped down into the desert. He took a short cut across one corner of it. Jim-Dandy laboured across a waste of white silt so finely powdered that the hoofs left no track. From this the horse climbed to a mesa lit by far stars so deceptively that the freakish shapes of erosion took on weird effects of hobgoblin land.

He came upon a lonely sheep ranch. It was the Gifford place. The corrals, the shallow feed troughs, the long flat sheds emerged from the darkness like ghosts of reality. The rider left this behind and wound into the hills.

Doctor Sanders was smoking a pipe in front of Yerby's cabin when McCann dismounted. He was a picture of indolent placid content. The doctor was wont to say that he could do nothing, that is could refrain from all activity, better than any man in Arizona.

"How's Jim?" the horseman asked.

"He's taking a little nourishment Miss Julia fixed up for him. Says he wishes now he'd broke both legs so as to keep her here longer. He acts plumb satisfied. Claims he always wanted to read a book. Figures every fellow ought to read one some time or other. He aims to read his now. Got any books at the ranch, Wils?"

"Some."

"Well, you round up a good easy one for Jim— all about lovely soft-eyed señoritas and husky he-men lovers. He's certainly going to read a book if it's the last thing he ever does. . . . How'd you come out at the Circle Cross? I see they didn't scalp you."

"No," McCann said dryly. "They sent a messenger to meet me."

The doctor's sparkling eyes guaranteed attention. He guessed that something interesting had occurred and he was a born gossip. Wherefore he waited silently, sure that he would soon find out what he wanted to know.

"Jas Stark shot at me an' lit out. I followed him lickety-split to the ranch. We had a few pleasant words, the old man an' me."

"Shot at you? He didn't! How come he to do that?"

"You're as good a guesser as I am, Doc. I kinda gathered that maybe he doesn't like me—him or old Matt either."

"They don't like you a lick of the road, you or any of your kin. But—shooting! Who started it?"

In a few crisp sentences McCann told the story. The doctor listened, absorbed. Was this the beginning of the end? Would the smouldering feud break into open warfare, bitter and tragic? If he knew the McCanns—and he thought he did—they were not the kind to take this challenge tamely. They came of fighting Irish stock, upon which had been grafted four generations of American frontier life. There were likely to be reprisals.

Even now both camps were waiting tensely for the signal to begin hostilities openly. The death of Tom McArdle had brought them to the point of war. But the doubt as to who had killed him had made for delay. Matthew Stark had hesitated to give the word. He did not want to see any of his lusty young riders buried in the small graveyard on the hillside. While he brooded, willing to let events shape themselves, Jasper had fired a wanton shot that might be the first of hundreds.

The doctor rose and with a sigh of resignation knocked the ashes out of his pipe. He saw busy days and nights ahead of him. Once before he had lived in a feud district and knew what it was to have riders come racing for him on horses lathered with sweat. Sanders preferred his pipe and his fireside and his easy chair. Well, it was in the hands of the gods, or rather of two grim hard men with too much of the desert fierceness in their blood. He was a pawn in the game they played, just as were the rollicking boys who would ride out laughing to meet death at the lift of a hand.

"No use telling you so, of course, but it's all

wrong, Wils—this putting yourselves above the law and killing so free and easy. It's sure enough bad medicine."

"Have I been killin' anybody free an' easy, Doc? Better speak to Jas Stark about that, hadn't you?"

"I'm not meaning you, Wils. But someone shot Tom McArdle."

"None of our outfit, Doc. You don't mean we had anything to do with it." The eyes of the range rider were bleak. They thrust at Sanders a warning to keep off dangerous ground.

The doctor withdrew into himself. He had already said more than anybody else could safely have done. As physician to the whole community, allied to neither faction and necessary to both, he could be bolder than most men. But he knew when to stop.

"No, Wils. Nothing like that. But you know how the Starks feel. They're holding it against you boys of the Flying V Y."

Sanders knew by the other's face that they were no longer alone. He turned, to see Julia Stark in the doorway. She stood slim and straight, her black eyes flashing.

"Who else would we hold it against, Doctor?" she asked curtly, looking straight at the younger man.

There was a thin ironic smile on the brown face of McCann. He murmured, with the soft drawl of insolence to which he sometimes reverted,

"Nobody else would have dry-gulched him, would they?"

"What d'you mean?" the girl demanded.

The man in chaps said nothing, but he continued to give her that mocking smile. It was the doctor who answered at last.

"Tom was quite a boy for the girls, Miss Julia. Folks say—some folks do—that maybe someone who was jealous or wanted revenge might have laid for him. Of course that's just talk. I don' know a thing about it myself. Chances are nobody does, except the fellow who did it."

The girl's dark eyebrows gathered in a frown. "First I've heard of it—that Tom was so fond of the girls. And if he was—if he did like them—is that any crime, any reason why someone would want to kill him?"

"I reckon you didn't know Tom very well," the doctor said judicially with intent to hold an even balance between the Stark and the McCann. "He was a top hand and sure could ride the buck. Good-looking as any fellow I know. Likable too. But a mite wild, Miss Julia, by the stories I've heard."

"I don't know anything about that. I never saw him but once." She swept defiant eyes over the rider. "But I don't believe a word about a private enemy killing him."

"You wouldn't," agreed the younger man.

The implications of his smile stirred her anger.

Stiffly she changed the subject. "Did you take my message to my father?"

"Yes, ma'am."

"What did he say?"

"I didn't wait to hear, me being in a hurry."

She did not understand the hint of sardonic mockery in his tone and manner. None the less it annoyed her. She turned and walked into the house.

Those outside heard Yerby take up again the thread of his conversation with her.

"No, ma'am, I reckon there never was a savinger human than Mrs. Dubbs. Down in that Yuma country I usta wonder could I live till night come it was so dawggoned hot, an' that woman would set around the stove cookin' up a mess of stuff so's not to lose any of the heat—an' all the fuel she could use in a hundred years right there in sight free gratis, as the old sayin' is."

"Yes," the girl assented, her mind fiercely busy with thoughts of the young man outside who could smile so hatefully that it meant more than words.

"I recolleck oncet on the calf round-up I was ridin' a blue roan for the Hashknife outfit. Them days I was some bronco peeler. Well, this broomtail I was on stepped in a prairie dawg hole an' bust me up so the boys had to leave me at the Dubbs place. I like to a-starved to death before they rescued me."

"And now, poor man, another female has you at her mercy. No wonder you feel so worried. Did Mrs. Dubbs have a temper too?"

"No, ma'am, she didn't. An' I ain't worryin' about yore temper none. I'm in luck. Y'betcha! Sittin' high, wide an' handsome. All I'm scared of is you'll go home an' never drap in to see how the old man's makin' out."

"Well, I won't." She added, by way of explanation, "I mean I won't forget to come again."

"You're whistlin', ma'am. If I know when you're comin' I'll sure be waitin' for you in full war paint. . . . Don't I hear that Flying V Y boy chinnin' with the doc?"

"Yes. Want to see him?"

"I reckon. Before he goes."

Julia made things snug for the night. She arranged the blanket so that he could pull it up in the chill of early morning. She put water on a chair beside the bed.

"Hope you'll have a good night and sleep well," she said.

"I'll be fine an' dandy," he assured.

Outside the girl spoke indifferently to the night, "Mr. Yerby wants to see you before you go."

Since Doctor Sanders had just been explaining that he intended to stay all night with his patient, McCann was justified in assuming that this impersonal remark was addressed to him. He went into the house.

38

"How they stackin,' oldtimer?" he asked.

"I'll make a hand yet. What's worryin' me is I've got to lie here like a bump on a log an' let a kid like you see Miss Julia home."

"Don't worry about that. I'll make out to entertain her somehow." He added with a grin: "Course I'm no ladies' man like you, but she'll have to put up with me, I reckon."

"She's outa luck. Well, give my love to Pa Stark when you get to the Circle Cross."

"I'm not figurin' on meeting him to-night."

"Maybe you're right at that. He's some impulsive, Pa is. Kinda quick on the shoot. Like as not he'd mistake you for a curly wolf."

"Was that what you wanted to tell me?"

Little imps of deviltry danced in the beady eyes. "No, Wils. A wink is as good as a nod to a blind hoss. Scratch gravel, boy. You know the ol' saying: Opportunity is like a baldheaded guy with chin whiskers; you can catch him comin' but not going."

McCann's answer was direct. "I'm not liable to forget that she's Matt Stark's daughter, so you needn't look so blamed knowin', Jim. I don't like her any more'n she does me."

"Sho! She's a mighty nice li'l girl, an' the best lookin' one in Arizona."

"No Stark looks good to me," the son of Peter McCann said grimly.

39

CHAPTER V

Desert Animals

THEY were taking the short cut across the white powdered desert before either of them spoke.

"What did you say your name is?" she asked, rather imperiously.

"They call me Wilson."

The girl noticed the slight pause before he had drawled the answer. It probably was not his right name, she reflected. A good many men did not use the one to which they were born. In that country it was not good form to insist on particulars as to who a man had been or from where he had come. She did not look at him, but without turning her head saw the resolute square-cut jaw and the broad muscular shoulders. There was strength in him, whatever he might have done in his checkered past.

"You ride for the McCanns."

He assented, without words.

Silence fell again between them. They had come out of the silt and were threading a way among the steel-thorned yuccas. The moon and the stars were out, touching the land as by a magic wand. All harsh detail was blurred. Ten thousand years of drought were wiped out. A soft desert breeze was sighing gently across a sleeping world.

His words, when at last they came, were a surprise. "Why isn't it always like this?" he asked, speaking almost to himself rather than to her.

"How do you mean like this?"

But she knew, she hoped she knew, what he meant before he answered. For the desert had entered into her life too. She sensed its moods and reflected them in her own. Sometimes it was a hot devouring monster blasting all living things with its fiery breath; again at sunset, when light was flooding over the sheen of the mesquite, it might be a silver dragon less destructive. In the moonlight it was kind and lovely, all ugliness and threat obliterated. The hard dry mountains, the stratified earth vertebrae, the barren sun-cracked valley, all had taken the veil and retired from stark reality to cloistered solitudes of spiritual beauty.

A crouching animal slipped quickly across the trail into the chaparral.

"Coyote?" she asked.

"Wildcat," he answered. Then, with unexpected bitterness, "That's the desert for you."

Again she understood what he meant, and again asked, "What do you mean?"

"Survival of the fit."

"Isn't that true everywhere?"

"Maybe so, but the conditions are different. Everything that lives here is born and bred in hardship, trained for attack an' defense. Take that wildcat—lean, cunning, ferocious, a machine made to stalk and kill."

"Yes," she agreed.

"Same every way you turn. No escape from it. All the plants have thick an' callous rinds. They have thorns that sting. They have to push their roots 'way into the ground to get water. If they don't toughen they die. Tha's what's ailin' us humans. We're desert-bred."

"Aren't people the same everywhere?" she asked.

"No. Here we have to fight or go under. We fight the drought and heat of nature. We fight each other for the water holes. If we don't we lose out. Consequence is we get fierce and savage like that wildcat."

"Yes," she admitted with a sigh. "We're all under the spell of it, all hard and relentless, kinda. But we don't have to be—what is it you called that wildcat?—ferocious and sly. The desert shows its teeth most of the time. It's full of sting and barb and thorn. But that's only one side of it. All the time it's trying to tell us something else too, isn't it?"

His brooding eyes rested on her. So she, too, felt it, this wild young thing so full of contrary impulses, of passionate resentments, of brave elusive dreams, of mysterious cravings for goodness and beauty. He forgot that she was of the enemy. He did not question the influence that had for a moment brought them close. Something primeval stirred in him, a joy old as the race, that walked with Adam and Eve in the garden. Without taking thought of it he knew that they rode alone in a world wonderful.

"What's it tryin' to tell us?" he asked in his low gentle voice.

"I don't know—quite. But something good—and hopeful. The lovely flowers of the yucca and the cactus—aren't they a promise to us? This morning I rode out into the desert, and the air was all rose-coloured, except where there were little lakes of lilac and pink and fire-red in the hollows of the sierras and on the peaks." She laughed at herself, soft-eyed. "Maybe that seems silly to you. But it's the way I feel. To-night, now. In all this still moonlight the desert isn't threatening us, is it?"

They were drawing up into a country of creased arroyos. On the crest of a hillock they stopped and looked back across the Painted Desert. The man was for a moment carried out of himself. Looking at this starry-eyed girl, clean and innocent and rhythmic in the freshness of her youth, it seemed possible to escape the inheritance of his dark environment. There was something in life deeper than hate and selfishness and revenge if he could only find it.

Down the wind came drumming the sound of hoofs. The two listened in silence. In the land of far spaces the ear becomes finely attuned to distinctions. Each of those sitting poised and alert on their mounts knew that several horses with riders were moving rapidly toward them. The fact had its significance in a country where one might travel a day without meeting a human being. Voices became clear, a snatch of laughter, an oath. Silhouetted against the skyline, three cowponies moved along the ridge across the arroyo.

Julia gave a little cry of greeting, lost in the clip-clop of the hoofs and the chuffing of the saddle leather. She turned to her companion, to suggest that they canter down and intersect the riders. But the words died on her lips.

The man beside her was watching the riders as they descended from the ridge and disappeared. He sat crouched, eyes narrowed to hard shining slits of light, teeth clamped like a vise. The change in him shocked her. Like the wildcat they had seen, he had become a machine designed to stalk and kill, a desert animal savage and ferocious, the deadlier for the stillness of his emotion.

"Did you—know who they were?" she asked.

The eyes that looked at her were chill. He nodded without speech.

"I reckon Dad sent them to bring me home."

She knew he would not accept that explanation since she could not believe it herself. They had come through Tincup Pass *and were headed south.* Moreover, they carried rifles. Why? What did they want with them?

"Does it need three men to bring you home—two Texas hired killers like Stone an' Gitner, as well as yore brother?"

"Killers! Who says my father's men are killers?" she flamed. "Who are you anyhow?"

"Wils McCann," he flung back at her.

He could see her recoil and stiffen. "I might have known it. You liar!" She threw the epithet like a missile in his face.

CHAPTER VI

Wils McCann Lights Out

STORMY-EYED, she drove to beat down his hard level gaze by sheer dominance of will.

He laughed, shortly, without mirth. "That all yore schoolin' did for you? I've heard you rip loose a heap more efficient than that. Language used to come outa you like hot shot off'n a shovel."

Helplessly she glared at him. "If I were a man—"

"You've got an able-bodied brother," he suggested, ironically. "Maybe you could get him to take a crack at me from the mesquite. He might have better luck next time."

"What do you mean—next time?" she demanded.

"Some other day."

"I don't know what you're talking about," the girl said scornfully.

"Ask him when you see him again. He wouldn't lie, Jasper wouldn't. He's a Stark, you know."

She swung her horse and gave it a touch of the spur. Before it had gone twenty steps the man was riding beside her again.

"Hit the trail!" she ordered hotly. "I don't need your help to get home."

"I reckon not," he drawled. "But I promised Doc, so I'll mosey along."

She pulled up, a diamond-hard glitter in her eyes. "I'm going to my brother. I'd advise you to light out."

"After I know you're safe." His voice was cool and dry, his gaze level and unwavering.

"If I tell Dave Stone and that Gitner what you called them—killers—"

"Why, then they'll prove it to you right there," he cut in with a jeering laugh. "Seeing is believing. They claim we owe 'em one for Tom McArdle, an' they'll collect now."

A tempest of impotent anger surged in her. His words bore the mark of hardy insolence. They were meant to affront and challenge her. Not since she had been in her early teens had she felt so uncontrollable an impulse to break out in crackling speech that pelted like hail. What was there in this hateful man that stirred so deeply the wild and lawless elements of her being, so long dormant?

Turning swiftly, she galloped down into the draw through the rabbit-brush. She did not look round, but she could hear McCann's horse close behind. It followed into the greasewood and palo verde that grew on the hill slope up which her pony clambered. Before she reached the top her escort was again knee to knee with her.

Julia's glance swept the landscape. The last of the three riders was disappearing into an arroyo. Obligingly McCann pointed him out. In a weak voice she called to her brother.

Her companion's smile was mocking. "Lemme get him for you." Before she could stop him there came from his throat the far-carrying yell of the cowpuncher. "Yi yi yippy yi!"

She had a shaken sense of stilled pulses, the premonition of impending disaster. But it was too late to ride away now. Already the three riders were showing darkly in silhouette against the sky line.

One of them called and McCann answered promptly. She waited with dread beside this enemy of her family while the men rode toward them.

"Who is it?" Jasper Stark demanded.

Julia called her name to him. She heard him say to his companions, "Jule an' Doc Sanders." He was riding in the lead and it was not till he had pulled up his horse that his startled oath announced recognition of McCann.

Stone and Gitner ranged themselves beside him. Their eyes fastened to McCann, but neither of them spoke.

Hurriedly Julia explained. "Doctor Sanders had to stay all night with Jim Yerby. He asked Mr. McCann to see me home."

"Since when has Wils McCann been yore friend, Jule," her brother demanded harshly.

"He's no friend of mine. I didn't know who he was till he told me just now."

"The Starks know me well enough to shoot at

me but not well enough to pass the time of day," McCann added tauntingly. "An' that's about as well as I want to know most of them."

His gaze moved to the Texans. Gitner was a big rangy fellow with the appearance and manner of a bully. He looked dangerous, but not so much so as the man on his right. There was a deadly quality about the stillness of Stone. He sat as though carved out of marble. Only the chill light-blue eyes were quick with life. McCann knew his reputation and one long steady exchange of looks told him this small brown Texan would live up to it. On the draw he would be chain lightning, and he would fling bullets with machinelike accuracy. But there was one advantage in dealing with such a man as Stone. He would not get nervous and fire because of jumpy nerves.

"You didn't shoot at him from the mesquite, Jas, did you?" his sister asked.

"Been runnin' to you about it, has he?" snarled Stark. "Well, there's nothin' to it. I shot to warn him back, an' he's been bellyachin' ever since. He's got no kick comin'."

"I knew it was something like that," the girl replied quickly.

McCann laughed, softly and derisively.

"Something amusin' you?" Gitner wanted to know, heavy lower jaw thrust forward aggressively.

The Arizonan met him eye to eye. "Any law against laughing, Mr. Gitner?"

49

"Depends how you laugh an' where."

"If I could get Mr. Gitner to show me how an' where—"

Stone interrupted, quietly, each drawling word spaced evenly. "If my name was Wils McCann I'd light out now *muy pronto*." His eyes were slits of shining menace.

Julia, alarmed, moved her horse a step or two so that she was between the Flying V Y rider and his foes. "Yes," she said, and her voice was not quite steady, "I'd go now, Mr. McCann—please."

"Tha's good advice, I reckon," he agreed. "Or I might not go at all. Yore friends seem anxious."

He lifted his sombrero in a sweeping bow, swung Jim-Dandy, and moved away at a road gait. The thing was done raffishly and flippantly, with obvious intent to irritate.

Julia was relieved when the darkness swallowed him and his horse. "We'd better go home now," she said to her brother."

Jasper was annoyed and showed it. He looked at his companions, doubtful what to do.

With a dry ironic smile Stone settled the matter. They could not go about their errand now, since the information that they were night riding had become public property.

"Why yes, Jas. Might as well go home, I reckon, like Miss Julie tells us," the little Texan said with gentle sarcasm. "We taken all the ride to-night we need for our health."

CHAPTER VII

The Giffords

ON HIS way back to the Yerby place from the Flying V Y next morning Wilson McCann passed again the sheep ranch on the mesa. A young woman was in the yard giving directions to a Mexican herder, a wrinkled smiling old fellow who shambled off as the rider pulled up his horse for a word of greeting,

The place belonged to the Gifford sisters. They had inherited it a few years before from a stiff-necked uncle who had brought sheep in regardless of opposition from the cattle interests. It had been an ill-starred venture, followed by quarrels, warnings, raids, and bloodshed. Old Andy Gifford died while the trouble was at its height and the hostility had been passed on to his nieces. But it took the form of sullen aloofness rather than active warfare. The neighbourhood did not like sheep, was disturbed at the presence of these "hoofed locusts" eating up the range, yet could not bring itself to the point of driving out three defenceless women.

When their uncle died Ann Gifford had been twenty-two, Nora past nineteen, and Ethel sixteen. Far from friends, on the edge of the desert, the life of the girls was a lonely one. The ranchmen of the district looked upon them with ill-concealed resentment. Their wives and daughters paid no friendly visits. An invisible fence separated them from the world around.

But in a man's country these three attractive girls were a magnet not to be resisted. A few cow-punchers met them and broke down the barrier. Their ponies had been seen in the corral at the sheep ranch. Rumours began to fly, as they must when presentable young women are visited only by men. At last the wagging tongue of gossip found something tangible to whisper. Ann and Nora Gifford had taken the train for Los Angeles, while the youngest of the three was attending school at Tucson. Some months later the older sister returned alone, hard-eyed, close-mouthed, with the look of tragedy written in her face. No letters from Nora ever came to the ranch, it was observed at the post office. Where was she? What had become of her?

During Ann's absence a band of sheep had been harried and driven over a cliff by night riders. Ann's lips shut tighter, the lines about them grew harder. Since her return the ponies of no cowpunchers had been seen in the corral. She and Ethel lived alone. They saw nobody except their herder, save on the rare occasions when they went to Mesa.

McCann lifted his hat. "Howdy, Miss Gifford. What's the good word?" he asked.

Ann Gifford was thin, brown, dry as a chip. Her eyes blazed a burning bitterness. Resentment at life's injustice marred her dark good looks.

"What can I do for you?" she said bluntly.

"For me? Nothing, ma'am," he replied, disconcerted. "I reckoned there might be somethin' I could do for you."

"Well, you reckoned wrong."

"When there's no men folks on a place a husky willing lad comes in handy sometimes. If you need me—"

"We don't."

"Now or any time, why—"

"Not now or any time," she snapped.

McCann was embarrassed but persistent. He had met the Gifford girls only two or three times, and then casually. But he had thought a good deal about the hard lines into which their lives had fallen.

"I'd be pleased to help any way I could. A man—"

"That's what Tony's for."

"Sure, but oncet in a while maybe a white man—"

"We'll not trouble you, thanks." Her refusal of his offer had the crack of a whiplash.

This was definite enough. McCann searched for some meaningless phrase to soften what she had said. This done, he would ride away promptly enough.

"Well, it's an open offer, ma'am. I'll be movin' on now. Jim Yerby's done broke his leg an' I'm kinda lookin' after him."

His glance picked up the figure of a young girl in the doorway, a soft round little person with dimpled cheeks in and out of which the pink could pour at the least excuse. The mouth was childishly sweet, the hair abundant and fluffy. Men instinctively grew tender and protective when they looked at shy-eyed Ethel Gifford.

Again McCann bowed, this time to the girl in the doorway. He had a strong sense of frustrated good will. If they would only let him help, he could be of use to these young women who were isolated as effectually as though under a quarantine.

Ann faced him, inflexibly hostile. She did not speak.

"Well, so long."

Jim-Dandy felt the rein on his neck and turned toward the trail. From the ridge above McCann looked down on the low buildings of the sheep ranch. Ethel was still standing where he had last seen her. She seemed to him a lonely and pathetic figure robbed of the joys of youth.

Yerby was inclined to be querulous this morning. His sleep had been broken and he had suffered more or less pain.

"Doc's been worryin' for fear you wouldn't come, boy. Seems he's got another patient— mebbe two or three. What's been keepin' you?"

"Had to fix a fence. Pedro bring my roll an' some grub last night?"

"Sure did. Well, son, now you're here make yorese'f to home."

Wilson hung his saddle by one stirrup to a peg in the outside wall and turned Jim-Dandy into the corral. He saddled Doctor Sanders's horse and brought it to the door.

Yerby, as usual, was reminiscing. ". . . I done so, then druv to Tascosa hittin' the high spots. It was a sure hellpoppin' team of colts, an' when they got too frisky I sawed 'em off into the polecat brush an' the smartweeds. Them was the days, Doc, when the Panhandle was a he-country in pants. I was with a buffalo-huntin' outfit, an' we ce'tainly taken the hides off'n 'em. One hammered-down li'l runt I knew skinned 'most a thousand that summer."

"Yore hoss is served, Doc," McCann called in. "Course I don't aim to drag you away from any hammered-down li'l runt you may have for a patient. Take yore time. He can't any more'n talk an arm off you."

The oldtimer snorted. "Ever see the beat of them kids, Doc? They don't know sic' 'em, an' they don't want to learn from them that does know. They're like that peg pony of mine when I go for to saddle him—plumb full of wind."

Doctor Sanders laughed. He knew Yerby enjoyed rough repartee. That was why McCann "rode him," to use the phrase of the country. "You act like a pair of kids, if you ask me. Don't forget to give Jim one of these powders every four hours, Wils." He added his "So long" and bustled out to the horse.

Before he left, McCann offered a suggestion. He did not quite know the spring of the impulse that impelled it. "Wisht you wouldn't say anything about that gunplay at Tincup Pass, Doc. No use startin' trouble before it has to come."

Sanders assented.

McCann's eyes followed him as he dipped into the arroyo that would bring him to the mesa upon which was the sheep ranch. The young man smiled ruefully. He was thinking about the Gifford sisters.

It seemed to him that their lives were involved in tragedy. The desert had taken toll of their happiness. Why should they be pariahs, outcasts from the society of those living near? What had they done to deserve it? That they ran sheep was an unfortunate incident and had nothing to do with what they were. Young McCann, with the hot temper of his age, rebelled at such injustice. No wonder Ann had become embittered at the destiny that pressed upon them. Nora had vanished, the bloom brushed from her life, if the dark rumours he heard were true. But his thoughts dwelt on Ethel, so unfit to cope with the harshness of this dry and cruel land. The soft warmth and shy charm, the whole unarmoured tenderness of her youth, were heavy handicaps for one within reach of the Jornada de la Muerte. It would inexorably wither the joy and gayety of her girlhood.

CHAPTER VIII

Peter McCann Tacks Up a Notice

ON THE porch in front of Basford's Emporium, which was also the post office, Mesa and the adjoining country met to discuss the news and formulate views. It was the official clubhouse of the frontier town, as Martin's Gilt Edge Saloon and The Legal Tender were the informal ones.

To-day conversation was engrossing but guarded. For the feud between the Starks and the McCanns had broken out again. During the night a cabin far from the main ranch house of the Flying V Y, one used by line riders in the foothills of the Sierra Mal País, had been raided and burned by armed horsemen. Two punchers had been sleeping there, and in trying to escape through the window one had been wounded. He had slipped away into the chaparral and hidden. After daybreak his companion had brought help from the Flying V Y and carried him to the ranch.

Mesa buzzed with excitement. Peter McCann, two of his sons, and his foreman Wes Tapscott were in town. They had come in force, so the story ran, to find out what the sheriff intended to do about it.

Curt Quinn, to two safe friends confidentially summed up public opinion. "Old man McCann ain't expectin' Hank to do anything. I don't reckon Hank got elected sheriff to pick a row with the Starks. No, sir. Hank will go out an' look the ground over an' scratch his haid. He won't look oncet at the Circle Cross ranch, an' I don't know 's I blame him. Nor old Pete won't blame him either. He come to the law to make the proper bluff, but he'd be plumb disappointed if it interfered in his own little private feud. The McCanns will play out the hand their own selves."

The town looked with respect and awe upon the four lean brown men who dismounted at the sheriff's office. All of them carried rifles as well as side arms. It was known they would use these if they held it to be expedient. Peter himself was of strong build and slightly bowlegged. Hard-eyed and imperious, a fighter from his youth, he asked no odds of any man. If he was a leader it was not by chance, but by reason of the dominant force in him. Hawk-nosed and shaggy-browed, the chief of the McCanns bore in his face the look of heady and ungovernable temper. One glance at the three was enough to show from whom his lithe and keen-eyed sons had inherited.

"Chips of the old block, Wils an' Lyn are— about as tough propositions to bump into as a fellow's liable to meet," Simp Shell commented as he watched the four riders leave the sheriff's office. Tilted back against the wall of the store, in the spot which would be reached last by the sun,

Simp was lazily rolling himself a cigarette. He was a middle-aged man with no business except everybody's business. Of late years, from sheer indolence, he was running to an overflow of flesh. He bulged prodigiously. "Except the old man. He's got a leetle the edge of the boys yet. When he gets on the hook I ce'tainly want to be lookin' for a tree to climb."

"How about exceptin' Matt Stark an' them Texans, Stone an' Gitner?" Basford murmured significantly. His gaze, too, was fixed on the horsemen moving toward the post office.

"They're no pilgrims," admitted Simp.

"Well, I don't claim to be no prophet, but someone's going to hell on a shutter one o' these days," spoke up a young man standing in the doorway.

Quinn looked at him quietly, judicially. The last speaker was Basford's clerk. He had come from St. Louis for his health two years before. Already the climate had healed his diseased lung.

"Young fellow me lad, if I was figurin' on stayin' well I'd be kinda careful how I drapped them dynamite remarks around. They're likely to go off onexpected an' blow someone up. If a guy padlocks his tongue it won't get him into trouble. I knew a man lived to be 'most a hundred oncet by travellin' right on his own range an' never crossin' to his neighbour's only when he was lookin' for some of his own dogies."

The clerk looked at the cattleman, flushed, and suddenly remembered business inside the store. He was not used to the ways of the Southwest and he had more than once talked himself into trouble. In a country where it is an open question whether a newcomer left his former habitat just ahead of a sheriff curiosity is a dangerous attribute. Men are taken for what they give themselves out to be and no questions are asked. Medford still remembered with acute humiliation an occasion when an innocent *who* and *where from,* addressed to a hard-bitten stranger, had brought him to precipitate grief.

The quartet of riders swung from the saddles and grounded the reins. Peter McCann nodded grimly to those on the porch and walked into the store. Tapscott followed him. The others stayed to exchange a word with Quinn and Shell.

"I seen that top horse of yours with a bunch of my broomtails the other day, Lyn, down on Dry Creek," Quinn told the younger of the brothers.

"That so? If you're roundin' up yore fuzzies wisht you'd run him into the corral for me, Curt."

"Sure will. Anything new?"

He asked his question casually and just as casually Wilson answered it. "Not a thing, Curt—not up our way."

"Tapscott was tellin' me the other day he figured we'd better start the beef round-up earlier this fall."

"Maybe so. I ain't heard the old man mention his plans."

Lyn sat on his heels and from his hip pocket drew the "makings." There was nothing to show he was not at perfect ease with the world—except the long rifle he had just propped against the wall. He was a good-looking lad, just turned twenty, slender and graceful as one of Praxiteles's models.

The talk drifted. It touched on the long dry spell and its effect upon grass, on a group of mustangers in the north who were walking down wild horses, on the *chaparejos* of a passing *vaquero*.

From out of the store came Peter McCann with a square of wrapping paper, a hammer, and some tacks. To the wall he nailed the coarse paper. Those on the porch watched him silently and read the notice roughly printed there.

$1000
REWARD
For information identifying
All or any of the Night Riders who
Shot Joe Walters at the Cass Cabin
Will be paid by
PETER MCCANN

This called for comment. After a long moment of waiting Quinn spoke. "How *is* Joe?"

"He'll make it, Doc says."

"Good. He's one tough customer, Joe is. I kinda figured he'd fool 'em. Nell was allowin' to ride over to-day an' see if they was anything she could do."

"Not a thing, Curt. But tell her much obliged."

That was all. McCann's spurs jingled down the steps. His sons and his foreman followed. They swung into their saddles and rode away.

"Short an' sudden," commented Simp. "The old man don't orate much, but his actions talk mighty loud. I notice he ain't offerin' no reward for the arrest an' conviction of them night riders. Not none. He aims to do all the arrestin' that's needed an' he don't reckon any convictin' will be required."

Quinn nodded. Simp's remarks had been addressed in a low tone to him. He was of the same opinion. McCann would go his own way, regardless of the law. If any one protested he could point out how he had first appealed to it for protection. But there would be a grim ironic light in his eye when he mentioned the fact.

CHAPTER IX

Wils McCann Uses His Quirt

THE MCCANNS had not been out of Mesa ten minutes when another group of horsemen were seen approaching by the Tincup Pass road in a cloud of dust. They drew up in front of the Gilt Edge Saloon and left their mounts at the hitching bar.

Jasper Stark straddled into the gambling house, his brother Phil and Carl Gitner at his heels. Stone stood on the porch and looked round leisurely in his cool measured way before he passed through the door into the Gilt Edge. Killer he might be, but he was an individual first. He did not follow at any man's beck.

The Stark brothers and Gitner were at the bar celebrating.

"Come an' wash the dust outa yore throat, Dave," invited Jasper, in no subdued voice. "It's on me to-day. Bet yore boots. Come on up, boys. Name yore poison." This last was addressed to the two or three loafers hanging about.

Stone's cold blue eyes looked at Jasper with no warmth in them. As a boy the Texan had ridden with Mosby in his border raids. There were rumors that at one time he had been one of Quantrell's guerillas. The habit of his life was to

64

consort with danger. It seemed to him child's play and worse, an indication of arrant weakness, to wear such a manner of exuberant triumph as Jasper Stark displayed. What had they done but drive two frightened cowpunchers into the chaparral, wound one, and fire an empty cabin? If the faction with which he was allied called this a victory there would surely be trouble ahead. The McCanns were fighters.

"I wouldn't choose to drink," he said.

"Different here," retorted Jasper. "Set 'em up, Hans. The lid's off to-day."

The older of the Stark brothers was large and muscular, but he carried himself slouchily. His physical strength was not convincing because it had back of it no mental or moral force. The younger son was of a different type. Phil was only eighteen, but he had been brought up in the school of the frontier which has no vacations. Already the softness of youth was hardening to manhood. Stone judged that he would go through when the call came.

The Gilt Edge was the usual resort of the Stark faction as The Legal Tender was of the other side. Hans now gave information to Jasper as he set out glasses and bottles.

"The McCanns wass in town to-day already yet."

Jasper stopped, glass poised. "Here now?" he asked.

"Nein, not now."

"How many of 'em?"

"Four. Old Peter, Tapscott, andt two of the boys."

"Hmp! What they doin' here?"

Hans shrugged his shoulders and lifted the palms of his hands. He had told all he knew.

"Got out, eh? Musta known we were headin' this way," Jasper boasted.

Stone laughed, softly, ironically. "Where do you get that line of talk, Jas? Are you foolin' yoreself too or jus' trying to fool us?"

"What's eatin' you, Dave?"

"Ever hear of old Pete McCann givin' the middle of the road to anybody? He's there both ways from the ace, if you ask me."

"We'll show him how much he's there before we're through."

"Yes?" drawled the Texan, lazily and insolently.

"I'll tell him so, right off the reel, him or any of his outfit soon as I meet up with 'em," the young man bragged.

He was irritated at Stone. Was the gunman on the Stark side of the feud? He was taking old Matt's money. Well then, why did he talk like that?

"Better tell 'em kinda slow, so's they don't hear, Jas. A few of 'em are curly wolves. Leastways they've got that rep."

"You scared of 'em, Dave?"

Jasper was alarmed at his own question. His eyes fell before the chill steady regard of the little

66

man. It was not safe to resent outwardly Dave Stone's scorn.

After a moment the Texan spoke. His words lessened the tension. "I reckon my six-gun will have to talk for me when the time comes, Jas. Only fool kids get all het up with talk so's they have to steam off," he drawled.

After some time of rapid refreshment at the bar the Circle Cross riders moved out again to the main street of the little town. Stone had already departed temporarily to buy a shirt. Gitner and Phil Stark had business at the blacksmith shop. Jasper strolled across to Basford's for the mail. Inside, he caught a glimpse of the little Texan at the dry goods counter.

Public opinion, represented by Quinn, Shell, and others, still sat on the porch and awaited developments. It watched Jasper Stark now to see what he would do about the placard on the wall. It had watched Stone too. The Texan had read it with an expressionless face and offered no comment. Nobody could have told from his manner that it held any interest for him.

Jasper swelled, evidently steaming up to blow off. He could not resist taking the centre of the stage. In the safe middle states he might have been a ward boss. Unfortunately for him leadership in the Southwest demanded first of all gameness. He was always trying to fill a place he had not the stark courage to hold.

"Hmp! Wants information, does he? An' he'll pay a thousand dollars. What's he aim to do with this information when he gets it?"

Jasper's voice was heavy, his manner abusive as he turned to Quinn. The cattleman did not look at him. His expressionless eyes were on a cloud of dust far down the road ribbon. A rider was cantering toward Mesa.

"Why, he didn't tell me, Jas. Yore guess is as good as mine," Quinn answered evenly.

"Thinks he'll run on us maybe. Figures he'll cook up a lot of lies an' then do us some meanness whilst we're not lookin'. I'll tell him not to fool with us any more 'an he would with the business end of a diamond back. We'll burn powder quick."

Jasper was "wilding up," as Simp Shell expressed it later. He was full of bad whiskey and a sense of his own importance. He strutted, moving up and down the porch as he boasted. The silence of the listening men exasperated him. He wanted applause.

"Don't amount to a hill of beans, this don't." The drink-excited man snapped his fingers contemptuously at the poster. "Say he knew. What then? What then?"

His back was toward the man coming down the road. If he had been observant he might have seen an odd change in the gray eyes of Quinn, a flicker of subdued and wary excitement.

"I'll show Peter McCann where he gets off,"

68

Stark went on, vanity overriding caution. "I'll sure learn that *hombre* not to run on the rope." He took two swift strides forward and with one sweeping gesture ripped the reward placard from the wall. Tearing the paper into fragments, he flung them down and ground them under his heel.

At the same instant a rider pulled up in front of the store and swung from the saddle. Stark turned, the anger he had worked up burning in him.

On the lower step a man was standing, his quirt dangling by the loop from his wrist. He was watching very quietly and steadily the impotent fury of the stamping rowdy.

Under his ribs the heart of Jasper Stark died within him. For the man looking at him was Wilson McCann. He had a feeling as though the ground were falling from his feet, a shocked certainty that he had been delivered into the hand of his enemy. His arm made a motion toward the revolver at his side, a hesitant and indefinite gesture.

"Don't you!" warned McCann, and his steely eyes did not for the thousandth fraction of a second release the other.

Stark dropped his hand. In his eyes was the look of the trapped rat. Actively his brain was searching for a way out. His brother and Gitner were nearly half a mile away, but Stone was here, not twenty yards from him. The Texan would pump lead into McCann if he got gay. With the thought came a resurgence of courage. He had nothing to fear.

His voice was loud, to attract the attention of his companion. "You pull yore freight, Wils McCann, if you know what's good for you. Get me. *Poco tiempo.*"

McCann came up the steps toward him, evenly and without haste. There was that in his face at which Jasper took alarm.

"Keep back. Hear me? Keep back, or I'll—" Jasper retreated to the door, his voice rising to a shriek. "Don't you dass lay a hand on me."

His enemy plucked him from the shelter of the store as though he had been a child. The quirt in the hand of McCann rose and fell, rose and fell again. Jasper cursed, threatened, wept. He called to Stone for help, tried to break away from that iron grip and escape, did all he could to save himself except stand up and fight. The swishing lash burned like a rope of fire. The tortured man howled in agony and begged shamelessly for mercy. Into his flesh the rawhide cut with inexorable cruelty.

He flung himself to the floor and McCann released him. The man with the quirt was panting from his exertions. He looked down scornfully at the quivering mass of wheals at his feet.

"You'll learn to—let my father's placards alone. Understand? An' not to shoot at me from the brush, you damned jayhawker."

McCann looked up. From the windows, from the door, from both sides of him the eyes of silent men were focussed upon him and Stark. Against the jamb of the door Stone was leaning, muscles at indolent ease, only his cold eyes warily intent. At the first glance McCann knew that the Texan had elected not to take up Jasper's quarrel. The thumb of his right hand hitched in the sagging belt was close to the handle of the revolver only for protection in case battle should be thrust upon him.

To Medford, the store clerk, Wilson spoke. "Father forgot the mail. Left it in the store. Get it for me."

Medford's excited eyes were withdrawn from the window. Presently the clerk appeared with a package of letters and newspapers.

"Much obliged."

The Flying V Y man turned. Jim-Dandy was standing near the porch, parallel to it. With one quick leap McCann was in the saddle. His feet found the stirrups and the pony went pounding down the road at a gallop.

Presently Simp eased himself out of his chair and waddled across to the braggart huddled on the floor.

"Better get up, Jas. He's gone," Simp said.

He lent a hand to get the other to his feet. Jasper looked round, furtive-eyed, and knew he had been weighed and found wanting.

"If I hadn't slipped—," he began, and stopped. His breath was still ragged with dry sobs. "He took advantage—with his quirt."

"Yes. You only had a gun," Stone answered contemptuously. "A gun an' yore fists."

The beaten man, trying to save his face, flared to weak and passionate resentment. "You stood there an' let him beat me up—after I fell," he accused.

The Texan looked at him stonily.

"I was hearin' how quick you burnt powder an' how you was allowin' to learn the McCanns not to run on the rope. From yore say-so I figured you'd make this Wils look like a plugged quarter. Anyhow, where I come from a grown man plays a lone hand when it's one to one."

"Tell you he took advantage. I slipped," whined Jasper.

"You sure done so when you picked on this Wils McCann to raise a rookus with," Stone agreed.

Jasper limped painfully into the store and sank down into a chair. "I'm sick," he whimpered.

Medford brought him water. After a time he was helped to the hotel. He was not able to ride home and in any event he had not the nerve to face Matt Stark with even a doctored story of his humiliation.

The old man would be in a blaze of fury at him.

CHAPTER X

Matthew Stark Serves Notice

JASPER HAD not in his mind overstressed the effect upon his father of the public disgrace his conduct had brought upon the family. Matthew Stark was game to the marrow and inordinately proud. That a Stark should show the white feather to a McCann, that he should be whipped like a peon without offering fight, filled him with a bitter despair he could not endure. If Jasper had gone to his death with guns blazing he would have sorrowed for him and been proud of him. But this degradation was unspeakably horrible to him. It was gall and wormwood in his mouth.

He ordered Phil to saddle his horse and rode to town alone. Fast though he travelled, the dusty road seemed interminably long. He craved action drastic and swift. First, a settlement with the weakling who had dishonoured him, then battle with his enemies to revenge himself upon them. He would have Wilson McCann's blood. Nothing less would satisfy him.

The old man strode through the hall of the Mesa House and into the room that served as an office.

"What room is Jas in?" he demanded of the proprietor.

"Why, he's in the front room upstairs, Mr. Stark.

I give him the best room I had. Doc Sanders has been lookin' after him."

Stark was already taking the stairs. Collateral information did not interest him. He always had been a man of one idea and had gone straight to the thing he wanted.

The man lying on the bed heard a heavy tread. The door burst open and his father stood before him, the fires of eruptive wrath blazing in his eyes. Jasper knew his day of judgment had come.

Matt Stark stood, feet well apart, leathery jaws clamped tight, and looked at his unworthy son. "Well?" he asked harshly at last.

"I slipped. He got me down," Jasper whined.

"Don't lie to me. I've seen Stone."

He had, and from the disgusted Texan had heard the plain undiluted truth.

"I was kinda dazed. He hit me first off with the loaded end of his quirt an' I didn't know what I was doing. He 'most killed me."

"I wish he had," the father retorted bitterly. "If any one had told me I'd raise a coward for a son—" He broke off, to deny his own claim. "But I knew it. I've known it for years, only I wouldn't let myself believe it. You were always a puling quitter. No sand in yore craw. Never was. The first Stark I ever knew without guts. I'd rather you'd died—a hundred times rather. But I'm through with you. No son of mine can stand up an' take a thrashin' without fightin' like a wildcat."

"I was sick anyhow, an' I wasn't noticin' when he knocked me kinda senseless," Jasper whimpered.

"You're lying. An' what if he did? Pack a gun, don't you? After he'd taken the hide off, you still had yore forty-five, didn't you? Think Phil would have let him get away with it an' not pumped lead? Not for a minute. But you—you're gun-shy. All you can do is drink an' brag. Why, you flabby weakling, they'll laugh at me all over the country. The McCanns'll never quit grinnin' about it. By God, I couldn't a-believed it—even about you."

It seemed to the writhing man on the bed that his father's eyes smoked, they were so full of burning fires of fury. He knew his protests were useless, that nothing he could say would blot out the unchangeable facts. But he continued to plead his excuses, because there was nothing else to do.

The old man cut him short. "I'm through with you—absolutely. Right now I'm going over to Fletcher's office to change my will. You don't get a cent—not a red cent. An' you get out of Arizona. I'll give you a week to settle yore affairs. You'll pull yore freight an' change yore name. From now on you're no Stark. Understand?"

"I've got to sell my stock," Jasper said sulkily. Already he was sketching a campaign to mitigate the old man's wrath. Julia was his favourite. She could do anything with him. He would have her talk to her father and get him to be reasonable.

"I'll buy it. Name yore price. See Fletcher about it. I don't want any dealings with you myself. Don't you ever cross my track or I'll make you think this Wils McCann was only playin' at quirting you."

Matthew Stark left the room and the hotel. He walked down the street to Fletcher's office and found the lawyer was at Phoenix and would not be back for several days. The owner of the Circle Cross hesitated. He was half of a mind to go to Tucson and have a new will made at once. Any kind of delay annoyed him. But he had reasons for not wanting to leave the valley just now. The new will would have to wait till Fletcher returned.

Across the street he could see the editor of the Mesa *Round-Up* sitting at his desk. Jackman was editor, news-gatherer, composer, pressman, and office boy of the weekly sheet. The chains of his spurs jingling, Stark strode across through the dust and entered the little frame building. He brushed aside the greetings of the newspaper man and ordered brusquely what he wanted.

Within the hour printed posters had been tacked up in each of the saloons, on the wall of the post office inside and out, on the door of the false-front town hall, and at a dozen other conspicuous places. They bore this simple legend in blackface type:

This Is To Serve
NOTICE
That I will kill Wilson McCann on sight.
MATTHEW STARK

This attended to, Stark mounted and rode out of town. From his favorite chair on the porch of Basford's store Simp Shell watched him go, a grim and menacing figure of wrath. To Basford and another crony Simp offered the opinion that hell was liable to pop mighty soon.

"The old man's called for a showdown. It's up to Wils now," he concluded.

"To Wils an' old Pete. Don't forget him. He's likely to sit in an' take a hand, the old man is." This from Basford.

"Sure is," the third man corroborated.

"Matt's crazy mad because Jas showed a yellow streak. He'll not rest content till guns get to fogging," the fat man added.

"Funny about Jas," Basford mused aloud. "Reckon he weighs twenty pounds more than Wils. Husky too. Big an' rawboned. Comes of good game fighting stock. He's been fed on raw meat too, as you might say. What ails him?"

"He ain't worth a continental ding an' never will be. You can't make a silk purse outa a hog's ear any more'n you can train a coyote to be a wolf even if it is of the same family. No, sir. No can do. That fellow Jas has had all kinds of chances, but

77

he's what he is. I've always kinda suspicioned he wasn't nothing but cock-a-doodle-do."

There was no dissent from Simp's verdict any more than there was from another opinion he voiced, that his father had kicked him out and taken upon himself the care of what he considered the family honour. It was agreed that Matthew Stark and either Wilson or Peter McCann would clash at their first meeting and that from it one or both would be carried away dead or mortally wounded.

CHAPTER XI

Yerby Offers Literary Criticism

WILSON drew up among the scrub pines on the side of the hogback across from Yerby's cabin. These days he followed roundabout trails and moved with extreme caution. For his life had been posted by a man who never made vain threats. It was the sight of a white-faced bay standing in front of the house that brought him up short now.

With the trained eye of a cowpuncher he recognized the horse instantly. He had last seen it on a certain moonlit night and Julia Stark had been in the saddle. But he had no certainty that she was using it to-day. Someone else might be waiting for him in Jim's cabin—say Jasper Stark or his father or that Texas killer, Gitner. Hs decided to play safe.

From its place beside the saddle he drew a rifle and tested its mechanism. This done, he crept on all fours through the greasewood and the yucca till he had put a long hundred yards between him and Jim-Dandy. Behind a clump of *cholla* he squatted and watched the house patiently. For nearly half an hour he did not stir. Except his eyes he was motionless as a statue.

A girl came out of the shack and hung a few pieces of washing on the limb of a live oak.

Wilson would have known the trim straight figure among a thousand.

He did not intend to take chances. Julia Stark might not be alone with Yerby, though the fact that he could see only one saddled horse pointed to that conclusion. With the greatest care, availing himself of every shrub that offered cover, he worked toward the house from the rear. Voices drifted to him, those of the old settler and Julia. Apparently nobody else was there.

When at last he reached the window Wilson raised his head slowly and looked inside. Julia had seated herself and was evidently just about to read aloud from a book. Jim was sitting in a chair with his leg propped up in another chair in front of him. The oldtimer was getting in a few words while there was still time. The theme of his talk was the book in the girl's hand, which was *David Copperfield*, brought by McCann according to the doctor's orders from his own small private collection. As a literary critic the old nester was original in expression if not in thought.

"This Steerforth guy, ma'am, he's sure enough one bad actor—about the worst I ever did see. I don't reckon he could a-got away with it in this country. I'd think some of the friends of this li'l girl would oil their six-shooters an' go gunnin'. Yes, ma'am, they'd ought to a-fixed it so's he went to sleep in smoke *muy pronto*. I recolleck oncet when we drove a beef herd up the trail from

Clarendon we jumped up three campers one night. They was headin' for the Cherokee Strip, an' I kinda got a notion one of 'em, a smooth black-eyed fellow, was in quite some hurry. He looked plumb worried when I give 'em 'Hello the camp!' till he seen I was a stranger. Along about three A.M. in the mawnin' whilst I was night herdin' I heard guns poppin'. This girl's brother had arriv onexpected an' let daylight through the black-eyed guy."

Julia did not ask what girl. Yerby's stories were likely to leave something to the imagination and in this case details were unnecessary. She settled herself to read.

Wilson went back to his horse, rode across the *arroyo*, and shouted, "Hello the house!"

Miss Stark came to the door. She stood, erect and uncompromisingly hostile, watching him as he dismounted. Her dark look was like a flashing sword.

He nodded good morning without response.

"How's Jim?" he asked.

She stood aside to let him pass into the house, gathering her skirts close so that he would not brush against her as he went by. Nothing could have expressed more positively her detestation of him than that disdainful gesture.

No discomposure showed on his aquiline face. Seamed and darkened by wind and sun, it had the immobility of the stark sierras.

With jingling spur he moved across the room. "How are you, Dad?"

"Fat like a match. Whad you know that's new?"

"Not much. Gather of beeves on Poison Creek next month. Some more rustling up in the hills, they say."

McCann chatted easily, casually, with the nester, ignoring the burning resentment that held the girl passionately silent. His manner was coolly indifferent, but not for a moment was he off guard. He sat astride a chair, back to the wall, so that his eyes could command both window and door.

Watching him covertly, Julia saw a sudden change in the lounging figure. The back straightened and the muscles grew taut. Every sense had quickened to life. For someone was coming up the path toward the house.

Julia moved quickly to the door, then drew a breath of relief. She had dreaded and half expected to see her father. But the approaching figure was that of a young woman.

The new arrival was Ann Gifford. She had brought with her a cake. Since Yerby's accident she had been in the habit of coming every day to supply his simple needs. Even her fierce aloofness had not been proof against the little man's good will. Nobody who knew him could continue to dislike Jim Yerby. She had capitulated, reluctantly and stiffly, on the tacit understanding that it was only while he was bedfast. She would give kindness if she must, but she would not accept any.

"Meet Miss Julia Stark, Miss Gifford," their host said, and after pronouncing the formula added: "Miss Julia she's jest back from Los Angeles where she's learned 'most everything they is to know outa them schoolbooks, I reckon."

Julia laughed at this testimonial as she stepped forward to shake hands. She had wanted to meet the Gifford girls ever since her return. Ann was still holding the cake and she did not put it down. Coldly she bowed.

"I called the other day, Miss Gifford, but you weren't at home," Julia said. "May I come again—some day soon?"

"We're often out with the sheep," Ann replied.

It was a rebuff, but Julia refused to accept it. "You can't be out all the time. I'll try my luck again," she said.

Yerby tried to cover Ann's discourtesy by a flux of words. "Miss Julia she was jest startin' to read to me from this here David Dickens book."

"David Copperfield," Julia corrected.

"Sure enough. Dickens he's the fellow that owns the brand. Well, I was sayin' that this Steerforth duck, the one that done li'l Emily dirt, why someone had orta hung his hide out to dry, seems like. If them fellows had been he-men some of them would have fixed him good an' ready for a

83

funeral. I don't hold with dry-gulching, you understand, but there's times—"

The nester stopped abruptly, the springs of his garrulity dried up. A glance at Ann Gifford's frozen face had done it. He recalled the rumours that had come to him as to the reason why Nora had gone to Los Angeles and embarrassment flamed in his countenance. He felt as though conversationally he had stepped off a precipice and was sinking in a gulf of space.

McCann rescued him by commenting on the number of characters in the book. "I never did see so many footloose folks trailin' around. There's David an' Peggotty an' Miss Betsy an' the Murdstones an' Barkis—"

Yerby jumped at this diversion as a terrier does at a rat. "You're whistlin', boy. There's li'l Emily too an' that Steerforth an' Mrs. Gummidge—"

"And Micawber and Mr. Dick and Uriah Heep and Ham and Traddles," Julia contributed, speaking to the man on the bed and not to his friend. "Then there's Agnes and Dora of course and Rosa Dartle."

"Looks like he'd have trouble with all them folks millin' around in his haid whilst he was writin'," the oldtimer mused aloud. "But this Dickens guy sure knows how to throw a rope so as to cut out any of 'em from the herd when he's good an' ready."

Ann Gifford did not stay. Her manner implied

that she wanted to have nothing to do with any of them except Yerby.

The nester spoke first. "I'd like right well to do something for her an' her li'l sister if I knew what," he said, wrinkling his forehead in thought. "O' course sheep are pests. I ain't denyin' that none. But seems like these girls ain't hardly to blame because old Andy Gifford was so mean and obstinate he plumb wasn't contented till he'd started trouble."

"Exactly how I feel," McCann agreed.

Julia had opened her lips to say substantially the same thing, but she closed them again without speaking. She did not intend to be of the same opinion as Wilson McCann on any subject.

Nevertheless she had a word to say to him, and before she left she said it. He had stepped out to bring a bucket of water from the spring. She met him under a live oak a few yards from the house.

"You know my father is looking for you?" she said abruptly.

He put down the bucket, an ironic smile on his face. "Someone did mention that to me," he said.

"Why don't you go away? Why don't you leave the country?" she demanded.

"Because Matt Stark has served notice on me of his intentions?" he asked grimly. "What kind of a man would I be if I ran away after that?"

"He's an old man—twice your age." Her voice

85

trembled and broke for a moment. "I should think—you'd be ashamed to hurt him."

"Am I the one lookin' for trouble? Did I print bills sayin' I'd kill him on sight?" His face was hard as hammered iron.

"You know why he did that—because you jumped on Jasper when he wasn't looking and beat him when he couldn't defend himself." The flash in her eyes warned him that she was restraining herself with difficulty, that if it had not been for the dread in her heart she would have let herself go in denunciation.

He laughed, scornfully. "That's the story he's telling, is it?"

"And now Father's crazy mad. If you don't go away—"

"I'm not going," he cut in harshly.

"Then someone will be killed," she cried despairingly.

"Yes."

His brown competent fingers were on the barrel of the rifle he had been carrying in one hand. Again, as once before, there flowed through her a sense of his virile power. This man was dangerous. His force expressed itself in the cool quiet eyes, in the clean lines of the face and figure, in a certain wary stillness that meant reserve strength.

She had a momentary picture of him lying still in the dust, all the vigour and potency of him gone limp and flaccid; and on the heel of it another one, this time of her father, being carried into the ranch house with his eyes closed forever. Both flashes of imagination were horribly clear to her. She shuddered.

"If you'd only go—while there's still time—"

Her distress touched his not very accessible heart, the more because he knew her capable of fierce and primitive passion. She was far from the clinging-vine type. Independence and courage were of the essence of her. But her pride could not stand out against the shadow of tragedy hovering in the background.

"I can't go. What would folks say?"

"Does it matter what they'd say if you were doing right?" she asked eagerly.

"It would matter to me. Besides, I'd not be doing right to go. This is where I live—the only country I know. I can't let any one run me out. I've got to go through."

"Why have you?" she pleaded. "It's all wrong, this feud. If you'd just go away, for a while, maybe things would quiet down. Then you could come back."

He shook his head. "No, I can't go. I don't want to have any trouble with yore father, but if he's hell bent on it, why it'll have to come."

With a little gesture of hopelessness she gave up. It was of no use. Before making the attempt to move him she had known it would be. For according to the frontier code he was right. None but a weakling could run away after an enemy had served notice that he was looking for him.

As she turned away his voice stopped her.

"I'll promise one thing. It'll be a fair fight far as I'm concerned—no layin' in the bushes an' waitin' for him."

Her dark troubled eyes rested in his. Their appealing beauty disturbed him. He would have liked to give peace to her worried soul. But he could offer no assurance. When the hour came, if it lay within his power, he must strike her to the heart.

Much stirred, he watched her lissom young body as it moved with light rhythm toward the house. She belonged to the enemy clan, but he could not hold her in cold disapproval. There was something fine and exquisite in her, something radiant and warm. An enemy, yes! But already he knew her a very dear one whose presence filled the secret places of his being.

CHAPTER XII

Birds of a Feather

AS JASPER STARK moved about the streets of Mesa with his slouching gait his eyes furtively questioned public opinion to discover what it thought of him. His manner of braggadocio still sat on him, but it was a hollow mockery. He was full of shame, resentment, and self-pity. Hatred surged in him. It was characteristic of the man that he was ashamed not so much of the weakling's part he had played as of being found out.

He sent for Gitner. That hardy ruffian straddled into an upstairs private room of the Gilt Edge and looked at young Stark with a scarcely veiled sneer. "Want to see me?" he asked.

"Yep. Heard the old man say anything about me, Carl?"

"The old man don't mention yore name. It's understood at the Circle Cross that Matt's through with you. Why?"

"Sit down," Jasper growled, with annoyed impatience. "I wantta talk." He pushed the bottle on the table toward the other man.

Gitner took a chair and a drink. He was willing to listen. Whatever developed would be to his advantage, for he knew he held the whip hand. Stark would have to come to his terms if he wanted anything—and of that the Texan had no doubt whatever. Jasper had not sent for him merely for the pleasure of his company.

The gunman offered no comment. There was a tactical advantage in forcing the other to lead and he availed himself of it.

"Shove that bottle north by west," Stark said surlily, and then poured himself a large drink. He tossed it down at a gulp and almost at once replenished the tumbler. Morosely he eyed the liquor. "The old man been to town this week?"

"No. Last time he was in was the day he read the riot act to you," Gitner grinned maliciously. "But he's had Fletcher out to the ranch an' they spent 'most a whole mornin' together. Miss Julia was with 'em a while an' she had quite a set-to with the old man by what I've heard tell."

"What day was that?"

"Lemme see. That must 'a' been Thursday."

Jasper gloomed at his drink and poured it down his throat without visible pleasure.

"He was making a will, don't you reckon?" he said at last.

"I reckon."

"Question is, has he signed it yet?"

"If you want to know, why don't you go ask him?" suggested the Texan with sarcasm.

"I don't need to ask him. He hasn't. Fletcher would draw it up when he come back to town. That would be the way they fixed it. But Fletcher

90

had to leave Thursday night again for Phoenix to argue a case before the Supreme Court. He got back this afternoon, not more 'an an hour ago. He'll finish writing up the will to-morrow."

"Looks like," agreed the man from the Lone Star state. "You got it all worked out, Jas. Ought to 'a' been a lawyer."

"An' he'll take it out either in the afternoon or next day."

"Sounds reasonable. Better kiss the ranch good-bye, Jas."

Stark moved the bottle toward Gitner, folded his arms, and put his elbows on the table. "Have another, Carl."

The eyes of the two met and held fast. There was something of crouched significance in Jasper's narrowed gaze. It brought the other man to a wary and alert attention. He knew that he was going to find out now why he had been asked to come here.

They talked, in whispers, for an hour, their heads close and the door locked. Not once, though they drank much, did their voices lift. It might have been noticed, if any one had been observing them, that Gitner left the Gilt Edge half an hour before his companion. Nobody but Hans the bartender knew that they had been in the room together.

At the hotel waiting for him Jasper found his sister. They walked a little distance down the road to be alone.

"No use, Jas," she told him. "I've fought it out with Dad and he won't listen to a word. You've disgraced the family, he says, and you're no longer a member of it. He's cutting you out of his will."

"That'll suit you an' Phil," he sneered. "What do you care if I do get a rotten deal?"

Her scornful eyes flashed anger at him. "That's a nice thing to say, after I quarrelled with Dad about it for you. But you always were a poor loser."

"I haven't lost yet," he snarled. "If you think I'll sit down an' let him cut me outa my share of the ranch, why, you've got another guess. I'll not stand for it."

"You can't help yourself," Julia told him curtly. His boasting was an old story with her and she gave it no weight. "After a while maybe he'll not be so bitter, and if you behave yourself we may be able to get him to put you back in the will. What's the matter with you anyhow, Jas? Why didn't you stand up and fight Wils McCann?"

"Tell you he hit me when I wasn't lookin'. Tell you I was dazed an' I fell. He jumped me when I was down."

"I don't believe it," she flung at him. "He's not that kind of man."

"Course you won't believe yore own brother against a McCann," he reproached her bitterly. "You're every bit as bad as the old man."

"I asked Dave Stone how it was. He told me the truth."

"He's a liar if he claims it's different from the way I tell it," he cried with weak violence. "He come at me, McCann did, an' hit me with the loaded end of his quirt. I kinda fell against the wall, stunned like, an' then he knocked me down. That's all I knew till he was ridin' hell-for-leather down the road. It's the honest-to-God truth."

She was convinced he was lying to save his face, but there was no use telling him so.

"When are you going?" she asked.

"Going where?"

"Away from here."

"Who said I was going?"

"Why, I thought—Dad said—"

"I don't care what he said. He's not runnin' me. When I get good an' ready maybe I'll go an' maybe I won't."

She came to a subject that never was long from her thoughts. The fact that she mentioned it at all to her brother, from whom she could expect no help, showed how much the dread of it obsessed her.

"I'm worried about Dad—awf'ly worried. Every time he rides away from the house my heart sinks. If he should meet that Wils McCann— and of course he will some time—"

"Does he always carry his rifle?"

Jasper's eyes shone with interest. His sister was

surprised and gratified at this evidence of filial concern. She had expected him to be sullenly indifferent.

"Yes. Wherever he goes. It's dreadful, Jas—to sit at home and wait—and never know till I see him again whether—"

She broke down and cried a little.

"Does he ride alone?"

"Not if we can prevent it. I go with him when he'll let me—or Phil—and once or twice Dave Stone. But if Dad sees we're trying to protect him he gets wild and won't have it for a minute."

"Sure. That's the old man for you. Well, you tell him something for me, Jule. He's not the only man that's lookin' for Wils McCann."

Her startled eyes fastened to his. "What do you mean?"

"What d'you reckon I mean? I'm a Stark, no matter what the old man says—an' he's a McCann an' on top of that he's done me dirt. I'll fix him, sure as he's a foot high. But keep it under yore hat. I ain't gettin' out any bills about it. Not none."

She was torn by conflicting emotions. That Jasper had spirit enough to fight his own battle, if he really meant it and would not weaken when it came to the test, was news that warmed her blood. The danger in which her father stood might be averted if her brother met McCann first. Yet this was cold comfort. After the first flush of gladness for Jasper she knew by the chill that

94

drenched her heart how dreadful it would be if any of her family killed Wilson McCann or were killed by him.

The whole thing was a tragic dilemma, one from which there was no escape. It was all wrong, yet disaster was inevitable. Till now the strong and vital energy in her had never recognized defeat. With youth's egotism she had thought herself able to overcome the current of life upon which she floated, and she found she was a helpless chip tossed aside by the sweeping tide.

"Isn't there any way out, Jas—any way at all but this?" she cried, almost in a wail. "Do we have to start this—this awful feud? Surely there must be some way I could stop it if I only knew how."

Yellow lights gleamed like sinister beacons in his cold eyes. "No way. The McCanns started this an' it'll have to go through now."

Julia turned back toward the hotel with sick foreboding in her heart.

CHAPTER XIII

Red Tragedy

PHIL was blabbing a calf when his father came out to the porch.

"Going to Mesa, son. Hook up the team for me, won't you?"

The boy tied the bleating animal to the snubbing post, but before he went to the stable dodged for a moment into the kitchen. Julia was making pies.

"He's going to Mesa," Phil said quickly.

Julia at once unfastened her apron. "Keep him here till I'm dressed," she told him, and moved in her swift light way to the bedroom she used.

While Phil, with the assistance of a wrangler, was hitching to a buckboard the half-broken colts his father drove, a rider jogged up and stopped to pass a word. The man worked for an outfit down the river.

"'Lo, Red!" Phil greeted him. "How they comin'?"

"No complaint, as ol' man Peters said when his third wife died. Everything fine an' dandy with you?"

Red eased his weight in the saddle to relax stiffened muscles and rolled a cigarette. Time was not of the essence of his contract and he was ready to gossip as the fractious colts were being patiently reduced to harness.

"Miz Rollins jes' got back from Los Angeles, and she happened on a piece of news out there right interestin'," the cowboy volunteered. "She was takin' care of her daughter whilst an interestin' event was occurrin'. They was a nurse there to meet the li'l stranger the stork was bringin', an' it seems she was hired awhile ago to look after Nora Gifford, one o' them sheep-ranch women. The Gifford girl she had a hard time of it an' died—her an' the baby too. Folks have kinda figured they was something wrong when the oldest sister come back alone. There's been right consid'rable talk."

Phil flushed angrily. "Why don't folks mind their own damn business?" he blurted out.

"You a friend of the Giffords, Phil?" asked Red.

"Maybe I am; maybe I ain't. That's not the point What I claim is that we're in big business when we pick on some lone girls an' make their life hell for them." The generous indignation of youth flamed in him.

"Tha's right too," agreed Red.

"I knew Nora Gifford—some. She was a mighty sweet girl. The lobo wolf that ruined her life had ought to be hunted down an' shot in his tracks."

"Y'betcha!" agreed Red with the easy variability of the cowpuncher. "Dry-gulchin' wouldn't be none too good for him."

"Well, if you ask me, I'd kinda like to know

the circumstances before I pass judgment so prompt," the old wrangler differed. "An' I don't reckon any of us is never liable to find out. That Miss Ann Gifford is a mighty closemouthed lady. Say, I'd smoke a cigareet if someone would feed me the makin's."

From his hip pocket Red dragged a sack of "smoking." The wrangler rested from his labours and lit up.

"I seen Wils McCann as I come up the road," Red said, in a carefully casual voice. "He was fixin' the head gates of that ditch runnin' along the ridge to his father's place."

"Right now?" asked Phil instantly.

"Well, it's a good four-five miles from here. Say an hour ago."

Matthew Stark came out from the house and swung across the yard toward the stable with his strong bowlegged stride. As usual he carried a rifle. He had not covered twenty yards before Julia appeared.

"Oh, Dad!" she called.

Stark stopped, waiting for her. But before she could frame her request he refused it.

"No, you can't go to town with me. I don't care how many dofunnys you got to buy. No use you pesterin' me either."

"But Dad—"

"You heard me, Jule. You ain't going. That's settled."

"We're out of salt, Dad, and canned tomatoes, and lots of things."

"You make a list. I'll get 'em."

"But I've got to match that goods for my new dress. Why can't I go?"

"Because I say so. Now, honey, don't you argue with me about it. It won't be a mite of use."

She came up close and took him by the coat lapels. She had always been the centre of his dearest love. In his heart he thought her the most beautiful and wonderful creature under heaven.

"I want to go—awf'ly," she whispered, her deep dark eyes appealingly earnest.

Because he found himself weakening he took refuge in temper. "Well, you'll not go. You'll stay right here at home. I'll show you whether I can't go off this ranch without being tagged by you or someone else. I claim to be a full-grown *hombre* an' I don't need any nurse. Not in this year of our Lord. You drop this interferin' in my affairs, Jule, an' behave yoreself. I won't have it."

He swung her round by the shoulders and started her toward the house.

As he got into the buckboard Phil gave him information. "Red says he saw Wils McCann at the ditch gates above the Three Cottonwoods. He may not be alone. Better let me go too, Dad."

Matt Stark flung a couple of crisp questions at the cowpuncher and announced his decision. "You'll stay here, Phil. This is my job, an' I'm going to attend to it right now if he's still there. Let go." This last to the wrangler at the head of the dancing colts.

The young horses dashed down the road, racing at top speed. The gravel flew as the wheels crunched through it.

Already Phil was saddling a horse he found in the stable. He rode to the house, swung off, and ran inside.

Julia met him coming out of his room carrying a rifle.

"Where you going?" she asked breathlessly.

"Wils McCann is down above the Three Cottonwoods. Pretends to be fixin' up the ditch gates. When he came by awhile ago Red saw him. Likely he's waitin' to get Dad if he comes along. I've got to get there before Dad does, so I'm takin' the hill trail."

Her heart contracted with a swift spasm of fear. "Let me go too, Phil."

"No. What can you do? Besides, I can't wait."

He brushed past her, pulled himself to the saddle, and was off instantly at a gallop.

For a moment Julia stood, palsied by dread. Then, with a strong resurgence of courage, she followed Phil out of the house and ran to the stable.

"Get my saddle all ready," she cried to Sam Sharp the wrangler as she snatched up a rope and flew to the corral.

Here she lost precious seconds. At the first cast

the rope slid down the back of the pony. She had to rewind, did the job bunglingly on account of her hurry, and the loop missed again. The ponies raced around the corral, but at the third throw the riata fell true over the head of the bronco and tightened. The horse gave up at once. Julia led her mount to the gate where the wrangler was waiting with saddle, bridle, and blanket.

The man slapped on the blanket, adjusted the saddle, and cinched it expertly. Julia kept urging him to hurry.

"What's all this racin' an' hurry about?" he wanted to know.

"That Wils McCann is down the road waiting for Dad. We just heard it."

"Where?"

"At the ditch above Three Cottonwoods."

She called this back over her shoulder as the pony found its stride. When she passed the clicking windmill it was at a gallop.

The sun was high in the blue bowl above and the atmosphere was aquiver with light and heat. The ribs of the porphyry sierras stood out stark and gaunt. Spiral dust whorls danced down the valley like great tops set spinning by Olympians.

Julia swung into the cut-off that led to the hills. She rode fast, not sparing the horse, for an urgent spur was driving her. If she could arrive in time she might avert a tragedy. Just how, she did not know, but she would find a way. It was not possible that they would kill each other if she flung herself between them. Surely they would not do that.

But the hope that had swept her into swift action was ebbing. She was oppressed by the deep conviction that calamity impended. Within there rang a bell of dreadful doom. She knew her father, how implacable and overbearing he was. She began to know Wilson McCann's quality of mind. If they met nothing could prevent an explosion. One or both would fall.

The buckskin she had roped was a good traveller, but she seemed to crawl over the ground. The hills were steep and rough, the declivities sharp. Catclaw bordered the path and prickly pear clutched at her skirt. She deflected, trying to save a few hundred yards, and presently found herself in a thicket of cactus and mesquite that grew more dense as she proceeded.

Out of this she worked, desperately aware that she had wasted invaluable minutes. An open draw offered promise of faster progress. This led to a pocket, the sides of which were so precipitous that she had to dismount to find a way up.

It was just as she reached the summit that the sound of a shot appalled her. She leaned against the saddle for a moment, shaken to the soul, before she could remount.

Julia spurred the buckskin in the direction from which the report had come. She rode recklessly, careless of danger of a fall from the plunging horse. All her being was obsessed by terror. Fear for those she loved rose in her and choked her.

The irrigation canal appeared below and presently the ditch used by the McCanns and their neighbours to carry water to their ranches. Automatically her brain registered the fact that while the canal was half full of water the ditch was empty.

The pony swung round a clump of bushes and shied so violently that Julia was almost unseated. A man was stooping over something that lay huddled on the ground. The girl dragged the animal to a halt and flung herself from the saddle. As she ran back she noticed that the man held a rifle in his hand. He straightened and turned toward her.

The man was Wilson McCann.

In his rigid face her fear-filled eyes read confirmation of what she had dreaded. She looked down—and from her throat there leaped an anguished cry. The stricken figure at their feet was that of her father. In the centre of his forehead was a small round hole. He was dead beyond any question of doubt.

CHAPTER XIV

A Good Samaritan

JULIA wailed, "Oh Daddy—Daddy!" as she went down to her knees beside the lax body.

Upon it she lavished the exuberance of despairing grief. The death of him who had always been the outstanding figure in her world, the embodiment of stark and ruthless strength, was so unthinkable that she tried to push away the fact, to blot it out of being by the vehemence of denial. It could not be true. It could not. Yet she knew beneath the violence of protest that it *was* horribly true. In an instant of time he had been stricken out of life.

Wilson McCann waited for the first emotional outburst to spend itself. This was no place for him. He knew that. The drumming hoofs of his horse should be putting miles between him and the scene of this tragedy. But first he had something to tell her, as soon as she was in a condition to listen. Besides, he could not leave her alone with her dead while she was still hysterical.

A twig snapped. Instantly McCann stiffened to alert and crouched wariness. The weapon in his hand shifted ever so little, but that scarcely perceptible movement meant that he was ready. His eyes searched the chaparral foot by foot.

The sun glistened on a rifle barrel. At once McCann moved swiftly so as to place the girl's horse between him and that shining tube of steel.

Out of the brush a face peered, searching the landscape. The shifting eyes found in the same instant of time both McCann and the grief-stricken girl, and a second later the supine figure over which her grief was spending itself. The surprise of the combination of the three paralyzed momentarily thought processes.

Julia had looked up when McCann ran for the shelter of the horse's body. She glanced round quickly, caught sight of the gleaming gun barrel, and rose hurriedly.

"Look out, Phil. He's killed Dad," she cried, in a panic of terror.

Without a thought for her own safety she ran straight across the open toward the mesquite thicket to protect her brother.

A shot rang out. McCann crumpled up behind the horse. Julia heard herself cry out, and even in that moment of fear felt a sense of puzzled wonder. For she had been looking at Phil and she was sure he had not fired.

Phil dragged her down behind him. "He's layin' a trap for me," he told her, almost in a whisper.

But Julia, looking over his shoulder, knew this could not be. For the man's head lay in the sand, his rifle flung six feet away by the fall.

Again there came the crack of a rifle.

"He's dead, but you didn't shoot," she murmured, horrified.

"Can't be dead," the boy answered. "How can he?"

"Some one shot—and neither you nor he did. I'm going to see."

"No," he protested.

But she was gone before he could stop her. Phil scrambled to his feet and followed.

One glance at McCann was enough to show that this was no ruse. He lay still, either dead or unconscious. The boy stooped and found where a bullet had gone through the shirt.

"He was shot from behind, looks like," he said.

"But—who?" Julia asked, white to the lips.

"Jas maybe." Phil said it reluctantly.

"Why Jas?"

"That's what made me late. I saw someone dodging in the chaparral. Looked like Jas, but maybe it wasn't. Anyhow, I stopped to find out an' he slipped away. I wish to God I hadn't. I might a-been on time."

They had walked over to the place where their father lay and were kneeling beside him. With her handkerchief Julia wiped from the forehead of the cattleman the little stain of blood showing where the bullet had entered his head. Her slim body was shaken with sobs. The face of the boy was working with emotion. For the first time in their lives they had been brought very close to death in swift and tragic form. The blow was staggering. The virile dominant personality of their father would never again rule their activities. He had gone out of life as the flame of a blown candle vanishes.

"One of us 'll have to go get the wagon," Phil said presently in an unsteady voice. "Dad musta left it somewheres near."

"Yes. You go, Phil."

She was clinging to him, quivering with grief.

"Now don't you, Jule. Don't you," he begged, and denied his own counsel by breaking down unexpectedly.

They cried in each other's arms. After a little, Phil spoke gruffly, ashamed of his own distress. "I'll be moving. Sure you don't mind stayin' alone, Sis?"

"No. But don't be longer than you can help."

"If you'd rather not stay—"

"No. I want to stay."

"I'll leave Dad's rifle with you. Not that you'll need it." He tested the mechanism to make sure it was in order. "He hadn't fired a shot. McCann got him from the chaparral, don't you reckon?" Then, with a high sobbing note in his voice, "By God, this'll be a bad day for the McCanns."

"Yes." In that monosyllable she concentrated all the passionate desire for vengeance in her young heart.

"My horse is in the brush," Phil said in

anticlimax. "I'll go to the road an' have a look-see for the buckboard."

He disappeared among the mesquite bushes, and after a minute Julia heard the sound of a moving horse threshing about in the brush.

The sun was shining on a land peaceful as old age. She could hear the faint twitter of birds. A cottontail hopped from behind a clump of cactus and looked at her. On a flat rock ten feet away a swift lay basking. Nothing had changed, yet everything had changed. Something had gone out of her life that would never come back. An hour ago she had been a girl, gay and carefree, singing at her work. That happy irresponsibility was gone forever. She was no longer a girl but a sad-eyed woman. With youth's lack of perspective, she was sure that she would never laugh or sing again.

Julia covered her father's face with his own bandanna. She did it to keep the sun out of his eyes, even though no light could ever be bright enough now to trouble them.

A slight stir made her turn. Wilson McCann had rolled over and was looking at her. For a moment the two gazed at each other, neither speaking.

"I didn't kill him," he said at last, feebly.

"You murdered him from ambush," she charged.

"No. I heard a shot. I came an' found him lying there." The weakness was wholly physical. The steely eyes did not flinch in the least.

"I hope you'll die as he did, without a chance for your life," she cried in a low bitter voice.

"I reckon I'll do that . . . soon. But first . . . I'd like to set this straight. I didn't kill yore father."

"What's the use of saying that?" she wailed, struck anew as by a knife blade at thought of her loss.

"You don't believe it. Look at my Winchester."

"Couldn't you have reloaded?"

"I could, but I didn't. Oh well! What's the use? I'm a McCann, so I must a-done it."

"Weren't you waiting here to—to murder him?" she cried in a passion of horror.

There was a look in his eyes she did not understand. It was as though he knew something he did not mean to tell her, as though he were actually pitying her.

"I told you . . . if I had to do it . . . that it would be in the open. He was shot from the chaparral."

She did not believe that he was guiltless. She could not think that. And yet—

"What do you mean?" she asked.

His head sank into the sand and his eyes closed.

Reluctantly she moved toward him, drawn by his great need. He was the enemy of her house, the one who had brought disaster irretrievable to it. But he was, she believed, a dying man. The eternal mother was in that hour stronger in her than the daughter of her father.

She knelt beside him, looking for the wounds. A

stain of wet blood in the back of the shirt showed that he had been shot from behind. The sight of it gave her a little shock, for she recalled what Phil had said about seeing someone who looked like Jasper. And he had told her, Jasper had, that he intended to get Wils McCann. Had he done it? She hoped not. Even though this man had killed her father she shrank from the thought that her brother had fired the bullet that had so quickly avenged Matt Stark. Murder from the chaparral was a dreadful thing, a crime wholly alien to the frank and passionate temperament of the girl.

Water was needed, and Julia had not brought a canteen. She took the dusty hat of the man and ran to the canal, where she filled it with water. This she carried back carefully, picking a way through the brush so as to avoid the prickly pear and the cholla.

In one of his pockets she found a knife and used it to cut away the soaked shirt clinging to the wound. With the handkerchief taken from her neck she bathed the muscular back. Apparently he had been shot through the lung, well up near the shoulder, and in the right side.

Julia worked with her father's rifle at her side. The man who had shot McCann might appear out of the chaparral to find out how well he had done his work.

The eyes of the wounded man flickered open and fastened on her. She was now sponging his face and temples with a clean strip torn from the handkerchief. Silently he watched her. The touch of her cool fingers was comforting. As he lay there weakly it seemed to him that some healing property passed from her to him through them. It came as a conviction that he was not going to die, that he would get well.

She knew that he was conscious, that his eyes were absorbing her. The knowledge of it was vexing. Whatever service must be done for him she would rather were done without his being aware of it.

"My brother has gone for a wagon," she said coldly.

He did not ask what she meant to do with him. It was possible she might think she had answered sufficiently the call upon her humanity and leave him here to perish. It was possible that after she had gone the man who had shot him would creep up through the bushes and make an end of him. But he did not believe that either of these would occur. She would look after him somehow, even though she thought he had killed her father. He must set her straight on that. He could not let her go on thinking it.

"I didn't kill yore father," he said a second time.

"Even if you didn't, what's the difference? Your friends did. You were here waiting for him."

"No," he denied. "I was alone—none of my folks with me."

"I don't believe it. If you didn't fire the shot you know who did." She said it in all the bitterness of green young grief.

And instantly she knew, as her eyes challenged his, that she had hit upon the truth. He had not himself shot her father, but he could give her the name of the man who had done it. Her heart hardened. She rose, turned her back upon him, and walked away. He had lied to her. He was as guilty as though his own finger had pulled the trigger.

The minutes dragged. Julia could not get the wounded man out of her mind, even when she was stooping over the body of her father and brushing flies from the folded hands. Did he need her? She had heard that wounded men became terribly thirsty. He might be suffering now. Or perhaps he had died since she had left him. She found herself turning, so that she could get a sight of him out of the corner of her eye.

He lay still. Suddenly she could stand it no longer. Quickly she walked back to him. His quiet eyes met hers.

"Are you thirsty?" she asked.

"Yes."

Again she took his hat for water. She held it to his lips while he drank, supporting his head with one arm beneath it.

His thanks drew from her no comment. Apparently she did not hear him. But presently she bathed again the hot face and afterward stood between him and the burning sun.

There came at last the sound of wagon wheels. She called, to direct the driver of the buckboard. The rig jolted into sight. Her brother Phil had brought with him Sam Sharp, the stableman. The old wrangler had been hurrying to the scene armed for battle and the boy had met him.

They put the body of Matthew Stark into the wagon.

Hard-eyed, Phil looked at his wounded enemy. "What about him?" he asked harshly.

"We'll take him home with us," Julia said.

"No," he demurred.

"Yes, Phil. We can't leave him here. He's a dying man, you know. We'll take him to the ranch and send word to his father."

"What for?" the boy wanted to know. "We can send word he's here."

Unexpectedly McCann opened his eyes and spoke. "That would be better."

"A damn sight better, an' if you die before he gets here it'll suit me fine," Phil flung out bitterly.

"We're going to take him with us, Phil," his sister answered. "We can't leave him here. That's all there's to it. I hate him as much as you do, but it would be inhuman to go and leave him. I'll not do it."

Sharp backed his young mistress. "Tha's right, Phil. I reckon we got to take him."

They lifted him up and put him beside the dead man.

McCann's face was touched by an acridly sardonic smile. "You're all plumb good Samaritans," he murmured.

CHAPTER XV

Wes Tapscott, Diplomatist

WHEN the buckboard drew up at the Circle Cross a small group of grim-faced men were waiting to receive its grievous load. For Phil had galloped ahead to prepare the ranch for the homecoming of him who had ruled as autocrat for many years. Among those gathered on the porch were Dominick Rafferty, the foreman, and the Texans, Stone and Gitner. They were a lean brown hard-bitten lot. The desert had claimed its toll of them.

Rafferty scowled at the wounded McCann. "What about this buzzard?" he asked callously. "What's the idea in bringin' him here? Couldn't you bump him off where he was at?"

Julia was white to the lips. The ordeal of bringing back her father had proved almost more than she could endure. She had ridden close to the wagon and seen it and the road through a mist of tears all the way. Matthew Stark had been so big a figure in her young life that the thought of existence without his protective love was terrifying and appalling. It shook her courage and drowned her heart in woe.

"Don't talk like that, Dominick," she begged tremulously.

"How you want him to talk?" Gitner asked with

an ugly sneer. "Do you figure we'll let this *hombre* get away with what he's done?"

Julia flashed one look of anger at the Texan. "You'll do as you're told, Carl Gitner, or you'll get your time."

"You're boss now, are you?" the big Texan snarled.

"Don't push on yore reins, Carl," advised Rafferty.

Boy and man, the foreman of the Circle Cross had been with Stark for more than thirty years. He was devoted to him and his family. Even though he might not approve of what they had done he had no intention of siding with any body against them.

Julia took control of the arrangements. "Take Father to his own room," she gave orders. "And carry this man to Jasper's room. Will you send someone for Doctor Sanders, Dominick?"

In the country of wide spaces news travels on the wings of the wind. Before Doctor Sanders left town on his way to the Circle Cross it was known all over Mesa that Wils McCann had got Matt Stark and that he was himself desperately wounded and a prisoner in the hands of the enemy. Within two hours it had reached the Flying V Y and Peter McCann was organizing a rescue party.

"Better go kinda easy to start with," Wes Tapscott suggested. "I figure we're aimin' to spy out the land this trip an' not exactly call for a showdown. This business asks for some deep-plomacy, as the papers say."

"We'll three of us go—you an' Lyn an' me," McCann decided. "An' Dusty will follow with a wagon to bring the boy home."

"If we get him," amended the foreman.

"If they don't give him up I'll round up the boys an' tear the ranch house to pieces," Peter answered, his mouth set grimly and his eyes hard as jade.

"Sure you will, an' we'll find the boy's body when we finally get in. There's more'n one way to skin a cat, Peter McCann."

"I'm aimin' to get my boy," the cattleman said stubbornly.

"Dead or alive?" asked his friend. "Seems to me, Pete, I'd use a little horse sense. We ain't lookin' for trouble now—not whilst Wils is a prisoner, as you might say, at the Circle Cross. They got the dead wood on you. Our play is to be reasonable till we get the boy safe home. Tha's how it looks to me."

"What's yore notion then of what we should do?" McCann inquired surlily. He did not want to talk softly to any Stark. It went against the grain that he could not drive ram-stam to his end.

They were on the way by this time, moving at a low daisy-clipping road gait. To save time they were cutting across country, a rolling land creased by arroyos and washes dry as a lime kiln.

"Well, if you set any store by that boy—an' I reckon you do—I'd not run on the rope to-day, by gum. I'd jest naturally act like I was mighty sorry the way things had turned out an'—"

"You want me to tell the Starks that Wils was to blame—after the old man had posted him all over the country? That it?"

"Not exactly, Pete. But play yore cards close. Lemme ride ahead an' see how things stack up. I'll bring Doc Sanders out to you an'—"

"I'm not going home without seeing Wils. You can't talk me outa that, Wes."

Privately Tapscott was of opinion that the Starks would never let McCann into their house alive. It was not reasonable to expect it, with old Matt lying there dead at the hands of Peter's son. But he did not say so bluntly.

"We'll see how it works out. Maybe they'll be willin' to let us move Wils. First off, we gotta find out what their intentions are. I aim to do that, if you'll stand back an' let me."

"I can do that my own self *muy pronto*."

"Sure enough, but I reckon their intentions might be different by the time you'd ripped loose with a few comments. Tell you our play is to smooth down their fur till we got Wils safe in our hands. A deef an' dumb blind man would get that without argument, Pete."

The owner of the Flying V Y looked across the soap-weed and the arrow-weed thickets to a grove

118

of giant saguaro on a hillside. The scenery did not interest him. It is doubtful if he saw any of its details, for his mind was wholly absorbed with his problem.

"Have it yore own way, Wes," he said at last. "An' if it don't work out I'll ce'tainly be right there with fighting talk."

"Don't I know you?" the majordomo went on patiently. "But I expect we'd better look at this from the Stark point of view jest a mite. The way they look at it we started this killing when we bumped off that rider McArdle."

"What's the sense in sayin' that when you know damn well we didn't?" Peter cut back irritably.

"I ain't claimin' we did. I'm tellin' you that *they* claim it. I'd give a plug of chewing if I knew who did dry-gulch him an' could prove it. But we'll never know, I reckon. Well, then Wils up an' gives Jas Stark the bud till the big bully-puss yelps like the cur he is. That don't set well with the Starks, who are proud as that Faro King Moses had to sic' the plagues on because he wouldn't give his folks a square deal. Top of that Wils kills old Matt. The whole clan of 'em are likely out for blood."

"What do they expect? Matt Stark served notice he would shoot Wils on sight, didn't he?"

"Yep. But you're not askin' them to be fair, are you? The point that sticks out like a sore thumb to them is that old Matt is dead an' Wils killed him. They won't look back of that an' in their place you wouldn't either. Use yore brains, Pete. Their fingers are itchin' to pull a trigger when they've got a bead on some of us. They're fightin' crazy likely. An' if I'd let you alone you'd play right into their hands."

McCann recognized the justice of his foreman's views. The situation was so delicate that it must be handled with wisdom to prevent an explosion that might be fatal to Wilson. Figuratively speaking, he threw up his hands.

"All right, Wes. I reckon you're right. You run it an' let's see where we get off at."

CHAPTER XVI

An Arrangement Is Made

PETER MCCANN and his son Lyn waited at the pass above the Circle Cross while Wes Tapscott rode down into the valley alone. They drew off a little way into the brush in order not to have to answer inconvenient questions in case someone chanced to come along the road.

The foreman held his horse to a steady road gait as any other traveller brought here on business might be expected to do. He had left his rifle with the McCanns. On his present errand it could not be of use to him and might serve to anger the enemy. His six-shooter he had thrust between his trousers and his shirt in front, for he wanted it very handy in case of need. He hoped not to have to use it. A gunplay would not only mean the failure of his mission but would probably be disastrous for him at such odds.

The afternoon sun was heliographing signals from the blades of the clicking windmill. A line of cattle, led by one bawling cow with neck outstretched, moved toward the watering troughs. Under the great live oak at one end of the house four or five saddled horses were hitched to the rack.

Wes rode leisurely across the open and swung

from the saddle. He was conscious that at least two men watched him. One was at the corral, the other lounging in the doorway of the house. Tapscott did not tie to the shiny bar, even with a slip knot. He might have to leave in a hurry. So he dropped the reins to the ground. Practically speaking, this would fasten the cowpony until he gathered up the reins again.

The Flying V Y man took a plug of tobacco from his hip pocket and helped himself to a chew. He saw without any visible concern that the man at the corral was running forward and drawing a revolver from its bolster.

Tapscott jingled his way houseward with the bowlegged swing of the dismounted horseman of the plains. "Hello the house!" he called.

The man in the doorway was Phil Stark. He was no longer lounging. He stood straight, face keen as a blade.

"What you doing here?" he demanded.

Then, before the words had died on his lips, he ran swiftly down the steps and joined the Flying V Y man. For there had come a puff of smoke, the spit of a bullet striking sand. The man running from the corral had fired.

Tapscott turned swiftly, hand on gun. But he did not draw. Phil Stark was between him and Carl Gitner.

"Put up that gun," the boy ordered the Texan. "Don't you see he's here as a messenger?"

"I see he's Wes Tapscott. Tha's enough for me," the hired bully answered heavily. "Get outa the way there, boy, or I won't be responsible."

Light footsteps sounded on the porch and the stairs. A slim figure flashed past Tapscott and joined Phil.

"Don't you dare shoot," Julia cried.

Out of the men's bunkhouse came Stone and at his heels Rafferty.

"Don't get on the prod, Carl," the ranch foreman shouted. "No sense in pumpin' lead till you know where you're at."

Gitner blustered, but he put up the weapon, growling something about a herd bossed by a cow.

To the Flying V Y man Rafferty put a blunt question: "What d'you want here?"

"I drapped in to see if we couldn't fix things up an' to get the correct facts. I'm hopin' the story we've heard ain't true," Tapscott replied amiably.

"What have you heard?"

"Well, mostly rumours, I reckon."

"If you think they're rumours what are you worryin' about?" Phil asked with a flash of bitter anger.

"Well, I ain't exactly worryin', but we've heard stories and o' course we're not lookin' for trouble, so we figured I'd better come to headquarters an'—"

Rafferty ripped out a sudden savage oath. "That lowdown mangy coyote Wils McCann waylaid

123

an' killed Matt Stark this mo'ning, since you're here for facts."

Mildly Tapscott protested. "I don't reckon Wils would waylay any one, Nick. Was any one else present? Who says he waylaid him? I know for a fact that Wils wasn't lookin' for trouble."

Phil's voice broke shrill and high. "Wasn't he? Well, he's found it. You go back an' tell them so that sent you."

"Meanin' he's been hurt?"

"Meanin' he's lying in the house here shot through an' through."

"Tha's bad."

"Bad for the McCanns," retorted Rafferty. "I reckon you ain't worryin' none about Matt."

"Tha's bad too," Tapscott replied. "I was hopin' we could patch up this range war before it got too late."

"You can't," Phil interrupted, with a touch of hysteria in his boyish voice. "Not till I've got two-three McCanns."

The foreman of the Flying V Y ignored this. He had not come to make or receive a declaration of war. "What does Doc Sanders say about Wils?" he asked.

"Gives him a day—or maybe two," Gitner cut in triumphantly, with a raucous laugh.

Tapscott looked through the Texan without apparently seeing him. But the blank hardness of his gaze softened as he turned to Julia. He had an appeal to make and he hoped that she would back it.

"How can I go back an' tell his old dad that? It'll sure break his heart. He sets the world an' all by that boy. What can we do? Does Doc think we could move Wils?"

"You'll not move him. He'll stay right here." Rafferty announced.

"Old Pete can have his body after he's dead," Gitner said brutally.

Julia addressed herself to Tapscott just as though the two men had not spoken. "No, Doctor Sanders says he can't possibly be moved."

"Then you'll let Pete see him, won't you, ma'am? You wouldn't keep an old man away from his boy, not at a time like this. That wouldn't be hardly human, I reckon."

"How about killing from the chaparral? Is that human?" Phil asked harshly.

"No, but it ain't proved he done that," Tapscott demurred. "I've knowed that boy since he was knee high to a duck, an' I can't believe it of him. But that ain't the point. His old dad is out there in the mesquite waitin' for me to bring him news of his son. What am I to tell him, ma'am?"

Julia's eyes were on a sudden little wells of brimming tears. She thought of her own father and of how he would have felt if she had been dying in the house of an enemy. She hated the McCanns, every last one of them. They had struck at her a mortal blow from which she would never recover. All her life she would cherish revenge. But even so she could not keep a father from the son whose life was ebbing. If she did that she would always despise herself.

"Tell him he can see his boy."

"If he feels like he wants to take the chance," Gitner added with an evil sneer.

For the first time Stone spoke, in the low drawl of the Southland. "If Miss Julia says Pete McCann can come here, why I reckon it'll be all right with you an' me, Carl, won't it?"

Gitner's eyes met his reluctantly. There was something compelling in the cool steady gaze of the little man, something that was a menace if not a threat in the even murmur of the voice. The big Texan said no more, but he said it sulkily.

Julia drew her brother aside and urged upon him impetuously her point of view. He listened, half resentful, half consenting. The trouble was that he did not know how under these difficult circumstances to live up to the responsibilities of the situation. The youth in him, the milk of his tenderness not yet dried up, appreciated and shared her feeling. But he had to remember his loyalty to the dead father within. He must not forget that for the hour at least, until Jasper should arrive on the scene, he was head of the clan of Stark. He was conscious of his inexperience, but he could not ask any one for advice.

Would it be construed as weakness for him to let Peter McCann into the house? Did his honour not rather demand that he shoot the man on sight?

The boy in him was for the moment dominant. "All right. Have it yore own way. I know you will anyhow," Phil said, a little sullenly. "Tell Tapscott to have him come down."

"No, that won't do, Phil. I don't trust that Carl Gitner. We'd better go and meet him, you and I. We'll ride one on each side of him."

To this Phil assented. He might be in doubt as to the right of permitting McCann to step upon the ranch, but he was quite clear that if the man came he did not want him shot down from the bunkhouse or the corner of the stable. Before he and his sister rode away with the Flying V Y man he had a few words with Dominick Rafferty, whom he knew he could trust regardless of the foreman's private feelings.

The three rode up to the pass and Tapscott waved his bandanna as a signal to the McCanns. There was an answering handkerchief, and presently Peter McCann and his son Lyn came out of the brush to meet them.

CHAPTER XVII

Enemies Meet

"MEET Miss Julia, Pete—Mr. McCann, Miss Julia. Her brother, Mr. Phil Stark—Lyn McCann."

Thus Tapscott, as self-elected master of ceremonies, by way of breaking the ice of a cold silence.

None of those named acknowledged the introduction in words or by an inclination of the head. They looked at each other with chill and bitter hatred. Steely eyes met rigorously, as rapiers cross, with ruthless hostility.

But, as the elder McCann looked at Julia, there came a change in his face. Beneath the shaggy brows she caught a glimpse for an instant of his soul. It was there, during the beat of a pulse, and was gone, a look that had amazingly softened the grim countenance. Later she was to puzzle over it and wonder at it. Now she could almost have believed herself mistaken. The brown rugged face was hard as chiseled marble.

"Well?" demanded Peter harshly.

"Doc Sanders is lookin' after the boy," Tapscott said.

"How *is* Wils?"

"Pretty bad, Doc says. Shot through the lung and in the side."

Not a muscle of the old cattleman's face twitched. "Can he be moved?"

"Not a chance. He's—a mighty sick boy, Pete."

"I'll go to him—right now."

Instantly Phil bristled. He would show McCann whether he could ride roughshod in this high-handed way to his end. "I'll have something to say about that."

Tapscott interposed, intent on keeping intact the truce he had arranged. "Hold yore hawsses, Pete. Tha's what we're here to see about. Miss Julia an' her brother here are actin' mighty reasonable, if you ask me. They say you can go down an' see Wils."

"One of you—not both of you," Phil cut in curtly.

Peter nodded. " 'S all right. I'll go."

"You'll go unarmed if you go."

There was a moment of significant silence while the eyes of the old and the young man clashed. "Let's get this right," McCann said. "If I go, do I go as a prisoner? Or am I free to leave when I want to?"

Phil's boyish voice lifted to a high note that was almost a wail. "My father's lying dead down there, killed by the son you're going to see. Some day we'll wipe yore whole damned outfit off the map. But not to-day. If you go in now you can walk out when you've a mind to."

"How do we know you'll play fair? How do we know some of yore killers won't shoot Dad?" Lyn asked.

"You don't." There was a flare of insolence in young Stark's scornful eyes. "We're not askin' him to come. It's his own say-so. If he's scared why he can stay away."

For the first time Julia spoke, eyes flashing, lips tremuluous. "We're not murderers like you."

"Now folks," interposed Tapscott hurriedly. "This is a mighty bad business all round. One thing's sure. We can't make it any better by that kind of talk. I'm dawggoned sorry myself, Miss Julia, about what's happened. I don't know the facts, but I'll bet my boots they ain't the way you think they are. I know Wils McCann. You don't. That's the difference. Now I reckon we got this all fixed up. You ride along with these young people, Pete, an' we'll stick around till we hear from you. So long."

They rode down from the pass in silence, the hearts of all three bitter with anger. In advance were the two young people, riding close together, without a backward look at their big bronzed enemy a few paces in the rear. But as they came into the valley the Starks fell back till he was almost abreast of them. They drew their ponies close to his, so that it would be difficult for anybody to take a shot at him without danger of hitting one of them.

Peter understood the manoeuvre and smiled sardonically. There was something amusing in this solicitude to protect him. In a day or two this boy and his allies would be laying plans to shoot him at sight.

As they came close to the ranch Rafferty cantered out to meet them. He looked at McCann with a hard defiant gaze, but he did not say a word to him. His horse fell into place beside that of the Flying V Y owner. The foreman was between Peter and the stable and corral.

In close formation the four moved to the porch and dismounted. Together they went into the house.

Julia led the way to the room where Wilson McCann lay. After stepping aside to let his father enter she left at once without a word. A Mexican woman was taking care of the sick man under instructions from Doctor Sanders.

"I'm making a nurse out of Ramona," the doctor explained. But his eyes were asking questions. They wanted to know by what means he had got here.

McCann moved forward and looked down at the restless figure on the bed. The young man's face was flushed. He was in a high fever and the glazed eyes showed no recognition of his father.

"Is he—so awful bad, Doc?" Peter asked, when he was sure of his voice.

"Mighty sick, McCann," the doctor answered gently. "If he wasn't an Arizona product, tough as cactus rind and clean-blooded as a young antelope, I'd say he hadn't a chance in the world. But he's liable to fool me yet."

"Don't you let him die, Doc," the father begged.

"Not if I can help it. If he lives you can thank Miss Julia. She looked after him fine till I got here."

McCann made no comment on that. "You'll stay right here with him?"

"Till morning anyhow. We'll see how he is then."

"How about sending for a doctor from Los Angeles or El Paso? It's not that I don't trust you, but if he'd have a better chance, why—"

Sanders considered. It would be two or three days before a specialist could arrive from one of the points named. The chances were that before that time the patient's life forces would collapse. But there was a possibility the boy might hold his own. Peter McCann would feel better if he had done all he could for him.

"All right. Wire for Doctor Elder from El Paso. He's a first-rate man."

Peter turned to the nurse and asked her in Spanish to bring Miss Stark.

Julia came. She stood in the doorway, straight as an arrow. Her dark eyes flashed defiantly into the light ones of the cattleman. She waited for him to speak, not asking what he wanted. And again, for an instant, she saw in his face the expression that had puzzled her before. All her life his name had been anathema to her. With youthful exaggeration she had as a child conceived him a prince of the power of darkness. Age had brought her a truer judgment, but she knew him to be hard and fierce as the Painted Desert. What was back of this look in his eyes, almost wistful and yearning, that broke through the cold mask? If it had not been for her father's body lying in the next room it would have disarmed her, for it undermined her prejudices. He was not an ogre, not a cold-blooded destroyer of her happiness. Or at least if he was that he was more, she suspected. She did not want to believe it, but she knew that there was a side of him human and probably likable.

"Miss Stark, I want to send to El Paso for another doctor, an' I want to stay here all night with my boy," he said.

It was on her tongue tip to tell him that he could not possibly stay, that neither she nor her brother would consider it. But her eyes were drawn past him to the stricken figure on the bed. Something in her that was deeper than hate, than the demand in her for revenge, stirred within her heart. She resented it bitterly, but she could not refuse.

"If you'll give me the message to your son I'll take it myself," she said.

Doctor Sanders wrote the telegram so that there might be no mistake in verbal transmission.

Julia took it and walked out of the room without another look at either of the McCanns. The circumstances which forced her hand were intolerable, she felt. But there was no escape from them. She was made to do things that looked like treason to her love for her father. But what else could she do?

Her pony was still saddled in front of the house. She rode out of the valley toward the pass, her body shaken with anguished sobs. Never before to-day had life seemed to her so empty and so futile.

A sound startled her. She turned, to see Stone riding just behind.

"Thought maybe I'd better drift along," he drawled. "You never can sometimes tell."

She choked down a sob and nodded thanks.

"I don't reckon I could help you any way," he suggested gently.

"No, it's—just the way things are. We have to let those McCanns stay here after—after what they did—"

The little Texan studied her a moment before he spoke. "It ain't been proved, Miss Julia, that Wils McCann did it."

"If he didn't, who did?"

"I'm not offerin' any opinion on that."

"Then why do you say maybe he didn't?"

His stony eyes were opaque. "Only a notion of mine."

"He told me he didn't do it," she replied. "But of course he'd say that."

"Would he? I ain't so sure. If he did it he'd keep

his mouth shut or justify himself. There's points about this thing that ain't clear to me yet."

"What do you mean?"

"Things I've noticed."

"Oh well! If he didn't do it he knows who did. It's all the same. They were lying in wait for Dad—he and his friends. What's it matter who fired the shot?"

Stone looked at her, strangely she thought, and looked away. "Maybe so."

CHAPTER XVIII

Cutting Sign

AFTER Julia had delivered McCann's message to his son she returned with Stone to the ranch. The Texan left her there and jogged down the valley along the road which Matthew Stark had followed a few hours earlier. It wandered up into the hills presently in the careless fashion of Western roads which do not have to remain on section lines but can travel all over the landscape.

Out of the brush a man rode to meet Stone.

"'Lo, Sam," the Texan said. "I asked you to be here because I want you to show me just where the old man was standin' when he was shot."

"Sure," agreed Sharp. He had not the least idea why the other wanted to know this, but he supposed he would find out in good time. If not, it did not matter. Sam was rather thick-headed. A good many fine points got by him unnoticed.

The two riders left the road at the place where Stark had hitched his horses and disappeared into the mesquite. Five minutes later Sam was showing Stone where they had picked up the body of his employer.

"Here's where he lay—an' Wils McCann was right over there. Miss Julia, she was lookin' after Wils. Say, I'm right sorry for that li'l girl. She

136

must be a sure enough Christian, her hatin' that McCann like she does an' having to save his life after he'd shot her paw."

"*If* he shot Stark," the Texan amended.

"Why, there ain't no question about that, is there? Miss Julia found him right there standin' over the old man."

"Which is exactly where he wouldn't a-been if he'd shot him. Maybe he would a-pumped another bullet or two into him from the brush after he fell. Then he would a-lit out. Looks to me like McCann heard the shot an' went to see who'd been hurt."

"Someone shot the old man. It don't look like if some of the rest of the McCann outfit did it they'd go away an' leave Wils wounded without lookin' after him."

"That's a bull's eye shot, Sam. They wouldn't. So we know Wils was alone."

"I reckon."

"Another point. Who shot Wils? Matt Stark didn't. Phil didn't. Miss Julia didn't. You hadn't got here, so you didn't."

Sam scratched his head. If this was a riddle he did not know the answer. "Blamed if I know. Who did?"

The Texan was quartering over the ground, examining it carefully. He looked up now to answer. "I don't claim to know—yet. But I'll say one thing. It ain't proved to my satisfaction that the same man didn't shoot both the old man an' Wils McCann."

"What would he want to do that for?" Sam asked, more puzzled than ever.

"I don't say any one did. I say it's possible."

"Now looky here, Dave. Looks to me like you're lookin' for Mr. Killer in the brush when you already got him rounded up. I ain't talkin' about the fellow who shot McCann. But take the old man. He gives it out in cold type that he aims to kill Wils McCann on sight. All right. He hears Wils is fixin' up this head gate an' he lights out hell-for-leather to get him. We all figure there's liable to be trouble between them an' we get busy to head it off. But we're too late. When we get here the old man's dead an' Wils McCann is standin' over him with a rifle in his hands. Great snakes! If I was on a coroner's jury I sure wouldn't bring in a verdict come to his death at the hands of a party or parties unknown. Not none. I'd name Wils McCann *muy pronto*."

"An open-an'-shut case, a fellow would say first off," the little Texan agreed with a smile. "But look at the other side. McCann's rifle was full up with shells. Not one gone. Are you askin' me to believe that he was packin' one extra shell in his pocket an' that he waited to put it in the magazine after he had shot Stark before comin' into the open? It don't look hardly likely, does it? Another thing. Do you figure *two* men, neither knowin' the

138

other was there, were lying in the brush at the same time an' about the same place to kill from ambush? Ain't that stretchin' this here long arm of coinsydence too far?"

"Well," demurred Sam, not convinced but for the moment empty of argument.

"This Wils McCann. I size him up a fighter but a game one. If he killed Stark it was in the open, an' I don't reckon the old man was give a chance for his white alley. He was plugged when he wasn't expecting it."

"We don't even know that. Maybe they met right here an' Wils beat him to it."

"No. He was shot from that ditch likely."

"Why from the ditch an' not from the brush?"

Stone showed his companion a clump of prickly pear standing on a sand hillock. Through two of the thick leaves a neat small hole had been bored.

"Here's where the bullet went after it passed through Matt's head."

"Great snakes! I'll bet you're right." The wrangler's forehead wrinkled in thought. "An' if it did the fellow must a-been lying in the ditch over there or mighty close to it."

They walked over to the irrigation ditch.

"Water runnin' in it," commented Stone. "D'you happen to notice whether there was any in it when you drove across with the buckboard?"

"Nary a drop. The ditch was dry as that wash there."

"Funny. Who opened the lateral headgate, do you reckon? An' why?"

"Ask me something easy, Dave. What the Sam Hill does it matter anyhow who turned in the water? Likely someone who needed it."

"What did he need it for?"

"Why, to irrigate."

"Might be so, but not likely at this season. The McCanns have a field of alfalfa they might be irrigating. I'd like to know if they are. You could ride over an' see, Sam."

"Sure. But why do you care?"

"I wouldn't hardly think they would be so keen on takin' care of that patch of alfalfa right after the rookus when young Wils was shot up. Here's the point, Sam, an' it sticks out like a sore thumb. The slit-eyed son-of-a-gun that shot the old man left a heap of tracks here in the soft sand at the bottom of the ditch an' in the clay just above. He had to light a shuck real sudden when Phil an' Miss Julia drapped in on him onexpected. But he was a heap worried about them footprints. So he beats it back later an' turns the water in to the ditch so nobody can cut sign on him."

"You figure maybe the McCanns—"

"Did I mention the McCanns?" the little Texan asked in a soft drawl. "Well, maybe I did. If they let the water into the ditch, Sam, why they'll carry their bluff through an' you'll find it trickling all over that alfalfa patch. But if some other mangy coyote did it, likely you'll find that grass still dry. Drift along, oldtimer, an' have a look. I got another hen on. *Adiós.*"

Stone rode slowly up to the headgate of the ditch, his keen eyes watching the ground every foot of the way. Once he dismounted for a closer inspection. At the junction of the ditch and canal he went over the sandy soil and studied it almost in microscopic detail. He spent nearly an hour at this before he remounted and rode away.

CHAPTER XIX

A Family Talk

JASPER STARK appeared at the Circle Cross toward evening. He swaggered into the house with the manner of a master.

Julia met him and drew him into the big room that served as the family gathering place. She could tell by his breath that he had been drinking. Yet she went into his arms and began to cry. There was no close bond of the spirit between her and this brother, but the terrible thing that had taken place drew her to him now.

"Oh Jas," she wailed. "Isn't it awful?"

"I just heard," he told her. "Been roundin' up cattle all day to sell. Fellow told me when I got back to Mesa. I came right out."

Her memories flashed back to what her younger brother had said. "Phil thought he saw you near the Three Cottonwoods. Were you up that way?"

He swept her face with a look of quick and sullen suspicion. "No, I wasn't. Nowhere near there. Why?"

"That's where Dad was killed. Someone shot Wils McCann there afterward. We thought maybe—"

"Well, you thought wrong," he interrupted

harshly. "But I hope whoever shot him did a good job."

"He's alive, but awf'ly badly hurt. He was shot through the lung and the side. Doctor Sanders thinks he hasn't much chance."

"Bully! Where is he at?"

"He's here."

"Here! Whacha mean?"

"I mean he's here in the house, too sick to move."

"You talkin' about Wils McCann?" he demanded.

"Yes."

"Who brought him here?"

"I did."

He exploded in a roar of rage, in crackling oaths of anger.

When for a moment he ceased to bellow Julia mentioned more information that added fuel to his fury. "His father's here looking after him."

"Pete McCann!"

"Yes. And there's no use shouting, Jas. Dad's lying in the next room, you know." She spoke quietly, looking straight at him.

His comment was at first both incoherent and violent. He stamped up and down shaking his big fist. It was not till he came to a specific threat that she interrupted.

"No, you won't, Jas. You'll not touch him. I told him he might come and stay."

"*You* told him. Goddlemighty, what you got to

do with it? Claim you're boss here now, do you? I'll show you about that."

Phil had come into the room and was standing beside his sister. "Gettin' down to cases, just what d'you mean, Jas?" he asked.

"Mean? Why, ain't I the oldest son? Ain't I runnin' the Circle Cross now? You can bet yore boots I am." He strutted up and down the room triumphantly.

"We'll probably run the ranch together, all of us. But that don't give you any license to cuss Jule an' you'll not do it."

The first sentence was the one Jasper's mind seized on. "Run it together. I guess not. Think I'm allowin' to have girls an' kids tell me where to head in at? I'm boss here now an' don't you forget it."

"Are you?" The eyes of the boy consulted those of his sister before he fired his bomb. "I reckon you're mistaken, Jas. Mr. Fletcher sent his black boy Tom out here last night with Dad's will. Right here in this room Dad signed it before witnesses. Jule an' I tried to get him to put it off, but he wouldn't listen to a word."

Jasper's face had turned a sickly yellow. "Cut me out of it, did he?"

"Yes." The boy did not add that Matthew Stark had said publicly to those present that Jasper was no son of his.

The older son snarled his resentment, using an

expression about what his father had done that set a spark to his sister's anger.

"You'll take that back, Jas Stark, or you'll walk right out of this house," she told him.

"Will I? Who'll put me out?" the man sneered. He was beside himself with disappointment, ready for any display of bad temper and malice.

"Don't get on the hook," his brother advised. "Say you act mean an' vicious. What good'll it do you? Soon as the will gets into court you'll be kicked out anyhow."

Jasper choked down his passion. What Phil said was true. He had no case for a fight in court. His only chance was that the other two children of Matthew Stark would reverse the action of their father. Sullenly he back-tracked.

"I didn't mean to roast the old man," he apologized ungraciously. "But it's rotten hard luck. I'll say that. Jule, you an' Phil wouldn't keep me outa my share of the property, would you? That would be a low-down trick, jus' because Dad got sore at me an' hadn't time to forget it."

"Phil and I haven't talked this over. We haven't even thought about it." She broke into sudden passionate protest. "I'd think, Jas, you'd have the decency to forget it till—for a few days anyhow."

"Easy enough for you to talk," he grumbled. "You haven't been kicked outa what belongs to you. Nobody's done you a meanness like they have me."

"We'll do what's right, Phil and I. But you can't come here and bully us. We don't want the McCanns here any more'n you do. We hate it—especially—"

She bit her lip to keep back a sob. Both the men knew she was thinking of her father. He would never storm at her again. He would never more take her into his arms and look at her with eyes of deep affection.

"Well, then, why not throw 'em out?" Jasper wanted to know.

"Because we're not savages. Because one of 'em is dying—and the other is his father. Can't you see, Jas? It's not what we want to do, but what we've got to do."

Her explanation was tearful. Why did she have to keep explaining this over and over to everybody she met? Why could they not understand?

"Folks are liable to do a lot of talkin'. I'll say that."

"Then they'll have to talk. We can't help it."

"I don't *sabe* this business, Jule," he told her, narrowed eyes full in hers. "What's back of it? What game are you playin'?"

A flush swept the girl's cheeks and died away leaving her white and still. She knew what he meant—that this was a covert insinuation of a love affair between her and Wilson McCann. A wave of nausea engulfed her.

"I think you're the most hateful man I ever

knew," she flamed, and went out of the room on a crescendo of sobs.

Phil missed the point but knew that his sister thought Jasper had insulted her. He asked a question bluntly.

"What you drivin' at anyhow?"

"Don't you get sore too, kid," the older brother answered. "I got eyes, an' I use 'em. She's mighty high-heeled, Jule is. But she can't draw the wool over my eyes. It ain't all Christian kindness that's moving her. Not on yore sweet life. You know what a li'l spitfire she is an' how loaded with temper. Well, she ain't turned angel all of a sudden. It's that Wils McCann. She's in love with him."

"What!"

"Sure as you're a foot high. There's somethin' doin' between her an' that lobo wolf that killed Dad." Jasper nodded malevolently and triumphantly.

His brother recoiled, hard hit. "I don't believe it."

"You'll see," Jasper promised, wisely.

CHAPTER XX

An Offer of Friendship Rejected

TO THOSE stricken by grief it seems at first that death has dammed the river of life and that its channel must be forever dry. But it is of the fortunate essence of our being that life flows on in spite of us. We are swept into the current, dragged out of the eddies into the swirl of the rapids. The very detail of existence so absorbs us that our sorrow is pushed into the background.

Thus it was with Julia in the days after her father's body had been laid to rest. Her time was very fully occupied, for she had inherited the joint management of large interests. Jasper still called the ranch his home apparently, though he was of no use whatever in looking after it. He was so sullen, his frame of mind so peevish, his nerves so jumpy, that he was much more of a liability than an asset. Julia did not understand him at all. It was not only that he considered himself ill-used. There was something on his mind that made him savage and irritable.

She found it quite impossible to discuss anything with him, for almost at once he flew into a rage. His idea of justice was that Phil and she should make out a deed to him of one third the property left by their father and should let him run the ranch according to his fancy without interference.

If he had been at all reasonable Julia would have been tempted to join with Phil in acceding to his demand. She wanted to be generous, to heal the breach. But she knew in her heart that if she gave way it would be weakness. She considered herself a trustee of her father's wishes and she did not intend to reinstate Jasper unless his conduct should justify it. In this Phil concurred. He knew, better even than Julia, that Jasper had flung away the reins of all self-control, that he was drinking heavily and spending his time with worse than worthless characters. In Mesa was a Mexican *tendejón* that had become a sink of iniquity where the scum of humanity gathered. It was known as Pedro's Place. Here Jasper went every morning and remained most of the day. If he returned to the Circle Cross it was late at night or in the small hours of the morning.

Wilson McCann and his father were still at the Stark ranch. The Mexican woman made the meals for Peter and helped wait on the son. Slowly, inch by inch, the young man was beating back the tide that had almost engulfed him. His strength began to renew itself. He was so nearly out of danger that the question of moving him became imminent. The negotiation for this took place between the owner of the Flying V Y and Dominick Rafferty. The foreman's instructions were to cooperate with the enemy-guest in making the arrangements. Neither Phil nor Julia ever entered the sick room or exchanged a word with the McCanns. If they met Peter in the passage they drew aside in silence to let him go by.

On an afternoon Julia made a suggestion to Phil that flushed his boyish face with pleasure.

"Let's go see the Gifford girls. We ought to show we feel friendly. Don't you think so?"

"Sure I do. If Ann will let us."

"You used to know them, didn't you?"

"Yes, before—before Nora went away. I knew 'em right well. But now nobody's welcome there."

"And Jasper knew them too, I've heard."

"Yep. Quite a few of the boys went there. Tom McArdle did—an' Gitner—an' I've seen Dave Stone there. They don't any of 'em go any more. Ann won't have 'em. Makes it mighty lonesome for Ethel. She's a mighty nice girl, Jule."

"Is she?"

"This is no kind of a country for her, with everybody against her except a bunch of rough men an' the bars up so's even they can't come. If you could make friends with her an' Ann—"

He left his sentence unfinished, but it was expressive as it stood.

"I'll try," she promised.

They rode up out of the valley toward Tincup Pass. From the distance came faint voices. The foreman of the Circle Cross was making a gather of beeves for the trail. The plaintive bleating of a calf just reached them.

Julia sighed. All of this was associated in her mind with memories of her father from the time when she had first been lifted to the back of a horse. It seemed to her she had passed none but happy days in that sun-kissed valley. Now war and rumours of war filled the air. Her father was dead, her brother fast becoming a ne'er-do-well. If there was a momentary truce with the enemy it existed only because the chief of the McCanns and his son were still in their power. She could see nothing but trouble ahead. It filled the air. Even the dear boy riding beside her brooded on vengeance. Her heart was stabbed by the thought that he too might fall a victim to this lust for destruction.

Through the pass they moved down to the desert, following a dry water-course to its parched and desiccated terminus. Against the drought of centuries still fought thin mesquite, clumps of cacti, some greasewood and palo verde. The horses trod over hot sand in shallow beds, so fine in the draws that the wind had winnowed it in waves banked behind the cholla or the prickly pear.

The girl thought of almost the last time she had crossed it, in the moonlight beside her the strong sun-browned man who had become anathema to her family. She had talked with Dave Stone. In her heart she knew that Wilson McCann had not killed her father. He had given her his word that he would not wage any but a fair fight. In spite of her resentment against him she believed he would keep his word. He was master of himself, and he would run a clean race.

The horses climbed the mesa where the sheep ranch had its headquarters. The young people rode past the feed troughs and the corrals to the house.

A shy-eyed girl came to the door to meet them. At sight of Phil her cheeks flew a flag of colour.

The boy swung from the saddle. "Miss Ethel, meet my sister Julia. She'll be right glad to know you."

Ethel Gifford's blue eyes filmed with tears when Julia came forward and impulsively kissed her. She was starved for affection. There was none of it in her life except that which came from Ann, who jealously protected her from any chance of it on the part of others.

"My dear, we're going to be friends," Julia said.

The other girl's lip trembled. "Won't you— come in?" she invited dubiously. Ann was away from home, but the thought of her obtruded. She would not like her asking the Starks into the house.

The visitors followed her into the low-ceilinged room. It was a homelike place, Julia saw in the first swift glance. In the deep windows of the adobe walls were potted flowers, geraniums, begonias, and fuchsias. They were curtained with clean muslin. A piano filled one corner. There was a small bookcase, and a set of Shakespeare held a prominent place in it. Navajo rugs covered the floor. On the mantel were photographs and a framed print of a Del Sarto madonna.

There was a moment of silence before Ethel explained that her sister was out at one of the camps. "But I expect her back any time," she added.

"I think she must be a pretty good manager," Julia said. "I hear you are doing so well. I am glad."

"If we could only sell out and go away," Ethel wistfully replied. "Perhaps we can when folks find out we're making money here."

"You don't like the desert?" the older girl asked.

"I hate it. It's . . . cruel." The soft voice broke.

"Sometimes," admitted Julia.

"It's . . . horrible. It . . . takes us and . . . crushes our lives." She flung out her hands in a gesture of passionate despair. "Folks that are good and kind—they change—and awful things happen."

"Yes," said Julia, struck by a sudden depression of sadness.

Ethel's sweet mouth quivered. "Oh, I'm sorry. I forgot—about you. I was thinking of myself. It gets so terrible sometimes—when I let myself think—"

She broke off. In her eyes was an expression of fear, of some haunting dread too great for endurance.

Phil's heart was very tender to this charming creature so soft and defenceless. It ached for her now. He wanted to put his arms around her and give assurance of protection against the ills she apprehended. The generous youth in him was eager to defend her.

But defend her against what? Not grief alone for her sister Nora's death had brought that stricken look into her face. There was something else—something sinister and evil that she felt like a shadow of disaster hovering over her life. What could it be? What had so moved her to futile and protestant outburst? Was it possible that some threat still overhung, one of the nature of which he was in the dark?

He sat there awkwardly, twirling a dusty hat between restless fingers, his back half turned to her in the fashion of the embarrassed rider of the plains. Though he ached to befriend her, the dumbness of his tribe was on his lips. He would cheerfully have gone out to battle for her against long odds, but he could not speak a word of comfort.

"Couldn't you and your sister come and stay with us a few days?" Julia asked, her fingers caressing the soft and dimpled cheek. "We'd love to have you?"

"Oh, I wish we could. But we can't. There's no use talking," Ethel cried. "It's sweet of you to ask us, though."

"Why can't you?" Julia insisted stoutly. "Your man can look after the place a few days."

"Ann wouldn't want to go. I'm sure she wouldn't."

A shadow darkened the doorway.

"Where is it Ann wouldn't want to go?"

Miss Gifford came into the room, a quirt dangling from her wrist. In an unlovely khaki divided skirt and spurred boots, a revolver cased in the belt at her hip, she looked very much a denizen of the desert. Her clothes were dust-stained, her face keen and brown. She was lean and wiry as the dogies in the hills. But she had an aspect of efficient competence.

"I was asking your sister if you and she wouldn't come and stay for a few days at the Circle Cross. We're—lonesome just now," explained Julia.

"No, thank you," Ann answered bluntly. "Other plans make that impossible."

"We'd so like to have you come," Julia persisted. "There aren't many of us women folk in the desert. Don't you think we ought to be friends?"

"Friends!" Ann's voice carried a laugh of scornful bitterness, a dry laugh far removed from humour. "Why not? When we have lived here

155

two years and none of you have come to see us, when you've all treated us as though we had the plague, when you've harried our sheep over cliffs and poisoned them, when your vile men—" She stopped abruptly, to add a moment later contemptuously, "Yes, let's be friends."

"Phil and I didn't do any of this, did we?" Julia asked gently. "Oh, I know you haven't been treated right. But give us a chance now. If you're generous you'll give us a chance to make up for it. We'd love to try."

"I'm not generous," Ann Gifford replied, and in her eyes there burned sparks of anger. "The less we have to do with any of you the better pleased we'll be."

"That's plain enough," Julia said stiffly. "It doesn't leave much room for argument. If you won't have our friendship, why of course we can't give it. You seem to think all the wrongs are on one side. Have you never thought of what it means to the ranchmen to bring sheep in to destroy the range they occupied first?"

"I see nothing to be gained by discussing it."

Phil spoke. "Miss Ann, some time you might need friends, don't you reckon? You can't play a lone hand 'way off here. You ain't livin' in Denver or El Paso. You seen yorself how it was with old Jim Yerby. He bust his laig an' would of died if Sis hadn't drapped around an' took care of him. You went up there every day an' looked after him.

156

Folks are dependent on each other in this country. You gotta have friends here. It ain't reasonable to say you won't have 'em."

"Can we pick our own? Or have you got to choose 'em for us, Mr. Stark?" Ann asked with obvious sarcasm.

"We ain't pickin' 'em. We're tryin' to say, Jule an' I are, that we'd like to be neighbourly even if you don't exactly want us for friends. Miss Ethel an' you, why you need good neighbours—"

"When we're looking for someone to neighbour with, Mr. Stark," Ann cut in with a swift flare of feminine ferocity, "we'll not choose any of the Circle Cross outfit."

"Why?" Julia asked.

"I'll not tell you why."

There was nothing more to be said. Ann had closed the matter by imperative veto. Phil longed for a rehearing, but knew it would be of no use. Better than his sister, he guessed at the grounds of Ann's resentment toward the Circle Cross. Most of the cowboys visiting the sheep ranch had come from the Stark place. He had heard whispered comment at the bunkhouse. Probably she had reason to think some one of them was responsible for the trouble that had come to her sister Nora.

His troubled gaze clung to Ethel. She had curtained her telltale eyes and was looking at the floor. For her his heart was wrung. So soft and young she looked, so little able to cope with the harsh world into which circumstances had flung her. This dewy-eyed girl was by nature dependent. Since he loved her, he longed for a chance to stand between her and the buffeting of fate. Ann's attitude was unjust. He knew that. But he was still a boy, and he did not know how to cope with it.

Reluctantly he followed Julia from the house and swung to the saddle.

They rode across the mesa and dipped into a draw. Round a sharp bend they moved—and came face to face with Jasper.

The meeting was a surprise to all three, to Jasper a disconcerting one.

" 'Lo, Jas! Where you headin' for?" his sister asked.

He murmured something about a calf cached by its mother while the cow went to the nearest water hole. The relevancy of this did not quite reach Julia.

"Where's the calf?" she asked.

He waved his hand behind him vaguely. "I was kinda lookin' for the cow. Figured it might be up at old Yerby's."

Neither Phil nor Julia was satisfied with this explanation but neither voiced their doubts after they had ridden on. He was going to the Gifford sheep ranch. Both of them believed that. But why? Was it possible that in spite of Ann's watchfulness he could be holding secret meetings with Ethel? It might be so. He was good looking in his way. There was a swagger about him some women found attractive.

Both Phil and Julia hoped that little Ethel Gifford was not one of them. Though Jasper was their brother, they much distrusted him.

CHAPTER XXI

Blackmailing

JASPER DID not ride up to the house at the sheep ranch and announce himself. He turned up an arroyo that brought him unobserved to a pocket in the hills where sahuaros dotted the slope. Here he left his horse and climbed to the rolling ground above. Carefully, so as not to be at any time within observation from the house, he worked his way to a grove of live oaks in a draw. From this he could look down on the ranch.

He laced his hands around his mouth and gave the hoot of an owl. Twice, at intervals of half a minute, he repeated this.

Presently from the back door of the house a slim and graceful figure emerged. As she walked lightly up the rise toward the grove a little breath of wind brought the print dress about her limbs so that the skirt clung to her knees and remolded itself at each step. There was something in the gesture of her fine and exquisite. She was like the flowers of the desert, of the cacti and the yucca, a flag of colour surprisingly flung out against a background drab and hostile. Yet she was unlike them in this; the bisnaga, the ocotillo, the prickly pear have their spines and thorns and barbs for protection, but this child had none. She was

160

wholly defenceless but for the quality of innocence in her that appealed to the chivalry of all decent men.

The man waiting for her in the live oak grove was not decent and he had no chivalry. His narrowed eyes gloated over the fluent grace of her young body. He absorbed her with his gaze possessively, ruthlessly. The clean sting of shame would never touch him.

Momentarily she stood silent, her breast rising and falling fast from the climb. After one swift glance her eyes had fallen before his.

"What do you want with me?" she asked at last.

The hateful note of triumphant victory was in his laugh. "What do you reckon I want with you?"

Voice and manner were so ribald that again the long lashes of the girl fluttered down to the hot soft cheek. A chill passed through her blood and left her drenched with dread. She knew measurably what manner of man he was—a coward, a bully, one who traded on a girl's fears to win his way with her. But because he was what he was, wholly unscrupulous, his lower instincts in the ascendency, she knew him to be dangerous as a rattlesnake. If he were frustrated he would strike to destroy.

The look on his face sent the colour flying to her cheeks. There was nothing in the armoury of her innocent and girlish coquetry to protect against such grossness.

"You—keep at me," she faltered. "You won't let me alone. If I had anything to give you—anything at all—"

She was considering in her mind, as she had done a hundred times, whether there was any way to raise money enough to buy him off, and she knew as she had each time decided that there was no chance of this unless she made a clean breast of her dilemma to Ann.

"I ain't onreasonable," he said. "I'm askin' you to marry me, girl. Do that, an' what I know will be buried. Fair enough, ain't it? You'll be makin' a good deal. I'll be some husband, if I do say so my own self."

At this she flared out. "Never! Never! No matter how much you bully me."

"Think not?" he jeered. "Lemme tell you this, Missie. I'm the kind of man gets what he goes after. I'm aimin' to get you like I done told you fifty times."

"I'd rather kill myself," she passionately cried, with the unconscious melodrama of youth.

"It ain't a question of you killin' yoreself, but of you sending yore sister to be hanged, or least-ways to the pen for life. You'll throw in with me or I'll sure enough put her through. I never rue back. Not me." He emphasized the claim with an oath. "You can't help yoreself. I got the dead wood on you, an' I'll certainly go through."

"You wouldn't do that," she begged, one hand

clasping the other small knotted fist in an agony of indecision. "No man would do that to two lone girls when—when things were like they were."

"Wouldn't I?" He thrust his face forward, lids narrowed so that his eyes were mere points of glittering light. "Grab it from me I would. I been done a heap of meanness lately an' I'm playin' my own hand."

"We've never done you any harm," she wailed.

"*Chieto, com padre*! What's eatin' you anyhow? Ain't Jasper Stark good enough for a sheep-woman?"

"I didn't say you weren't good enough. I don't want to—to marry you."

"Why don't you?"

"Because."

"That ain't a reason."

"I don't—"

She stopped. Her mind refused to let her utter the word love even in denial to him. It seemed a desecration.

"I'm mighty fond of you, honey, more'n of any girl I ever did see." His words were suave and his manner insinuating. He moved close and put his arms around her.

She shivered but offered no resistance. He was stronger than she. The weapon he held was one she could not parry. If he insisted on using it she must surrender, though the very thought struck all the warm joyous life out of her body. His ravenous kisses fell on cold lips and cheeks, on a soft throat line from which the pulse seemed to have died.

With a curse he released her. Ethel turned. Her sister was swiftly breasting the hill toward them. She must have seen, she could not have helped seeing, what had taken place.

Ann stood before them panting, eyes furious.

With an awkward swagger the man strode forward a step or two. "Pleased to meet up with you," he laughed. "We hadn't aimed to make any announcements yet, but since you drapped in why we gotta admit the corn."

The older sister looked at Ethel, standing there white and stricken. She did not understand, but she knew instinctively that the girl hated this bully and was afraid of him. Her fierce eyes went back to Stark and stabbed at him.

"Get off our land," she ordered in a low tense voice. "If I ever see you on it again I'll kill you."

"Like you did Tom McArdle," he suggested significantly.

The blood ebbed from her face, but the hard and shining eyes did not falter. "Who says I killed him?" she asked, almost in a whisper.

"Why, I'm sayin' it right now, an' I know another fellow who could say it," he told her exultantly.

"You're a prince of liars," she told him.

"Thought you'd get away with it, didn't you?

Thought nobody knew how you'd dry-gulched Tom at the cutbank? Pretty slick work, eh?"

"What do you mean?"

"You know what I mean all right."

He straddled, bowlegged in his leather chaps, fleering at her exultantly. Standing there with hands on hips, big and raw-boned, he tried to dominate her by sheer malignant force. The slim brown-faced woman looked like a child beside him, but she faced him without quailing. She might have stood for a portrait of quiet defensive resolution.

"I'm asking you what you mean."

"An' I've done told you. Plain enough, ain't it? You shot Tom from the brush, an' I can prove it."

The older sister turned to the younger. "How long has he been meeting you?"

"He came the week after—after he was killed." Ethel spoke in a low voice of distress. The pronoun of indefinite antecedent was quite clear to all present as to who was meant.

"And he has been here since?"

"Four-five times."

"Threatening you?"

Ethel nodded. The burden had been lifted to stronger shoulders than her own and she was ready to break down emotionally.

"That he would tell—what he claims to know about me? Is that it?"

"Yes."

"If you wouldn't marry him? I suppose he does you the honour to offer marriage. Or does he?" Ann spoke in a low clear note of concentrated bitterness.

"Yes."

"I'm on the square with her," Stark said virtuously. "Tha's the kind of a fellow I am. Like I done told her already, I ain't aimin' to be anyways onreasonable. I'm here as a friend, understand."

"But if she doesn't marry you I'm to go to the penitentiary. Is that it?"

"She'll marry me. I ain't worried about that."

"Or you'll send me to prison," the older sister persisted.

"Have it yore own way," he laughed brutally.

The pupils of her eyes dilated as they blazed scorn at him. "You yellow coyote! If there's anything that walks as low as you—"

His teeth showed in a snarl. "Tha's no way to talk to me, you crazy hellcat. I got you where the wool's short—got you right. Get on the hook with me, an' I'll sure enough put you through. Seein' as I'm drug into it, I'll serve notice here an' now that you can't come no cock-a-doodle-do stuff on Jas Stark. Not in this year of Annie Dominick."

"Do whatever you've a mind to do. But get off our ranch and stay off. If I ever see you on it again I'll pump lead into you—as I would into a diamond back." Voice and manner were full of disgust and bitterness. She felt degraded at having

166

to wrangle with him. It seemed to put her on his level. She was afraid of him, of what he knew and could tell, but deeper than her fear was the protective mother love that watched over her little sister and would guard her at whatever cost.

"I'll get off when I'm good an' ready to go. But get it straight, girl. It's a showdown. I'm tellin' you. Me, Jas Stark." He swaggered into the shade of a live oak and rolled a cigarette for effect. "I'm tellin' you that either Ethel an' me take a trip to the sky pilot or you take one to the pen. Understand?"

"I told you to go," Ann warned.

"Don't run on me," he advised savagely. "I'm dangerous, girl. Don't fool yoreself till it's too late. I want the kid, an' I allow to have her in spite of hell an' high water. What's the matter with me anyhow? What's all this big talk about? Have you got it in yore cocoanut that I ain't good enough for a damn li'l sheepherder?"

"You'd better go."

"What's the sense of all this the-á-ter talk? I'm makin' a reasonable proposition." He turned to Ethel. "Look here, honey. She ain't in this á-tall. It's between you'n me. Listen."

"I don't want to," she cried at him, a little hysterically.

"Well, you're going to listen."

He moved toward Ethel in his heavy domineering way. What his intentions were perhaps he did not quite know himself. He meant to take her into his arms and by sheer momentum ride down her will; just how, he did not know.

But Ann was taking no chances. Out of its scabbard she whipped the small revolver she carried. "Stop right where you are," she said.

His stride faltered. He stood still, taken by surprise. There was about her such an air of tense feminine ferocity that his purpose was shaken. He remembered that she could use a gun and had given proof of it.

"I wasn't aimin' to hurt her none," he explained sullenly.

"Get away from here."

He hesitated, his vanity in arms. The position was a humiliating one, but he did not see any way out of it just now.

"All right. It's yore say-so," he admitted vindictively. "But don't come belly-achin' to me when you get arrested. I've done give you yore chance an' you wouldn't take it. Suits me if it does you."

He turned and walked down into the arroyo where he had left his horse.

Ethel looked piteously at her sister. "Is it true— what he said?" she asked.

Ann did not ask to what she referred. There was no need to specify. In the forefront of both their minds was the death of Tom McArdle and Ann's relation to it.

"It's true."

They stared at each other, horror in their eyes.

"I . . . I was afraid so," Ethel murmured. "It's been awful for me too. I was awake when you came in that morning—and I knew something was wrong by the way you looked. I pretended to be asleep, but I saw you clean the rifle. You acted so . . . so kinda dead for days . . . like you were numb. And when this Jasper Stark came and told me one day when you were out that you had . . . done it . . . why I just knew you had."

She ended with a wail of distress.

They went into each other's arms and sobbed together. After a time, when they had cried themselves out, Ann told her story.

She had spent the night at one of their sheep camps and was riding home in the early morning when she met Tom McArdle. He had stopped her, though she had tried to push past him, and she had lashed him savagely in a spate of words for what he had done to Nora.

"I thought of her, lying out there under the ground in California, and of him riding around big as Cuffey," Ann said to her sister. "But that wasn't the worst of it. You know how he kept coming to the house . . . afterward, pretending he wanted to hear about our dear girl and all the time trying to make up to you. You know how I told him never to come again. Well, after I had flayed him that morning he bowed and thanked me with a sneer and rode away. When he got to the edge of the road above the cutbank he called to tell me he'd be over to see you Thursday. You don't know how hatefully he said it. Something in me snapped. I didn't have time to think. I just fired at him and he threw up his hands and slid from his horse down the cutbank. I didn't wait to see any more, but rode away fast as I could. For I knew by the way he fell that . . . he was dead."

"You poor poor girl!" Ethel held the slender figure close as though to keep her from the cruel reach of the law that was going to snatch her away and lock her up for years. "Oh darling, why didn't you tell me?"

"I don't care if you don't hate me for doing it," Ann replied brokenly.

So, with love, they comforted each other.

CHAPTER XXII

"Whatever Suits You Suits Me"

IT WAS characteristic of Jasper that he did not at once go to the authorities and charge Ann Gifford with the murder of Tom McArdle. Instead, he wrote an anonymous letter to Sheriff Le Page and accused her of it.

He did not want to burn his bridges behind him. It would be better, he reflected, to see what the effect would be of a covert imputation. Hank would very likely go out to the sheep ranch and ask questions. This would frighten not only Ethel but Ann too in spite of the high hand she had taken with him. They might come to terms. Anyhow, it could do no harm to wait a few days and watch developments.

Most of his waiting was done at Pedro's Place, a bottle in front of him. He sat there sulkily, mooning over his wrongs and making dark threats about what he intended to do in revenge. But as the days passed he grew impatient and decided to talk the matter over with Carl Gitner. It might be a good idea to send the big Texan up to the sheep ranch just to show the Giffords that he really had the goods on them.

The clear pale wine of the morning air enveloped Jasper as he rode out to the Circle

Cross, but the purity of a young world washed clean escaped him. He was no more affected by it than he was by the cool flecked sky, blue and silver above the cedar hills, which still kept the deep quiet of the dawn, beneath the mist, coloured like the bloom on a grape. Out of the cup of such a day one might be expected to drink fine thoughts, true and lovely. But this slouching rider's mind was full of suspicion, hatred, and filth. God had said to-day, "Let there be beauty," and no consciousness of it touched the man's sordid heart.

He had come early to see Gitner before the latter left for work that might take him a dozen miles into the hills. The Texan was not a good cow-puncher. He was a poor roper and he did not understand the ways of cattle. Most of his life he had spent around the gambling halls of Austin, San Antonio, and El Paso. But Matthew Stark had given him employment because he knew the feud would soon become acute and a man of Gitner's type might be useful. The fellow would make smoke at the drop of a hat. He could shoot quick and straight.

Jasper pulled up at the bunkhouse and swung down. Inside he found Gitner and Stone. The former was riveting a stirrup leather.

"Come to say *Adiós* to yore dear friend Wils McCann?" he jeered.

"Whajamean?" demanded Stark.

"Why, ain't you heard the good news?" Gitner

affected polite surprise. "Our dear guest's done mended so much he's allowin' to hit the trail to-day. The old man's comin' with a wagon to get him. Pretty soon, if Mr. Wilson McCann continues to improve, as the papers say, he'll be able to bump off another Stark or two maybe."

Stone was honing a hunting knife. He had acknowledged the arrival of Jasper by a nod. Now he spoke.

"Wils McCann didn't kill Matt." He said it quietly, without emphasis.

"Like sixty he didn't."

"How in Mexico you know he didn't?"

Gitner and Stark had demurred together and instantly.

"I use my eyes an' my brains, boys."

"Hmp! Don' look thataway to me. He was caught, you might say, right in the act." This from Jasper, with exasperation. "What's the sense in sayin' he didn't do it?"

"I went over the ground soon as I could an' read sign. Wils didn't shoot yore father any more than I did."

"Phil tells me you gave her an' Jule that line of talk, Dave. Tha's why she's lettin' this murderer get away from us." He ripped out an oath of savage anger. "I've a good mind to plug him from the chaparral my own self."

"I wouldn't do that, Jas. I'd hire someone. Maybe you could get Carl," the little Texan murmured.

The words seemed to fall almost casually, except for the fact that Stone's eyes were full on those of the man he addressed. They had a surprising effect. The red of Jasper's skin faded to a sickly yellow. His jaw dropped. He stared at the little Texan with eyes grown suddenly panic-stricken.

Gitner was made of stiffer stuff. He turned snarling on Stone. "What the blue blazes you mean by that?" he demanded with a series of crackling oaths.

Stone's face was hard as jade and held as much expression. "Why, what could I mean, Carl? Only that you're a better shot than Jas, an' if he wanted any killin' done looks like it would be reasonable for him to hire you to do it."

"Say, what's eatin' you, Dave?" Gitner's eyes were closely slitted. He had dropped the stirrup leather and his hands hung free for action. "I can understand plain talk, I can. If you've got any-thing to say, why now's a right good time."

The conch shell of the cook sounded for breakfast.

A cold lip smile was on the face of Stone. He too was alert to the least motion of either of the men before him, and no man in the territory was quicker on the draw than this small Texan.

"Not a thing, Carl, except that the breakfast horn's done blown. Whatever suits you suits me, breakfast or—anything you say."

Slowly Gitner's rigidity relaxed. Stone had declined to force the issue. So much the better. He, Gitner, would choose his own time. "I wouldn't drap any more jokes like that around, Dave. They're liable to go off an' hurt someone, don't you reckon?" he growled.

"Maybe so, Carl."

Stone sat down on his bunk and picked up the knife and hone. He had no intention of walking through the bunkhouse door in front of Gitner. His fellow-Texan was too undisciplined a ruffian, would be quite capable on impulse of pumping lead into his back.

It was not often that Carl Gitner let anybody reach the breakfast table ahead of him. He was what he called "a good grubber." But just now there was something even more important on his mind. He had to find out how much Stone knew and had not yet told.

"Lemme get you right, Dave. What makes you figure Wils McCann didn't bushwhack the old man?"

"Several things, Carl. First off, if Wils did it he wouldn't 'a' been found lingerin' around. More likely he'd 'a' been hittin' the high spots for a getaway."

Jasper spoke. "Likely he was aimin' to do that, but he made one big mistake. He came out of the brush to make sure the old man was dead."

"Why come so close? Why not take a coupla

more shots from the edge of the chaparral an' then light out?"

"Wanted to gloat maybe."

"Not likely. Another point. His rifle hadn't been fired."

"Nothing to that a-tall. Prob'ly he reloaded."

"Not unless he was carrying just one extra shell in his pocket to reload with. Point three. I cut sign on the ground an' I know Matt was shot by someone lying in the irrigation ditch. The fellow got scared afterward an' turned water into the ditch to wipe out his tracks. We know Wils didn't do that."

"We ain't claimin' he wasn't hunting in couples. Some other of his outfit was with him."

"Think so, Carl, an' then ran off an' left Wils lying there without even takin' a shot at Phil?"

"He was plumb scared an' he lit a shuck *pronto*."

"Pass that then an' tell me who shot Wils."

A swift sidelong look passed between the others.

"How do *we* know?" Jasper replied.

"I'm not satisfied that the same guy didn't shoot both yore father an' McCann."

"Sounds reasonable," sneered Gitner. "Go ahead. Tell us who he is."

"I went up to the head gate an' studied the ground some. McCann's tracks were there. He'd been fixin' it. We know that. Covering his tracks in two places there was the print of a big boot run over at the heel with a nail sticking out."

The eyes of Stone and Gitner were fastened as

though drawn together by powerful magnets. Jasper felt a cold chill at his heart. He flashed one look at Gitner's boots.

"How d'you know which was Wils McCann's track an' which wasn't?" Gitner asked.

"I took his boots later an' fitted them to the tracks."

There was a moment of chill sinister silence. Not for a thousandth part of a second did either Texan relax the vigilance of his gaze.

"Did you take any boots an' fit them to the other tracks?" Gitner asked, almost in a murmur.

"Why no, Carl. *Whose boots would I take?*"

The issue between the men had come to a crisis. To Jasper it seemed that in the sunny bunkhouse a bell of death was tolling. No words were spoken. For that question was a low-voiced challenge. It called for an answer.

There was silence, heavy and oppressive, while one might have counted twenty. Watching Gitner closely, Stone could almost read his exact thoughts. Should he draw now and be done with it? Or had he better wait? The brutal impulse of the big man was to strike instantly, but the caution that had brought him through several killings urged him to wait. He was not looking for even breaks when he drew steel.

"Well, you know what you mean. I don't, an' I don't give a damn." Gitner turned, bravado in his manner, to Jasper. "Me, I'm headed for the chuck wagon. Get a move on you, Jas."

Stark breathed again. Carl had chosen to post-pone the question of the day to a more favourable time.

The two men left the bunkhouse together. Through the open door Stone watched them walk to the eating room. He had done an unwise thing, some men would have said. At least he had done it on purpose. He had smoked them into the open. Beyond a reasonable doubt he was convinced that he had found the man who had shot Matthew Stark and Wilson McCann. He had made a guess that was a centre shot.

That he had endangered his own life he knew. Gitner was a known killer. He would not rest until he had put an end to the man who knew too much, if it were possible to do it. The shot would be fired in the dark or from ambush probably, but that it would come unless forestalled was as sure as fate.

Grimly Stone smiled. He had carried his life in his hands for years. Come to that he was something of a killer himself. But he was at one disadvantage. He had never killed and he never would kill without giving the other fellow a show for his life.

Out of the situation he got one flicker of amuse-ment. He would be willing to give odds that when he saw Carl Gitner after his next visit to town the big man would either be wearing a new pair of boots or the heels of the old ones would be rebuilt.

CHAPTER XXIII

The Court of Public Opinion in Session

IT WAS Wilson McCann's first long ride since his recovery. The weeks had slipped away and his splendid vitality had asserted itself. Health had flowed back into his veins and he had gradually tested his strength by crossing his bedroom alone, by walking across to the stable of the Flying V Y, by taking short rides. Though still a little pale beneath the tan of his face, he was on the road once more to robust health.

To-day Wilson and his brother Lyn were jogging along toward Mesa. The fierce heat of summer was almost broken, but they still looked up into a brazen sky and clouds of alkaline dust choked them.

With an eye carefully measuring his brother's strength, Lyn suggested that they throw off and rest at the river.

"I'm kinda off my feed these days," he added apologetically.

Wilson smiled at this duplicity. "Suits me," he assented. "I'd hate to see you wore to a frazzle an' you with no more appetite than you got. I was worried about you travelling so far on nothing but nine flannel cakes, eleven biscuits, two-three eggs, one small steak no bigger than a plate, an' three cups o' coffee."

"It ain't what a man eats, but how it nourishes him," argued the bronzed young giant.

At the edge of the dry river, in a little group of cottonwoods a couple of hundred yards from the road, they dismounted and Lyn unsaddled. With their rifles by their sides they lay down and Wilson rested.

"It does kinda take the tuck outa me," he admitted. "I reckon I'm not right stout yet."

Purgatory River the Indians called it from the Spanish name, or the River of Lost Souls, but the unsentimental cowpuncher had corrupted it to Picket Wire River. At this place and season it was a wide wash of sand stretching from bank to bank.

Lying on his back, one leg cocked over the other, Lyn mused aloud. "Something's changed Dad. He ain't so rambunctious since you an' him got back from the Circle Cross. All the boys have strict orders not to get into trouble with any of the Stark riders. He acts like he's bumped up against something that set him thinking."

Wilson thought of his father, big, strong, slightly bowlegged, hard eyes set in a leathery face, a dominating man with many friends and some bitter enemies. What Lyn said was true. There had come a change in him. He spoke less. His manner was gentler at times. More than once his oldest son had come on him in the dusk brooding in an armchair. This was not at all like the Peter McCann he had known a score of years.

"Figure it out for yoreself, Lyn. Julia Stark an' that young brother of hers saved my life an' kept right on saving it. They scared off the killer. They took me home an' looked after me. They sent for Doc Sanders. She nursed me, that girl did, like I was her brother, though her father lay dead beside me an' she thought I'd killed him. They let Dad come an' live in the house, an' every minute of the time they watched to see we weren't shot while we were there. Do you reckon, if they had been given half a chance Jas Stark an' that Gitner would ever have let us get away from there alive? Not on yore tintype. But the girl an' young Phil an' Stone an' Rafferty rode with us, bunched round the wagon, till we met up with the boys. That puts it right up to us, don't it? Dad's millin' this over in his head. He's a white man, Peter McCann is. He's figurin' on finding a way out that won't leave him feeling like a coyote."

"How about you?"

"I'll not crook a finger against one of 'em. How can I now?"

"What kind of girl is she?" Lyn asked, his curiosity stirred. "She used to be a regular li'l catamount at school."

Wilson measured his words carefully to achieve a dispassionate manner of casual criticism. "I reckon she's got that temper yet. There's most usually a breeze around her neighborhood, I notice. A sure enough li'l ginger mill. She's let

181

loose on me some. O' course she hates the ground I walk on. Naturally she would, since she figures I shot her father. But she's all right, Lyn—there every way, high, low, jack an' the game. I don't quite know how to tell you what she's like. You remember that li'l palomino racer we usta have—what a fine high-strung, high-steppin' thorough-bred the filly was, game to the marrow an' true as steel. Well, that's Julia Stark."

Lyn rolled and lit a cigarette. "I ain't spoke a word to her since she was a long-legged colt with her mane all flying wild an' black eyes snappin' at you like live coals. But what you say goes with me. If she hadn't been there both ways from the ace she sure would have let you die the day of the rookus. Funny about women, how they tangle up the lives of he-men. When we was out on Tin Cup the other day Wes Tapscott got to talkin' about Dad an' Matt Stark. We was breakin' camp an' I was loadin' the crossbuck. He got to joshin' me while I was fixin' the lass rope to throw the diamond hitch an' somethin' I said reminded him of old days. Seems that Dad an' Matt usta run together when they were young. They skylarked a heap in Dodge an' Hays City an' Denver when they were out with trail herds. Seems they both fell in love with the same girl an' that busted their friendship wide open."

The older brother nodded. "Jessie Farwell her name was. She married Stark."

"It would be right funny if this Julia Stark was to put an end to this feud after her mother started it before any of us were born."

The brooding eyes of Wilson were not focussed on anything within range of their vision. He made no comment on what his brother had said, but his mind was full of it. Why not? Surely the thing she had done made it impossible for the McCanns to pursue the feud, to fight for hair-line rights bitterly and savagely. She had cut the ground from under their feet. If there was any generosity in them they would have to abstain from hostility even though friendship was not practicable.

"Do you reckon they're liable to push the case against you for killin' Matt Stark?" asked Lyn presently.

Wilson was out on bail furnished by his father. He had been formally arrested by the sheriff, even though it was understood that no conviction would be possible in Arizona after Stark had given public notice that he meant to kill young McCann on sight.

"I don't reckon," Wilson replied. "They haven't got a leg to stand on and they know it. Even if I had killed him I was justified."

"Who *did* kill him? You don't reckon any of our boys could of done it and be holdin' out on us."

"No, I don't. I'm not guessin', Lyn—not out loud."

Lyn suddenly sat up and listened. There had

come to him down the wash the sound of a horse's hoof striking a stone. Presently voices drifted to the two in the grove. In a feud country it pays to watch travellers whose intentions have not been declared. Both of the McCanns reached silently for their rifles.

Into view rode Carl Gitner and Jasper Stark. They crossed the dry river and passed into the desert landscape of light and colour and air. The McCanns watched them go.

It was Lyn who spoke first. "I'm wonderin', Wils," he drawled.

"Yes."

"Whether if those beauties had been here and we'd been ridin' across the river there we'd still be good insurance risks."

"One of us anyhow wouldn't; likely both of us."

"Both of us. They'd never a-let me get away to tell it. It's a cinch they wouldn't. That's one trouble in dealing with scalawags like them. You can't play the game their way, an' it don't make an even bet."

Presently Lyn resaddled and they took up again the sandy road. Bandannas covered their mouths like masks as a protection against the parching alkali dust. It sifted through, cracking their lips and burning their throats.

Half an hour later they rode into Mesa and drew up in front of Basford's Emporium. Public opinion sat on the porch in session. Simp Shell was there as usual, fat and overflowing, wielding a palm leaf fan when conversation momentarily ebbed. Basford lounged in the doorway. Doctor Sanders held down the top step, his back against a post. In a chair tilted to the wall, one high heel hooked in a rung of it, lounged Curt Quinn, just in from his ranch.

Simp was talking, guardedly. "Course I don' know a thing but what Hank told me. He got this anionymous letter an' he went out an' had a talk with her. She hadn't a word to say but just one thing: prove it." He broke off to greet the new arrivals. "'Lo, Lyn—Wils! How you makin' it? Doc here says you had a narrow squeak, Wils. Like to a-handed in yore checks."

"He ought to know," Wilson answered, smiling.

"Well, we're all mighty glad to see you 'live an' kickin', boy. Sure are."

"Same here," agreed the recovered invalid.

"How you feeling, Wils? Seems to me this is a right long ride for you to be taking so soon," Doctor Sanders said.

"Oh, I got restless to hear the gents' gossip circle," grinned Wilson. "What's the latest? After me comin' so far ain't you got a scandalacious story for me, Simp? None of the boys been misbehavin' a-tall?"

"Hmp! I reckon you know one of the boys who's been kinda in the public eye, as you might say, Wils."

"Maybe so. But he's an old story. Don't anything new ever happen?"

"Well, there's this anionymous letter Hank got."

"Hank who?"

"Hank Le Page—sheriff of this here county. Understand, I'm jest tellin' you what happened. Hank he got this anionymous letter tellin' him that Miss Ann Gifford was the person who shot Tom McArdle." Simp spread his fat hands in disclaimer. "Like I said before, I don't know a thing but what Hank told me. Course I've done heard rumours about reasons she might have for not liking Tom. I reckon you all heard 'em for that matter. Jas Stark says he heard her warn Tom never to show up at the sheep ranch again, or if he did she'd fill him plumb full of lead."

"Jas is tellin' that, is he?" Wilson's dry question implied a criticism.

"Told it right on this porch an hour ago. He acts sorta mysterious, like he could tell a heap more if he wanted to."

"I'll bet he could, too," Wilson said significantly.

"The sheriff went out to the sheep ranch and had a talk with Miss Ann," Doctor Sanders contributed. "She acted funny, he thought. Wasn't hardly civil. Good as told him to get busy and prove it if he could."

"Funny she didn't welcome him more cordial," the young man answered with obvious sarcasm. "You'd think she would ask Hank to stay to dinner when he come out merely to inquire if she murdered a man from the chaparral. I can't understand her being sharp about a li'l thing like that."

"Didn't know she was a friend of yours, Wils, or I wouldn't a-mentioned it." This from Simp.

"She isn't. Far as I know she's got no friends. You can put me on record right here as sayin' that this country here has been hog mean to those three girls on the sheep ranch."

"I've had notions that way myself at times," Lyn said, backing his brother. "We got off wrong foot first with 'em. Just because old Gifford was a stubborn cantankerous old son-of-a-gun don't prove his nieces weren't nice girls. We didn't give 'em any chance to show whether they are or not. Me, I got no use for a sheepman, but you got to treat women human."

"Because some darned fool writes an anonymous letter we've got to begin persecuting those two lone women again. We're certainly in fine business." Wilson spoke with heat.

"No use to get all het up, boy. We ain't persecutin' her none," Simp objected. "We ain't even sayin' she did it. What evidence there is against her is liable to come out now. Maybe she can prove an alibi. It's no penitentiary offence to talk, Wils."

"By Gad, it ought to be, for when you talk about a woman you damn her good name. What do we know about this? I don't suppose for a minute she did it. But say for argument she did. Maybe he needed killing. Maybe he wasn't a man but a coyote or a lobo wolf. You sit here like a lot of gossiping old women without any teeth. Give her a show, I say."

"You talk plumb eloquent, Wils," said Basford dryly.

"Say she killed a man, though I'd bet my boots she didn't. All right. What kind of man? How'd she come to do it? Why? What had he done to her or to those she was like a mother to?"

"We're not discussing the justification," Doctor Sanders replied.

"No, you're just hintin'. Come to that I've killed two-three men myself. So have you, Simp. An' you, Basford."

"I never did," Shell sputtered indignantly.

"Sure you have. Murder's in the heart. Tha's where it is. You don't have to pull a trigger to kill a man. You can kill him in yore thoughts. It's seein' red. It's bein' so crazy mad you'd do it in a minute if you seen a chanct."

"Oh, well!"

Young McCann had talked his indignation away. He relaxed to a grin. "Why, you bunch of onery old alkalis, that li'l woman on the sheep ranch is an angel compared to any one of you. I'll bet *you* never broke any laws, Simp, never did anything to go to the pen for. An' Curt, o' course *you* never helled around any, always led a nice quiet Sunday-school life when you was a colt. Stayed home nights. Behaved. You too, Basford. Walked the straight an' narrow trail, I'll bet."

Curt Quinn let down his chair and got to his feet. "The boy's right at that. Give the girl a chance. It ain't a square deal to go cackling round about this onless there's some real evidence. If Jas Stark claims to have anything up his sleeve let him play the card."

"You're damn whistlin'!" Wilson turned amiably on the fat man, his smile robbing the words of their sting. "Why, you durned old toughfoot, where did *you* head in from? I ain't ever heard tell of any pedigree you brought with you. You claim yore name's Simp Shell. Maybe at that it is. We ain't askin' questions about what yore oncet name is. We're givin' you the benefit of the doubt, old-timer. Not even inquirin' what penitentiary you registered at, if any."

Simp waved his fan, sputtering. "See here, boy, tha's fightin' talk if you only knew it."

Wilson's grin was friendly and disarming. "I don't really reckon they got the goods on you enough to put you behind bars. Likely you were too smooth to get caught. But oncet when I visited the pen at Santa Fé one of the prisoners sold me a wooden do-funny he'd carved out. There was some letterin' burnt on it. 'Them that hollers loudest for justice had ought to have it done to

189

them.' Me, I don't want justice done to Wilson McCann, an' I'm a tol'able white citizen at that. My point is that it ain't a man-size job to sit here on yore roosts gabbing about one poor woman who has had the cards stacked against her in this game of life."

"You make yore point stick out like a sore thumb, Wils," Quinn admitted without rancour. "An' before you begin on *my* pedigree I moves this gossips' aid society stands adjourned."

The motion appeared to be carried. Lyn passed into the post office, but Wilson stayed to talk of cattle and water holes and the fall round-up. He felt awkward and ashamed at his defence of the weak, as though he had been advertising his virtue. In this cynical old world no man likes to be caught doing good. Young McCann had much the same hang-dog abasement that he would have felt if he had been found stealing sheep.

CHAPTER XXIV

On the Homeward Trail

STONE HAD killed a white-tailed buck in the foothills of the Sierras. Phil was with him, and Julia. All three of them had left the ranch in the early morning, but the two younger people had not even had a shot.

They were homeward bound now, with night impending. In the valley darkness was beginning to fall, but long shafts of golden glow still ran along the mountain ridges and bathed their rocky slopes in splendour. To Julia the desert always symbolized itself in terms of life. She saw the flash of teeth in its eternal conflict. This little man riding beside her, so lean and sinewy and dangerous, so effective in meeting the conditions it demanded to endure, was a reflection of its gaunt persistence.

The long stratified escarpments of rock behind them began to lose their sharp outline. The lomas looked less stern, the mesas softer as detail blurred, touched by the velvet hand of dusk. Only the wine-red of the mountain silhouette, the terra-cotta yellow of an outstanding peak, still flung out the flag of waning day.

All day Phil had been preoccupied with an anxiety that now found words. For it is true that in the half lights and the darkness much is said that would not be uttered in garish day.

"I'm worried some, Sis."

"What about?" Julia asked.

"At Mesa yesterday I heard some gossip." He stopped, then added: "About Ann Gifford."

The Texan riding beside him gave by no outward action any sign of interest, but somehow Phil knew that he was intent on catching every word.

"Can't they let her alone?"

"It's something new this time. They say she shot Tom McArdle."

Julia flashed an indignant retort. "How outrageous! And senseless! What object could she possibly have?"

"They say—her sister Nora."

"What do you mean?"

"Why, that Tom was responsible."

"Oh!" The girl fell silent, her thoughts busy knitting together loose ends of gossip she had heard.

"They say she was coming back from one of her sheep camps when she met Tom. They had words an' she shot him."

"Who says so?" she demanded.

The boy hesitated. He could talk freely before Stone, for hard and tough though the Texan was, an accredited killer, both these young people sensed in him the same loyalty that bound them to Dominick Rafferty.

"Jas, for one," Phil gulped out.

"Jas!" Julia pulled up her horse abruptly. "What does he know about it?"

"Claims he practically saw her do it, him an' Gitner. They didn't see her shoot him, but they saw her ridin' away hell-for-leather right afterward, lookin' like she'd seen a ghost. That's the story."

Stone spoke for the first time. "Where'd you hear this, Phil?"

"In town—at Basford's, at the Legal Tender. Everybody knows it. They say when Hank Le Page went out to her place she wouldn't even deny it—jus' told him to prove it if he could."

"But Jas—I don't understand. If he saw her do it, or felt sure she had done it, why did he wait nearly three months to tell it? Why didn't he tell it then, or not at all?" Julia asked, greatly disturbed. She had a vague feeling that she was on the edge of a discovery that would still further discredit her brother.

"I don't know," Phil answered. "But what worries me is that the story is liable to be true. She might a-done it. She's thataway."

Out of the night came the Texan's low drawl. "You needn't to worry none, boy. She didn't do it."

"You think she didn't?" Phil turned with relief to Stone.

"I don't think. I know."

Julia turned white. "You don't mean that—Jas did it?"

"No."

"But you know who did?"

"I sure do."

"And you'll tell?"

"Yes, ma'am. I was tryin' to shield him, for Tom McArdle certainly needed killin'. But now that Miss Gifford's name has been brought into it I reckon he'll have to stand the gaff."

Both of the young Starks wanted to ask him who had done it. More than once the question almost passed Julia's lips. But there was something in the little man's manner that restrained her. If he wanted her to know he would tell her. She had a feeling that for the present the bars were up.

"Well, I'm glad Ann Gifford didn't do it," she said. "The poor girl's had enough trouble."

"Yes, ma'am," the Texan said gently. "She's had a right smart lot for a young lady who's certainly not deserving of it."

"If she wasn't so stiff with me—if she'd only meet me a quarter of the way—I'd ride over tomorrow and see her, just to show her we believe in her."

"I'd do that anyway. It would be right kind of you. She sure needs a woman friend. Old Jim Yerby is about the only one she neighbours with a-tall."

"Will you go with me?" Julia asked Stone. "You used to know her."

He hesitated. "I'll be in Mesa on this McArdle shooting business."

"Well, the day after—when you come back."

"I'll go with you if I'm footloose," he promised, rather evasively.

She laughed. "I believe you're afraid to go."

"Tha's no josh, Miss Julia. Ladies scare me."

"Some ladies," she corrected. "I notice I don't scare you any."

Snatches of thought began to race in the girl's brain. Usually when a man was afraid of a woman, unless he was her husband and had given offence to her, it was because he was attracted to her. She had observed a painful shyness on the part of the youths about her as a symptom of suppressed emotion. It was an unconscious warning they flung out to Julia to trim the sails of her manner to them. This Texan would not exhibit any awkward bashfulness. He was too self-contained, too much master of every nerve and muscle. None the less he might, within, be as much disturbed as they were. Why shouldn't he be in love with Ann Gifford? She guessed his age about forty, and in a man that is still young.

He had walked dangerous trails, had done dreadful things if rumours were true. But she knew instinctively that there still burned in him that dynamic spark of self-respect which justified him to himself. He had his standards, and he played the game by them. She had no more doubt of this than she had that such a man as Gitner had no standards.

Ann Gifford needed someone to take from her shoulders the heavy burden life had laid upon them. Stone was such a man, strong, quiet, self-reliant. He was dangerous to his foes, but it came to Julia with a flash of clairvoyance that the very qualities that had made his name notorious would be a sure protection to a woman like Ann.

When Julia looked at him again her eyes were smiling.

CHAPTER XXV

A Quiet Man Talks

STONE rode up to the office of Hank Le Page, sheriff, swung from the saddle, and dropped the bridle reins. The building was small and of one story, with the false front habitual to Western frontier towns.

The Texan walked with the slight roll of the dismounted rider of the plains, making music with his spurs as he moved.

Le Page looked up from the ledger in which he was laboriously entering some item of expense. "'Lo, Dave."

"'Lo, Hank!"

"How's everything?"

"Fine an' dandy."

The Texan found a chair, a cigarette, and a match.

For five minutes there was silence except for the scratching of the sheriff's pen and the gruntings with which he accompanied the manual labour of bookkeeping. Then, with a sigh of relief, the official closed the heavy volume.

He flung a leg over the arm of the chair and lit a cigar.

"Anything new, Dave?" he asked, relaxing.

"Not a thing with me. Hear you've hit a new trail in the McArdle case."

"Looks thataway. Some of you Circle Cross boys tipped me off that the Gifford girl was seen makin' a getaway from the place where Tom was shot. I went out to see her about it. She acted mighty funny."

"How?"

"Oh, kinda defiant. The li'l sister broke down an' cried. I couldn't get a thing outa her either."

"So you reckon Miss Ann did it?"

"Wouldn't it look that way? Tom McArdle had made his brags about the other sister. That was known. She'd warned him off the place, Ann had. Say they meet by chance an' quarrel. She's got a temper. Well, say it ripped loose an' she shot him."

"Looks reasonable."

"It does to me, Dave."

"Only trouble is, it ain't true."

"Think she didn't do it?"

And again Stone gave the answer he had given Phil. "I ain't thinkin'. I know."

The sheriff lost his manner of casual ease. His leg came down from the arm of the chair, the cigar out of his mouth.

"Did you say you *knew?*"

"Tha's what I aimed to say."

"How do you know?"

"Saw him do it."

"Who?"

"I'm allowin' to tell you who—presently."

"Hmp!" The sheriff looked at him, not without

resentment. "You've waited three months to tell me. Reckon I can wait another five minutes."

"Sure. Fact is, I didn't aim to tell you a-tall. But when I found out there was talk about Miss Ann —why, tha's different."

"Glad I started something at last," Le Page grunted.

"Might as well begin at the start," the Texan said. "I usta hang around the sheep ranch some my own self. Knew old Gifford when he lived at Santone, so I drifted in oncet in a while to advise Miss Ann. I got kinda suspicious of McArdle. He was one of these black-moustached lady-killers, good lookin' an' glib with his tongue. Nora was a mighty nice li'l lady an' I could see she had took a great fancy to him. What I was worried about was that she'd marry him, but that wasn't what happened. If I'd known what I knew later, that McArdle had a wife living at Prescott, well I'd sure have sat in an' took a hand. But you know how it is. I ain't any kin to them, an' anyhow I figured pretty soon Miss Nora would see how no-'count he was an' tie a can to him."

Le Page nodded. The Texan looked away dreamily and blew smoke wreaths. Presently he took up again his story.

"After Miss Ann came back from Los Angeles she wouldn't have any of us around. On top of the trouble about her sister some durn fools had killed a bunch of her sheep. So she jus' swept us all out.

Tom had been ridin' in to Tucson to see Miss Ethel while she was at school an' he tried goin' to the ranch. Wish I'd been there when he showed up, but I wasn't. Anyhow, Miss Ann gave him the gate. For that matter, the li'l sister was plumb through with him when she found out what he'd done."

"You're making' a long story of it, Dave."

"I'm comin' to business now. The mornin' Tom was killed four of us from the Circle Cross had a camp near the foot of Round Top. There was Tom an' Jas an' Gitner an' myself. We separated to pick up a bunch of *vacas* to drive back to the ranch. 'Long about sun-up I heard a shot right close to me, over to the left where Tom was. I rode thataway an' met Tom. He was laughing fit to kill an' right away began to tell me the joke. He'd just seen Miss Ann an' been devillin' her again. I didn't say a word but listened to him dig his grave with his tongue. What tickled him so much was that he'd riled her so that she'd shot at him an' he'd pretended to fall from his horse over a dugway like he was dead. I asked him what he'd said to make her mad. He'd told her he was comin' up to the ranch to see her li'l sister."

The Texan stopped. He looked out of the open door at a freight outfit coming down the dusty street. The mule skinner was using raucous and explosive language. Dave Stone did not see him except automatically. Another picture filled his vision.

"The Gifford woman shot at him an' missed," the sheriff prompted.

"Like I done told you. I said to him, 'You don't really figure on going back up to the sheep ranch after what you've done?' He come back at me right quick that he sure did. I taken a hand there an' then. I said he had another guess comin', that I wouldn't stand for it. He got mad an' wanted to know what business it was of mine. Then he began to lay the blame on what had happened on that li'l girl lying in her grave out in California. I told him what he was an' gave him first chance to draw. His gun was in the open when I killed him. It was me or him an' I beat him to it."

"I figured he'd been killed by a bullet from a rifle."

"He wasn't. My .44 carries the same bullet as a '73 Winchester. Tha's what fooled you."

"Jas Stark and Gitner didn't know you did it?"

"No. I couldn't prove it was a fair fight, so I rode back into the chaparral when I heard them comin'. Pretty soon I showed up an' they began to tell me how Miss Ann had shot McArdle. I'd a-told them how it was but I saw Jas was all for hushin' it up that she'd killed him, so I jus' told the boys I didn't believe she'd done it an' let it go at that."

The sheriff reflected. "I'll have to lock you up, Dave."

"I reckon so."

"Not that I don't believe yore story. But I'm sheriff of this county. It'll have to be looked into."

"Sure. But I've told you the straight of it. Would you mind sendin' someone out to the Gifford place to tell the young ladies that it's all right far as they're concerned?"

"I'll send someone soon as I can."

"Better jus' put it that we quarrelled an' I killed him. No use worryin' them with what I told you. I wanted you to know the facts, but there's no need of spreading 'em broadcast."

The sheriff assented.

CHAPTER XXVI

Gitner Makes a Suggestion

A PUNCHER riding the grub line passed the Circle Cross and stopped at the bunkhouse. Through the saffron-hued sand he looked at the shining mountains where the sun was sinking into a crotch of the saddle-backed range.

"I would of liked to a-got home, but I reckon I'll kick in here to-night," he told himself plaintively. It might be judged from the weak mouth and the retreating chin that he was the kind of man who rarely achieves his intention.

Jasper came to the doorway. "'Lo, Bud! Light an' look at yore saddle," he invited.

"I'd orta be pushin' on my reins," the puncher demurred. "My wife'll sure give me a cussin' when I git home. She knows I quit the Open A B three days ago because old Caldwell was in town an' seen me there. I had hard luck in Mesa. It's sure enough one high-tariff town."

His predicament pleased Jasper. He guessed that Bud had been "given his time" at the Open A B and had dissipated his check in drink and gambling.

"Chin Wong's restaurant is a two-bit one, ain't it?" he asked.

"Maybe so." Bud rubbed an unshaven chin.

"Say, I got kinda corned up an' I got a hangover this morning. Dog my cats, I'm dry as a cowchip. How about a li'l drink?"

"Might be arranged. Did you get nicked at Pedro's Place?"

"For forty plunks, in a stud game. My luck's something scand'lous."

The rider dropped from the saddle and came into the bunkhouse. After he had taken a couple of drinks he forgot the story he meant to tell about quitting his job because he didn't like the foreman.

"I'm sore as a toad on a skillet," he explained confidentially. "Me, I'm a top-hand with a rope. You know that, Jas. I aim to hold up my end always. I been through hell an' high water for that thirty-cent outfit. If I hadn't of I wouldn't make no holler at bein' give my time. Course I can get plenty of jobs. That ain't it. A friend of mine's brother wants me to take my roll over to the Diamond A an' go to ridin' there. 'Lo, Carl."

Gitner had drifted into the room and seated himself at the table. "Anything new in town?" he asked.

"Why no, I reckon not. Except about Dave Stone."

"What about him?"

Both of the cowpuncher's hosts had become instantly intent, but he failed to notice it.

"Why, he's been arrested for killin' Tom McArdle. Ain't you heard?"

"For killin' Tom McArdle. You crazy with the heat, man?"

"All right. If you don't believe me. He rode in to-day an' confessed to Hank Le Page that he done it. They had some kind of a row an' he plugged Tom."

Jasper drove a clenched fist down on the table. "He's lyin', to get that Gifford girl out of it. Why, he couldn't a-done it. We practically caught her."

The eyes of Gitner met those of Stark. A sly and furtive cunning filled them. The germ of an idea was filtering into that brutalized brain. It had not taken form yet, was still vague and uncertain.

"I dunno, Jas. Maybe he could. There was somethin' funny about the way he looked when he come outa that manzanita gulch, come to think of it."

"Whachamean?"

"Didn't you notice? He didn't really act surprised when he saw Tom lyin' there. He played like he was, seems to me. O' course if he waylaid Tom from the brush—"

Jasper started. The idea and its possibilities had come home to him. If it could be made to appear that Stone had shot Tom McArdle without giving him a chance for his life the Texan could be got rid of quickly. It was a country of swift action. Stone's reputation as a "bad man" would tell against him. Sentiment could be worked up. He had delivered himself into their hands.

If Jasper had not been thoroughly frightened he would not have jumped so eagerly at Gitner's suggestion. But he quaked like the coward he was at thought of what the little man knew. The terror of it walked with him by day and night. More than once he had wakened from sleep in a cold sweat under the delusion that an officer's hand was on his shoulder. Stone was dangerous, a ruthless tool of Nemesis dogging his footsteps to destroy him. He had followed Gitner's logic, that the only safety for them lay in putting an end to the man. But he had shuddered at the thought of actually doing it, of facing the danger that went with an attack upon so efficient an enemy as Dave Stone.

Now a way had opened, without danger, with no possible comeback. If Mesa rose up and lynched the murderer of Tom McArdle he could not be blamed in any way.

"Let's go to town, Carl," he proposed. "We gotta find just how things lay."

"Reckon I'll go back with you, boys," Bud said, willing to postpone indefinitely the meeting with his wife which promised to be a stormy one.

The three rode there together. They dismounted in front of Pedro's Place.

Gitner led the way to the bar. "Free drinks on me today, boys. Everybody welcome. Set 'em up, Pedro."

The process of working up public sentiment for a lynching had begun.

CHAPTER XXVII

Yerby Forgets His Snakebite Medicine

IN TOWN with a pack horse for supplies, Jim Yerby stopped at the Gilt Edge saloon to get a bottle of snakebite medicine. The oldtimer admitted that he never had been struck by a rattler but you never could tell when your luck would turn bad. He took the cure in advance to forestall the evil day.

"Three fingers of preventive, took twice a day, is better than a passel of cheerful remarks like, 'Well, Jim was a good ol' scout if he hadn't of been so onery,'" the little man remarked to the bartender with a grin. "Oncet when I was in the Strip trailin' a bunch of fuzzies I recollect a young fellow was in the rabbit brush clost to camp when a diamond-back got him. He passed in his checks before night. So I aims to be prepared."

While Yerby talked his quick beady eyes darted round the room on voyages of discovery. Something was in the air, something that caused unwonted excitement. The Gilt Edge was well filled and was doing a rushing business. This in itself was unusual for so early in the day. But that was not all Yerby observed. The patrons of the place were gathered together in knots, and at the heart of each group a man was talking in a low

urgent voice. Jasper Stark was one of the mur-
muring orators. Another was Carl Gitner.

The bartender took Yerby's money for the bottle
of liquor he bought but pushed back the quarter
proffered for the drink.

"It's on some of the boys to-day," he explained.

"A li'l celebratin'?" asked the nester with lifted
eyebrows.

"I reckon the celebratin' will be later," the man
in the apron said significantly.

Yerby sauntered to the outskirts of the nearest
group. It was the one in the centre of which Jasper
Stark sawed the air.

"You say he was our friend when he did it,"
Jasper was repeating, in a voice dry as a whisper.
"Leave it lay at that. Say he was. So was Tom.
But that ain't the point. I wouldn't make no holler
if he'd plugged Tom fair an' square in the open.
No, gents. I'd go through from hell to breakfast
for him. You're damn whistling I would. If it
had a-been thataway. Which it wasn't. Like I been
tellin' you, this Texas killer an' Tom had
quarrelled. Stone told Carl an' he told me that he
would sure get Tom. When we saw the Gifford
woman lighting out so sudden we figured
naturally that she'd done it. All the same both Carl
an' I thought Stone acted mighty funny when he
came outa the brush an' found us beside Tom's
body. He played like he was surprised, an' it didn't
get acrost to us. We suspicioned somehow he

208

knew more'n he said. Maybe he was in cahoots with Ann Gifford."

Yerby spoke up promptly. "Not on yore tintype. Miss Ann hadn't a thing to do with this. She's a right nice young lady."

Bleakly Jasper looked at him. He did not take kindly to opposition from one he considered a nonentity, but just now he could not afford to be deflected from the main issue.

"Sorry if I hurt yore feelings by naming yore sheepherding friends, Yerby," he sneered. "But leave that go. Say Stone played a lone hand. Question is: Can a Texas killer come in here an' shoot down our boys from the brush an' get away with it? I'll gamble on it he can't."

"Meanin'?" asked Yerby.

"Meanin' that the boys aim to take a hand *pronto*."

The nester knew the crowd had been drinking. He had met before the lust to kill that makes a mob cruel and inhuman. For some reason, he saw at once, young Stark was working up the men of Mesa to an act of summary vengeance.

"Hold yore hawsses, Jas. I'd like right well to hear Stone's story before you get rampageous. He's a killer, I reckon. Leastways he's got that rep. But he don't look to me like one of the kind that shoots you whilst he's shakin' hands with you. No sense in going off half cocked. It's mighty easy to bump a man off, but it would take God

Almighty to bring him back to life again. So I'm for going slow. Oncet at Tascosa, when I was a kid, we hung the wrong man by mistake—found him on a stolen hawss an' wouldn't listen to his story of how he got it. I wake up nights in a sweat about that yet."

"What's eatin' you, Yerby? This Stone has confessed he did it," Jasper interrupted rudely.

"Has he confessed he shot Tom from the brush?"

The shy and shifty eyes of the younger man met those of the oldtimer and slid away. "Not necessary. The facts show it. Carl an' I were the first folks on the ground. Tom hadn't fired a shot. The coward that shot him never gave him a chance."

"When you tell that to a jury—"

"We ain't aimin' to tell it to no jury. We ain't allowin' to let some slick lawyer talk him off. Not none. This town aims to see justice done, to show these bad men who come in an' kill our citizens that we won't stand for it a minute."

The gray-haired little man rubbed his unshaven chin and tried again. "Boys, it's a mighty serious business to make a mistake an' take a man's life without giving him a show to tell the courts his story."

A big hook-nosed man, the worse for liquor, laughed savagely. "You're right, it's serious. Dave Stone's liable to find that out. Jas is c'rect. This fellow had ought to be strung up to a telegraph pole. Me, I expect to do some pulling on the rope that's round his gullet."

The fierce murmur of assent told Yerby that opposition was useless. In the language of the house, he was on a dead card. Argument here was a waste of time.

He moved away reluctantly, forgetting to take his snakebite medicine with him when he left the saloon. For he was troubled. This thing was wrong, he felt. Yet he did not know how to prevent it.

At Basford's he found little encouragement. On the porch were Simp Shell, a cowpuncher whom he knew as Red, and Medford the tenderfoot clerk. The fat man wanted to know in his indolent drawling voice what was new.

"Why, nothing I reckon, except— Say, Simp, the devil's broth is brewin' in town to-day. The boys are aimin' to lynch Dave Stone."

"Looks thataway," admitted Shell. "I'm not for it myself after he come in an' give himself up— not till we hear the right of the story, but of course if they're hell bent on it—"

The nester shook his head. "Something queer about this deal. I don't get it a-tall. Me, I don't hold with these killers. Time we settled down an' became decent folks an' law-abidin' citizens. But there's somethin' about Dave Stone—well, I guess he's a killer all right, but I'd trust him all the way an' back. He's game an' he'll stay hitched. Tha's the way I size him up."

"But Jas Stark says—"

"I know what he says, an' wouldn't trust *him* any farther than I could throw a bull by the tail, neither him nor that Carl Gitner. They're bad eggs, both of 'em. There's somethin' back of this, I tell you, if we knew what it was."

"Stone had a talk with Le Page an' then shut up like a clam, I understand. Hank's gone to Tucson on business."

"He has?" Yerby's thoughts moved fast. "Then they aim—the Circle Cross outfit does—to get Stone outa jail an' hang him while Hank's away. They'll do it too, sure as you're a foot high." The little man's voice shrilled with excited protest.

"I ain't allowin' to stop 'em, Jim. Are you?"

"I don't know as I am," Yerby conceded reluctantly. "But looks to me like the decent citizens would get together an' serve notice that there would be nothin' doin' in necktie parties far as this case goes."

Simp's fat forefinger fanned the air. "Now tha's right where you're 'way off, Jim. If Jas was fixin' to hang *you* why I reckon some of us would wake up an' ask some questions. But this Stone—why, we don't care a billy-be-damn whether he gets hung or not. They're all in the same crowd— no'-count triflin' fellows hellin' around an' makin' trouble for the rest of us. If they string up this Stone, it makes one less of 'em. I wouldn't lose no sleep if three-four of the outfit was decoratin'

212

telegraph poles. Them's my sentiments, strictly not for publication. Wherefore I sits back an' watches events without being anyways on-easy in my mind."

"All I got to say is that Stone's sure gettin' a raw deal."

"Maybe, so, in this particular case. I don't claim to be a Bible shark, Jim, but you'll find it prophesied there that them who live by the sword shall perish by it. There's just one plain word for killers. They're cold-blooded murderers. Most of 'em would just as lief shoot a man in the back as in front. Point of fact they'd rather if they think they can get away with it, because there's less danger in it. You can't get me to shed any tears about this Stone."

Yerby tried one or two other representative citizens elsewhere and met with the same lack of response. The general sentiment was that neither Jasper Stark nor Carl Gitner were any good but so long as they confined their attention to Stone they might go as far as they liked.

The little man gave up with a shrug of his shoulders. The feeling of the town had its weight with him. After all Stone was a "bad man" and probably deserved the fate hanging over him. Yerby loaded his supplies on the pack horse, arranged the lash rope, and threw a squaw hitch. Presently he was out of town and headed homeward.

CHAPTER XXVIII

Ann Rides to Mesa

ON THE way home Yerby stopped at the sheep ranch to leave a sack of flour and some coffee he had bought for the Giffords. Ann came to the door at his call.

He carried the supplies inside.

"Miss Ethel not home?" he asked.

"No. She rode out with a message for Tony."

"Maybe just as well. I got news for you, Miss Ann."

A bitter smile broke the lines of her thin sardonic face. "News is always bad news for us," she said. "What is it?"

"I don't know as you could call this right bad news. That Dave Stone of the Circle Cross outfit has give himself up an' confessed that he killed Tom McArdle."

Ann was literally struck dumb with astonishment. She stared incredulously at the nester.

"That had ought to relieve yore mind some," he went on. "O' course I knew this fool talk hadn't a thing to it, but it's real satisfyin' to have folks know the truth an'—"

"Dave Stone says he killed McArdle," she repeated.

"Yes, ma'am. Come through clean as a whistle,

214

they say. Sheriff Le Page he give it out himself. I didn't get to talk with him because Hank's outa town. Gone to Tucson, I hear. I'm right sorry about that too, because he'll be needed in town tonight, looks like. Some of the Circle Cross outfit are makin' trouble."

"Trouble?"

"They're aimin' to break into the jail an' lynch Stone."

Beneath the tan the colour faded from the face of the young woman. "Because he killed Tom McArdle?" she asked in a hoarse whisper.

"Tha's why. Jas Stark is stirring up feeling. Him an' that Gitner. I tried to talk 'em out of it. Might as well have talked to a bunch of dogies. So I quits an' p'ints for the hills."

"I'm going to town," Ann announced. "Can you go with me?"

"Why, I reckon so," he replied, taken aback. "But Mesa ain't any place for a young lady like you-all—not to-night. The lid's off an' there's certainly going to be wild times."

"Will you saddle the buckskin for me!"

"Now looky here, Miss Ann—"

"No use for you to talk. I'm going."

"You can't do a thing. I know, because I did my darndest. They're hellbent on going through with this."

"I can tell them the truth—that I killed him myself."

It was his turn to stare. "McArdle?" he asked.

"Yes. You see why I've got to go. And hurry—please hurry."

"You killed Tom?"

"Yes. I'll tell you all about it on the way. But let's get started—please. We may be too late already."

Yerby went to the corral. He roped and saddled the buckskin while Ann changed her dress and wrote a hurried note to Ethel. This she left on the centre table under a paper weight made of petrified wood.

"Miss Ann, you ain't gonna be able to put it over," the oldtimer warned her. "I'm scared to death you'll git into trouble yore own self. A mob's a crazy thing. It ain't got any heart. It gets all het up till it hasn't got a lick o' sense. It's cruel as a bunch of lobo wolves. I hadn't ought to let you go to Mesa."

"I'm going," she told him with finality. "When I tell them I did it and why—"

"I've been in mobs," he persisted. "I've heard 'em roar when the pore devil they was waitin' to hang was brought out. It's awful. This one tonight will be full up with bad whiskey. I tell you it's dangerous to monkey with a mob—bad as it would be to go into a den of lions. They're liable to turn on you too, an' anything you say won't do Stone a mite of good."

"I've got to do what I can." She swung to the saddle and started down the road.

216

There was nothing for him to do but follow. But first he went into the house and got the rifle from the rack on the wall. Half a mile from the ranch he caught up with her.

When they came to a long hill and were forced for a short time to walk the horses he once more remonstrated with her.

"If it would do any good I wouldn't say a word, Miss Ann. But it won't. Like I done said before, they're liable to turn on you an'—an'—"

"Do you think I can sit still and let them kill a man I know is innocent?"

He knew by the set look in her young face, the intentness of her gaze, that she could not be moved from her purpose. But he could not consent in silence.

"He claimed he did it, Miss Ann—went in and told Le Page so. Whyfor did he do that if it ain't so?"

"I don't know." A faint flame of colour beat into the cheeks beneath the tan. "But how could he have done it when I—when I shot Tom McArdle myself?"

"If you'll tell me the story, Miss Ann—"

She told it, almost as she had done to her sister, just as she had gone over it in her own mind a hundred dreadful times. There was a relief in confession. The pent-up horror of her guilt seemed somehow not so awful after she had shared it with this simple man who understood and sympathized without exonerating.

His wrinkled leathery hand reached across to the pommel of the saddle where hers rested and gave a comforting little pressure. "I'm with you at every turn of the road, Miss Ann."

The young woman looked at him and nodded, a lump in her throat. Since life had wounded her so greatly she had tried to encase her heart in ice, resolved to fend off friendship. What others offered of kindly human contact she had rejected on the justification that in the end it would fail her and leave only more bitter memories. In the shame of her hurt she had hugged her passionate resentment, cherishing it as a virtue instead of the evil thing it was. To look at this brown-faced little cowman, whom she had helped in his need, was to know that his loyalty would never falter.

And there was another who had offered friendship and been rejected—the man who was lying in the jail at Mesa while the town seethed with propagated hate. Even now the mob might be storming the prison to blot out his life. In imagination she could see him, cool, quiet, master of himself in all the turmoil of the rage that surrounded him. He was dangerous, men said, of a cold and deadly temper it was not safe to cross. But the David Stone beneath this surface armour of defence was a wholly different one, Ann was convinced. She knew him kind and strong and steadfast. To save her he had taken on himself the burden of her guilt. He would not weaken. Even now, with the dread of his impending doom heavy on her, she thrilled with pride in him. If he died it would be for her.

They rode fast, for Ann was consumed with anxiety. She looked once and again at the ball of fire sinking behind the porphyry mountains. The fear flogged her that they would be too late.

Just before they reached the river a rider swung into the road twenty-five yards ahead of them. He had been cutting across country through the mesquite grass. At sight of Ann and her escort he reined up.

"Have you heard?" he asked.

"That you folks from the Circle Cross are workin' up the town to lynch Dave Stone? Yes, we've heard that," Yerby replied curtly.

Phil flushed angrily. He was much excited. "No such a thing," he retorted angrily. "There won't be any lynching if I can stop it. I don't get this business, but I'm dead sure of one thing. Stone never killed Tom McArdle unless he had it to do."

"He didn't kill him," Ann said quickly. "I did."

The boy's eyes grew big and troubled. "Then why did he say he shot him?"

"Because he was our uncle's friend and wanted to be ours."

Phil reflected on that and shook his head. It was an explanation that did not satisfy him. Stone was a hard citizen. He had lived among bad men and

219

been of them. Was it likely that out of Christian charity he would take the onus of another's crime? He said as much.

"Does it matter what his reason is?" Ann asked impatiently. "I tell you I did it. I shot the man and left him there. Surely I ought to know."

The horses were tramping through the heavy sand of the dry river bed. As soon as they had clambered up the bank the riders put them to a canter.

"We better slow up," Yerby said after a time. "Or our horses will be dead on their feet. My broomtail is 'most done now."

They did, for a few moments, then were off again. Half a mile from town, to Yerby's disgust, the young people urged their ponies to full speed. He tried to race in with them, but found it impossible to keep up.

The old ranchman pulled his horse to a walk. "I never did see such crazy foolishness," he fumed. "Kids! Tha's what they are. Just kids! An' they can't do a thing. Not a thing. I hadn't ought to have let that girl come. Sure as ginger's hot she'll get into a peck of trouble."

CHAPTER XXIX

Wils Promises to Try

ALMOST on the wings of the wind the news spread that the Texas killer was to be lynched for the murder of Tom McArdle. By word of mouth it came from the cowpuncher Red to Julia, who had just returned from a ride to the nearest neighbour to get a subscription for the new church fund. Red had wanted to stay in town and share the excitement, but he had agreed to skin a jerkline string to Monarch with supplies for the Ben Bolt mine. And he prided himself that he was a man of his word.

"Come night they'll sure put it up to Mike Rand to open the jail door an' turn over Dave to them. If he killed poor Tom McArdle like they claim he did hangin' ain't any too good for him. Jas has sure got the right of it when he says we hadn't ought to stand for them Texas bad men comin' in an' bumpin' off our own boys. Y'betcha! Mr. Stone can say *Adiós* to his enemies, for I reckon he ain't got any friends now."

The sound of her brother's name dragged Julia out of the shock the news had given her. "Is Jas mixed up in this?" she asked quickly.

It occurred to Red that perhaps he had been indiscreet. He went through the process of what he would have called stalling.

221

"Why, he's—he's in town, I reckon."

"That's not what I asked you."

"Well now, Miss Julia, I expect everybody's in it more or less."

He was putty in her hands. Inside of two minutes she had the truth out of him.

Julia was greatly troubled. In the past weeks she had come to know the little Texan. It was impossible for her to believe that he was a cold-blooded murderer. He had been a friend when she needed one, at a time when her own brother had failed. In the phrase of the Southwest he would do to tie to, she felt sure. Now, somehow, he was caught in this net and would be destroyed.

And Jasper was leading the mob against him— Jasper who had always claimed to be a friend of his. She knew her brother was not doing it because of his love of justice. Instinctively she felt, with dread, that there was some sinister motive she could not guess.

Like Ann Gifford her impulse was all for action. She could not sit down quietly and let events take their course. It was in her horoscope to be a good friend, to be no laggard in generous giving. Phil was not at the ranch. He could not go to town with her. But Dominick Rafferty could and would. She sent Red to find and bring him.

Unfortunately Rafferty was not to be found. Julia was sorry, for the foreman was a strong and forceful man. He would know what was best to do. She took with her instead the wrangler Sam Sharp, leaving word for Rafferty to follow as soon as they could get word to him.

They rode through the falling night. The stars were out when they drew in to the outskirts of the little town. An unusual excitement could be felt. Many people were on the streets. They gathered in small knots, their heads close together.

Julia stopped one hurrying man to ask fearfully if the jail had been yet stormed. At recognition of him she gave a startled little cry. The eyes that looked up into hers were those of Wilson McCann.

"Not yet, Miss Stark," he answered.

"And you—are you one of this brave mob?" she asked scornfully.

"No."

She forgot that he was a McCann, sealed of the tribe of the enemy. She remembered only that the life of a man she liked was in great danger. "Can't you save him?" she cried. "He didn't do it—not the way they say he did. I know better. He's not that kind of man."

Her appeal went home to him instantly. "I'll try."

"What can you do?" she asked eagerly, wistfully.

The sense of her sweet dependence flowed in on him like a stream of cold bracing water. He had not the least idea what he could do, but he was suddenly sure that he would find a way.

And Julia was sure of it too. This brown man with the steel-blue eyes, so light and strong of step, so perfectly poised that every attitude into which his powerful figure fell announced reserve strength, was one out of ten thousand. If it took a miracle to save the life of Dave Stone—well, somehow he would contrive the miracle.

"We've got to move fast," he said, his brain working as he talked. "I'll get myself appointed deputy sheriff by Mike Rand. You go to yore friends. Tell 'em what you've told me. Try to stir up an opposition sentiment. No use foolin' away time on yore brother Jasper or on Gitner. They're set on a lynching."

"If I could see Jasper—if I could talk with him—"

Even as she spoke an idea flashed into the mind of McCann. "Don't you," he urged. "I'll see him. I'll talk with him."

"You!" Her eyes dilated. "You don't mean—you wouldn't—"

"I'll not hurt him," he promised. "But there's just a chance I could persuade him to be reasonable. It may not work, but it might."

"You! How could you persuade him, when he hates you like poison?"

"I've got an argument that might work with him. No time to talk it over with you now."

"Well," she agreed doubtfully.

"That's my secret, how I figure on doing it." He

smiled up into the dark vivid eyes to assure her it was no dark and dreadful one. "Now we got to get busy right quick."

"Yes," came her obedient answer.

Afterward she was surprised at the meekness with which she surrendered to him, to the arch enemy of her family, the direction of her actions. It seemed natural at the moment to let this man decide what should be done and how. She did not question that he knew best.

"See everybody you can who might help," he told her. "My brother Lyn is in town, probably at the Legal Tender. He's a good man. Send for him. Tell him I'll be at the jail. If he can get half a dozen men with rifles it'll do the business. They'll have to come up the creek bed and in the back way. You keep off the streets yoreself. Outdoors in this town is no place for women to-night. Sam here will do yore errands for you."

"Sure will," Sam volunteered.

What McCann said was true. The streets were full of men loitering, men whispering together, men hurrying to and fro, but of women there was no evidence. More than one pair of searching eyes during that minute of hurried talk had challenged her right to be out.

"I'll stay in," Julia promised, an access of colour in her dark cheeks. "But you don't think—There won't be fighting, will there?"

"Maybe so. Can't tell yet. But don't worry.

Mobs most usually melt when they bump into someone who can't be bluffed."

He nodded, casually, and turned away. Her gaze followed him as he moved down the street, walking with the strong purposeful stride of one who knew what he was about to do and the best way to do it. A primal emotion, old as the race, surged up in her unexpectedly. It lifted her as the wave of a tide that crashes upon a swimmer. For the moment he was not the man she hated but the one who filled her life.

Before Wilson McCann put into execution the plan he had in mind he paid a visit to Mike Rand, jailor and deputy sheriff. There was a chance that a simpler method might save the life of the Texan.

The jail was already being watched, but after a few words with those in front Wilson was allowed to go in. The instructions of the armed men posted near were not to allow the deputy to pass out with his prisoner. Nothing had been said about people going into the jail.

"What you aimin' to do, Mike?" McCann asked the jailor.

"About what?"

"This lynchin' Jas Stark is workin' up."

"What do you reckon I aim to do?" Rand asked sulkily. "I'm sheriff here in Hank's absence."

"Meanin' that you'll fight, I reckon." McCann shook his head. "No chance, Mike. Let me light

226

out with Stone an' keep him hidden till this blows over."

The deputy rejected this proposition flatly. "No, sir. He'll stay right here. Hank left him in my charge, for me to keep in jail. That's right where he'll stay long as I'm runnin' the show. Once I turn him loose I'd never see him again."

"I'd agree to deliver him when he was wanted."

"Hmp! An' what would Dave Stone be doin'? No, sir. He'll stay right in his cell. That's where he belongs. If the mob takes him from me I can't help it."

From that decision Wilson was unable to move the deputy.

CHAPTER XXX

A Self-appointed Deputy

ON THE outskirts of the group that Jasper Stark was haranguing a Mexican appeared. He waited to edge in his message.

"Señorita Stark ees at the back door and weeshes to spik with you, señor."

Jasper frowned angrily. He understood what this meant. Julia had come to protest against the outbreak he was instigating. With the passing of the hours he had imbibed freely. A spirit of valiant Dutch courage animated him. He decided that he might as well put her in her place right now. She was always interfering with him, advising him, hectoring him. Once for all he would show her he intended to run his own business.

He strode out of the saloon into the starlit night all primed for a burst of indignation at her unwomanly conduct in coming to town on such an errand. It died away on his lips. Julia was not there. A man moved forward to meet him out of the darkness.

Jasper started. The heart died in him under his ribs. His valiancy was gone like the air out of a pricked bladder. The first swift impulse in him was to turn and run back into the saloon. But the man had stepped to the door and was barring the way.

"You lemme go, Wils McCann," he ordered. "I got no business with you." Voice and eyes both betrayed him. The one shook with fear, the others mirrored it. For it was in his thought that his enemy had lured him out to shoot him down.

"But I got business with *you.* Don't be so scared. I'll not hurt you if you're reasonable."

"W-what do you mean reasonable?"

"If you go with me quietly."

McCann had not drawn a gun. The only weapon in sight was the steady compulsion of two steel-blue eyes.

"Go-go where?"

"To the jail. I've something to say to you."

"Say it right here then." Jasper began to breathe easier. He was still very uneasy, but the panic that had taken him by the throat was subsiding. If McCann did not mean to destroy him, if no physical violence was intended, he could probably talk himself out of trouble.

"Not here. We might be interrupted."

"I ain't going a step with you." Suspicions were flying like blind bats through Jasper's brain. Perhaps McCann meant to draw him to a lonely spot and murder him. Perhaps he would step aside and let his friends pour buckshot into his victim.

"I won't hurt you if you come quietly," Wilson promised.

"You got no right to take me. You can't do it.

You're not the sheriff and you've got no warrant for my arrest," Jasper quavered.

"I know I can't, but I'm going to." Somehow a revolver had jumped into sight and was lying in McCann's hand, pointed groundward. "You walk on my right side, close to me, so's my arm will be under yore coat. If you try to run or call to any one, why I reckon that'll be suicide. I couldn't hold myself responsible."

"Wh-what do you want with me? Ain't we treated you decent? Didn't we let you live at the ranch whilst you was wounded? Now you come around all fixed to gun me," the big man whined.

"Tell you I don't aim to hurt you a-tall. Not if you don't start something. Walk beside me easy an' steady an' there won't be any trouble. Tha's right. I don't reckon the gun barrel will prod yore ribs to hurt."

They walked down the alley and crossed the street to the alley of the next block. This brought them to a dry creek.

"Go right ahead," McCann directed.

Stark drew back at the edge of the descent into the arroyo. His throat went dry. His stomach sank within him. Was he to be dry-gulched down in the cottonwoods at this lonely spot? Nothing could be more likely than that he was being led into a trap. It was the very sort of thing he would have contrived himself for an enemy.

Before he could speak he had to moisten his

lips. "You—you're aimin' to murder me," he managed to get out in a hoarse whisper.

"I told you I wouldn't hurt you if you were reasonable."

"Whacha want with me down here then?"

"I'm takin' you to jail, by the back way. Step lively. I've no time to waste."

The man in front of the gun shuffled down through the loose rubble to the creek bed. His fluttering heart was still panicky, for he did not entirely believe McCann. Nobody had seen them come here. It would be a good chance to get rid of him. All that was needed to destroy him was a crook of the finger.

But he had no choice. He moved up the creek bed in the darkness through the cottonwood grove, and as he stumbled forward he pleaded abjectly with the man whom he had more than once tried to kill.

"You wouldn't take advantage of me thisaway, Wils," he wheedled. "I ain't got a thing in the world against you-all. This family feud is plumb foolish. Tha's what I said to Jule. I says, 'Let's take Wils home an' nurse him.' I says, 'This shootin' was Dad's fault anyhow, an' Wils is a good fellow.' Honest to God tha's what I told her, Wils. We looked after you right at the Circle Cross, didn't we? Done everything for you that we could?"

"I'm not going to hurt you," the other said with

disgust. "No use lying to me. It don't buy you anything. . . . Move on up the bank here an' knock on the door."

Through the gloom the shadowy outline of a building had emerged. It was the back of the stone jail.

Jasper knocked on the iron-studded door. He knocked a second and a third time before the men outside heard steps in the passage and a cautious voice within.

"Who is it?"

"Wils McCann with a prisoner. That you, Mike?"

"Yep. It's sure enough you, Wils, is it?"

The deputy was already unlocking the door. His question had been surplusage, for he had recognized the voice. Nevertheless Rand's revolver covered the men as they entered.

"Whachawant?" he demanded.

"Why, I brought a trouble-maker along with me, Mike," answered Wilson. "I figured he was better here than shootin' off his mouth at the Gilt Edge. Got a cell handy for him."

"You've got no right to hold me without a warrant. I won't stand for it a minute," blustered Jasper, now much reassured as to his safety.

"Incitin' to riot, Mike. Better hustle him into a cell. This is liable to be our busy night. I'm going back to get that Gitner if I can."

"What for?" asked the deputy sheriff bluntly. "I

232

can't hold 'em. Think I can keep that mob from breakin' in soon as they get ready?"

"We'll talk about that later. I'll be with you an' likely some of the other boys. If we get these two birds in jail an' nobody knows where they're at the mob is going to drift around for awhile lookin' for its leaders. If we can stand 'em off a few hours there won't be any lynching. Mostly mobs are what you call temperamental."

Rand was Irish and ready to fight. If there was a chance to save his prisoner's life he was more than willing to take it. The appearance of a friend willing to play the game out with him was tremendously cheering. He knew the McCanns well. If they rallied to his aid there was a likelihood of success.

"Boy, I'm with you till Yuma gets snowbound," he cried with enthusiasm. "We'll put Mr. Stark in Number 40 an' give him a chanct to cool off."

Five minutes later a small coloured boy was giving a message to the big Texan. "Gen'lman says Mistah Stark would like for to see you at the back doah, Mistah Gitner."

Busy though he had been drinking and exhorting, Gitner had missed his fellow conspirator and wondered where he had gone. That Jasper should send for him to hold a whispered conference away from the crowd was quite probable. Gitner swaggered to the rear of the saloon without an instant of misgiving.

"Back in a minute, boys," he promised. " 'Bout time to start, I'd say."

He walked out of the back door straight into a forty-five, the barrel of which pressed against his stomach.

"Hands up, Gitner," came the hard crisp order.

The Texan had no option. His hands moved skyward.

Deftly McCann removed his revolvers.

"We're going down the alley," he explained in a low voice. "I don't aim to kill you unless you make some fool break. Do that, an' it will sure be yore funeral."

"What's the play, if you're not fixin' to kill me?" Gitner asked.

"You'll find out. Now move—not too fast—an' don't look back. I might change my mind."

The Texan moved. He never argued with a man who had the drop on him and meant business. It was safer to watch for a chance and plug the fellow when he was not looking.

Wilson followed at his heels, the gun under one edge of the coat he wore unbuttoned. They reached the street unnoticed, crossed it without observation, and passed into the gloom of the alley beyond.

"Where you takin' me?" Gitner growled.

"To jail."

"What for?"

"Raisin' a riot."

The prisoner made no complaint about the illegality of this proceeding. It was high-handed of course, but the man behind a gun has the privilege of being that if he chooses. There was no use trying to talk McCann out of the advantage he held. Gitner did not attempt it. His cunning mind concentrated on the practical problem of escape.

The chance came as they were picking their way down into the small gulch. It was so dark that McCann was following close on the heels of the other. Gitner stumbled and fell. His arm swept out, caught the younger man's legs below the knees, and dragged them out from under him.

The revolver flew out of Wilson's hand as he went down. Before he could stop himself he had rolled down the steep ground on top of the Texan. They went to the bottom of the incline together, now one and now the other on top.

In the scramble of wildly flying legs the two men clung fast. But in that instant, while they were locked in each other's arms, Wilson realized that he was no match for his opponent at this kind of rough work. He was lighter by twenty-five pounds and he was still weakened from the effect of his recent wounds. To survive, he knew it would be necessary to break the other's bearlike hug. Otherwise his ribs would be crushed and the breath driven out of his body.

They landed in the creek bed with Gitner on top. The Texan laughed in savage triumph. He had his enemy at his mercy and knew it, though Wilson was still trying with short arm jolts to the jaw to break the viselike grip that encircled him.

"I gotcha, by God," the Texan grunted.

He shifted his hold. One hand pinned down the fist beating like a piston rod against his face. The other found the throat of the prostrate man, the sinewy fingers tightening until McCann strangled for breath.

Wilson knew he was lost unless he could escape from the grasp of steel encircling his neck. Yet it was by no set plan that he hit upon a way of saving himself. In his agony he drew up his feet and straightened them with swift force. The effect was astonishing. Gitner let out a shriek of pain. His throat hold loosened momentarily. Again McCann brought up his heels and raked them savagely down the calves of the other.

Gitner tore himself free, cursing, and got to his feet. The man's trouser legs were shredded and his limbs bleeding. The sharp spurs on Wilson's boots had ripped through to the flesh and rowelled it mercilessly. He stood there cursing, furious with rage.

Before he recovered his reason the man on the ground covered him with his own revolver, drawn from the belt Wilson had fastened above his hips.

"Reach for the roof," McCann ordered.

The Texan glared at him savagely. His huge doubled fists worked spasmodically. He wanted to fling himself on this young fellow and stamp the life out of him. But under the menace of the forty-five he dared not attempt it.

McCann still struggled for breath in a world which swam in bubbles before his eyes. But Gitner did not know that. The big fists slowly moved up over the bullet-shaped Teutonic head.

"If I had a gun—"

The subordinate clause was a threat which needed no conclusion to be understood.

"I'm still borrowin' it. Don't you move."

Slowly Wilson rose. Every moment he was breathing less raggedly and was seeing more clearly. But he knew the pressure on his throat had been lifted not a second too soon.

"If you're quite sure—you don't want to start something, Mr. Gitner—we'll be moving on again," he said with an effort.

They travelled up the sandy wash, climbed from the creek bed, and were admitted into the jail.

"How's everything, Wils?" the deputy asked.

"Why, fine as silk. Brought you another prisoner, Mike."

"What's *he* been doin'?"

"Inciting to riot too. Can you give him a nice quiet cell all by his lonesome?"

"Sure can do." To his prisoner the deputy said: "Come right along, Mr. Gitner. Room 27 for you."

When Rand had locked up the Texan he led his friend down the corridor toward the office.

"You sure set a good example, Wils," he said with a grin. "Since you left I've had more visitors offerin' to help me outa the hole I'm in. Two of 'em."

"Good. If we get four-five fighting men—"

"One of these is a lady," the deputy explained dryly.

"A lady!" McCann's mind flew to Julia Stark. Had she been so unwise as to come to the jail with the idea that she could be useful? It would be like her. She was both impulsive and unselfish.

"Why yes, a lady! Come right in an' meet her."

Wilson followed him into the office.

CHAPTER XXXI

The Yell of the Man Hunters

BEFORE he had left for Tucson, Sheriff Le Page dropped in to Stone's cell. "If there's a thing more you need to make you comfortable, Dave— cigars or newspapers or a book to read—why, speak right up an' I'll see you get it."

"Not a thing, Hank. I'm doing fine. You're treatin' me like a parlour boarder."

"That's what I aim to do. You're no oiler in for stealin' a sack of flour like yore next-door neigh- bour. Well, if there's anything you want while I'm away holler for it to Mike. He'll fix you up."

Stone did not trouble the deputy with fussy requests. He was the type of man who lives within himself. Entertainment from outside was not essential to his well-being. Many a day and night had been spent by him alone in the Panhandle as a line rider. There had been times when after many hours of silence the sound of his own voice had almost startled him.

So now he read or lay on the iron cot and let his thoughts drift where they would. He found them turning, if he did not consciously direct them elsewhere, to a tightlipped young woman whose last word to him had been that she did not want him for a friend.

When Rand brought dinner in for him at noon Stone detected in his manner a note of silent evasiveness foreign to the temperament of the garrulous Irishman. Within five minutes he knew what was troubling the deputy. The town was "wilding up." Looked like Jas Stark and Gitner might get the boys to do some crazy thing or other. Everybody was drinking hard and talking foolishness.

Stone's impassive eyes fastened to his. "Meanin' just what, Mike?"

The jailor dodged. "You can't always tell what a mob will do when it lets itself loose."

"Allowin' to hang me, are they?"

"Well, Jas Stark an' that Gitner are tellin' how you dry-gulched Tom McArdle."

Stone nodded. "I know those birds. So they're fixin' to get rid of me? They would, of course. I've played right into their hands."

"They're hell-bent on it, looks like."

"What you going to do about it, Mike?"

"Well, I've wired Hank to come home an' I'm figurin' on swearing in some deputies to help me."

A sardonic smile touched the face of the Texan. "To help you protect Dave Stone, bad man' an' killer. I reckon you'll find the boys some reluctant."

It proved to be as the prisoner predicted. Rand returned to him in the middle of the afternoon. From the cot where he was lying Stone looked up and read failure in the deputy's honest face. The Texan put the open book he had been reading face down on the blanket.

"Well, you got the jail full of law-abidin' citizens?" Stone asked with gentle derision. "All of 'em anxious to go the limit for me?"

Rand's eyes confessed defeat.

"Don't worry, Mike," the Texan went on. "I knew it would be thataway. Question is, what do you aim to do now?"

"Darned if I know. This flimsy shack won't hold 'em out ten minutes," the jailor blurted.

"No. Do I get a chance for my white alley, Mike?"

"How d'you mean?"

"Do I get my guns back, so I can take Gitner an' Stark with me on this long journey?"

"I don't reckon that would hardly be right, Dave. You're a prisoner."

"You'll turn me over to be lynched, then, by two murderers who want me outa the way because they're afraid I've got the goods on them."

Rand had an inspiration. "No, sir. If it comes to a showdown I'll swear you in as a deputy," he promised.

"I'll promise not to throw down on you this time," Stone assured him with mordant irony.

During the long afternoon the deputy was in and out of the prisoner's cell a dozen times to consult him. The man on the bed looked at him, grimly amused.

"What's worryin' you, Mike? You're restless as grease in a hot frypan. They ain't fixin' for to hang you too, are they?"

The Texan himself showed no emotion or excitement. He faced imperturbably the shadows of darkness drawing closer to him. Whatever of despair he may have felt in his heart did not reach the chill mask of his face. When Rand came in he spoke quietly, in the low even drawl of the Southland.

"Grit clear through," the jailor thought admiringly. "He'll game it out without weakening."

Even when he was alone the prisoner did not allow himself the luxury of weak self-pity. His face had some of the expressionless self-containment of the professional gambler. Yet it had this difference; it was not a pallid bloodless countenance, but one into which sun and wind had beaten a smooth brown colour.

Through the window he looked down at Mesa, and he knew that the men hurrying to and fro on the streets were thinking of the fate in store for him. Above was a patch of Arizona sky, a vault of deep blue through which trailed shredded mackerel clouds. The sun rode high in it. When that ball of fire sank behind the porphyry hills he could just see over the high ground to the west, they would come to take him away and blot out his misspent life.

The chances were that he would never again see

the glory of a new day, the sunlight streaming across the silvery sage of the desert. Life was full of many pleasant things—of the song of birds, of the smiles of men he liked, of the dust of the drag drive with a saddle clamped between his knees, of camp fires when the darkness pressed in and restful sleep was near.

Sleep! Would he sleep forever after the next few hours? He did not know. It had always seemed to him that the future was a riddle man could not read. What was there beyond that great divide he would cross so soon? He paced the cell, brought sharply face to face with the question man has never answered wholly to his satisfaction.

He had lived hard, but on the whole clean. They had called him the good bad man because he never wasted his force in futile dissipation. Would that serve him where he was going? He smiled grimly, wondering.

Night fell. Stone walked to the barred window and looked out. The lights of the town were coming out one by one. He could see that the place buzzed with excitement like a hive of swarming bees. Main Street was full of moving people. They trickled in and out of the saloons constantly.

"Soon now," he told himself quietly.

He thought of many things almost forgotten—of schooldays in the small town where he had been born, of boys not recalled in years, of the scrape which had driven him to the Texas frontier. There came to him tender memories of the mother who had prayed over her wild son and passed on still hopeful of him. Scenes in his turbulent life, some of them detached and episodic pictures, jumped to mind vividly.

One of these showed a barroom, and inside it a swaggering bully and bad man "devilling" a boy of seventeen. It showed the flash of guns, the surprised desperado sinking slowly to the floor while the boy stared at him with fear-filled eyes at thought of what he had done. From the hour he had killed King Hill, in the eyes of the world David Stone had been marked with a brand he could not escape.

The door of the cell opened and Rand's head was thrust in. "Lady to see you, Dave."

Stone turned swiftly. A young woman was moving across the threshold of the room. He recognized instantly her slender erectness.

"You—Miss Ann!" he exclaimed, amazed.

She moved forward, and when she was close he saw that her face was working with emotion.

"Why did you do it?" she cried in a low voice.

"Do what?"

"You know. You know. Pretend that you shot Tom McArdle."

"Other folks were being suspected. I figured I'd better tell the truth."

"It's not the truth. You know it isn't. I killed him."

"No, ma'am. You thought so, but you didn't."

"How can you say that? I saw him fall from his horse when I shot."

"I'll tell you about that, Miss Ann," he said, and related to her the same story he had told the sheriff.

"I don't believe a word of it," she replied, and there was a sob in her voice. "You're doing it because I'm in trouble about it, and now—they're going to—to—"

"I know," he said gently. "Don't you worry, Miss Ann. I'm a hard citizen. Any one will tell you that. I'm only gettin' what's comin' to me. An' about McArdle—it's sure enough true. I killed him. If I hadn't of, how would I know he'd made his brags that he was comin' over to yore place even when you didn't want him?"

She could not wholly deny that bit of corroborative evidence. But she saw another possibility, a more likely one. "Maybe you found him before he—died. Maybe he told you."

He shook his head, meeting her eyes steadily. "No, ma'am. I told you the straight of it. He said something no decent man would say. I called for a showdown an' beat him to the draw. He had better than an even chance."

She threw out her hands in an impatient little gesture of abandon. "I don't care what you say. If you did it—and I don't believe it yet—you did it for me. You're shielding me now. That's why you gave yourself up, so that people wouldn't blame me. And I had treated you mean—wouldn't let you be my friend. Then you do this for me. But I won't have it. I'm going to stop it. I'll tell them I did it and they'll let you go." Ann ended on a rising note close to hysteria.

The gunman was close to death. The dull roar of its menace echoed up to him from the street a block away. He did not think of that now. In his blood there drummed a beat of joy. In that hour he was nearer to the woman he loved than ever he had been before. But no flicker of feeling was allowed to reach his poker face.

"Nothing to that," he said quietly. "This is a private grudge an' those holding it will git me if they can. You're not in this. What's the sense of you mixin' in? It won't help me any, an' you'll get in bad yoreself. It's right good of you to come to see me. I appreciate it. But it might make talk. If I was you I'd go straight home an' not say a word to any body. Maybe things will work out all right for me. You never can tell."

His coldness chilled her, but she would not give up. "Go home!" she repeated. "Leave you here to die when—when—" She put her hands up to her face and broke into violent sobbing.

The Texan stepped closer and touched her arm gently with his hand. "Don't you take on thataway," he begged. "Don't you."

After a time, through the catches of her breath he caught the answer. "What kind of a woman do you think I am—to go home and fold my hands while—while—"

"I think you're the salt of the earth, Miss Ann," he told her simply. "You've risked a heap in tryin' to help me—what folks will think, an' what this crazy mob would be liable to do if they found you here with me. It's the biggest thing any woman ever did for me—except my mother. But there's no way you can help me more than you've done already. So I say, don't get yore name mixed up with me in this. I'll likely make the grade. I've been in tighter places than this an' come through all right. Do I look like I was worried about it?"

Before he had finished speaking there rose a sound such as Ann had never heard before. It had in it something of the wild beast's triumphant scream when it has brought its kill to bay. At that yell of hundreds of voices answering the call of the old savage blood-lust she shuddered with terror. The dread of it crashed over her senses like a great wave lifting her from her feet. The room tilted and objects swam together in a haze of bubbles.

When her eyes opened she found herself looking up into the face of Stone. He was supporting her in his arms.

"You fainted," he explained.

An appreciation of the situation flowed back into her mind.

"I—was frightened. It's dreadful. If someone would talk to them, would explain things—"

He shook his head. "No use. They're beyond talk," he said quietly.

"But there must be some way. There must be," she pleaded desperately.

"We'll fight 'em off," he promised. "Time for you to go, Miss Ann. If Mike figures it's safe, have him let you out the back way. Then you go straight home. If they're all round the jail, go to the office an' stay there. Shut the door an' don't move from the room no matter what you hear. Folks may be runnin' round. Don't pay any attention to 'em."

She was pallid beneath the tan. Her lips trembled. He knew that she was shaky on her legs.

"If you die it will be for me," she told him in a whisper. "I'll never forget it—never as long as I live."

"I'm not figurin' on dying," he told her, with a steady cheerfulness designed to deceive. *"Adiós!* You'll have to hurry."

He had not removed his arms from her for fear her strength had not fully returned. Her eyes, with all the gift of her love in them, sank fathoms deep in his. Again he knew the exultant beat of drumming pulses. Unworthy though he was, he knew that she had given to him the inner citadel of her heart.

Because the end of the passage was so near for him and because he divined that in the years to come it would be a comfort to her, he drew her close to him and kissed her lips.

Then, without another word, she was gone.

Again there came to him on the light night breeze the ominous yell of the man-hunters.

Out of his eyes the tenderness died. They grew hard and cold as ice. Involuntarily he straightened his shoulders. Then he sat down on the edge of the cot to wait.

CHAPTER XXXII

Ann Tells Her Story

WILSON stopped in the doorway of the office, taken by surprise. The woman he saw was not the one he had expected to see.

Ann Gifford, pallid to the lips, came forward eagerly.

"Can you save him?" she asked.

"We'll try," he promised.

"He didn't do it. I did. I can't let them kill him. It's—awful." Her eyes closed for a moment, so that he thought she was going to faint. But she caught at the back of a chair and steadied herself. "I want to give myself up. If they must hang somebody, why—"

The young man's eyes picked up two others in the room, Jim Yerby and Phil Stark. He passed the question of her guilt as immaterial for the moment. The mob was in a hanging temper and would disregard any evidence she might offer, no matter whether true or false.

"You boys here to help Mike?" he asked crisply.

"Tha's whatever, Wils," Yerby answered promptly for both.

"Good." Wilson turned to Mike. "If Miss Gifford's story satisfies you, why don't you turn

Stone over to me as deputy to slip him outa town? I'll be responsible for him."

The jailor rasped his chin dubiously. "That ain't a bad idea either, if it's not too late. You mean for the rest of us to stay an' hold the jail."

"Make a bluff at it, yes."

"Question is, have they got the jail surrounded? They've got a dozen men with rifles strung out in front." This came from Phil.

"I just got in the back way, by the creek bed," Wilson said. "But we'll have to hurry. Get Stone, Mike—an' don't waste a second."

The Irishman nodded and left the room almost on the run.

To young Stark his inherited enemy gave orders. "Get Miss Gifford away from here. I'll have Mike let you out the front door. There won't be any trouble with the guards outside. They'll let you through, except maybe to ask some questions. Take her to the hotel. If yore sister isn't there they will know where she is at. Get hold of my brother Lyn an' tell him to come up the creek with what men he has gathered. The men on watch back there will figure they are part of the mob an' let them pass. When we hear an owl hoot twice we'll know he's there an' open the back door for him."

Ann demurred. "I don't want to go. I'd rather stay here so I can go out and tell the mob he didn't do it. I mean, if you and he don't get away."

"That would sure do a lot of good, about as

much as tryin' to persuade a hungry tiger not to make its kill." Wilson scoffed. His harsh voice softened. "If you want to help, there's a way. Go to the hotel and tell yore story. Or wherever Miss Stark is now. She's likely gathered a few good citizens. Stir 'em up to help."

"Well," she agreed doubtfully.

Rand came into the room with Stone. The prisoner's face was hard and impassive as rimrock. He looked round the room and nodded to those present.

"Ready?" asked Wilson.

The deputy sheriff handed a revolver to Stone. "Me, I believe this young lady's story. But I'm askin' you to give yoreself up whenever Hank calls for you, Dave."

"Yes," the Texan promised.

Rand led the way to the back door through the corridor. He unlocked the heavy door and stepped outside. A bullet flattened itself against a boulder two feet from him.

"Nothing doing, Mike," a voice called from the brush across the creek. "We've got you covered good an' plenty."

The deputy stepped back into the corridor and closed the door. "Too late. They'd get you both sure," he said.

"Yes," agreed McCann. "No chance."

They returned to the office. "They're watchin' the back way," Rand explained. "Now what about

Miss Gifford? Do you reckon she had ought to go?"

Stone and McCann answered "Yes" simultaneously.

"The sooner the quicker," Yerby added.

"Sure it would be safe for her?" Phil asked in a low voice.

"We'll call out first an' tell those in front she is coming, so there won't be any chance for a mistake," McCann said.

Ann looked piteously at the Texan and followed Mike without a word of protest. Her heroic gesture to save the man who had come to play so large a part in her life was under a veto of general masculine opinion. No doubt their view was a common-sense one, that the mob would listen to no explanation she made, but none the less she longed to try what still seemed to her the only simple way that might save bloodshed.

To the watchers outside, the deputy sheriff explained in a shout that a woman was leaving the jail accompanied by a friend.

"Let 'em come straight down the walk an' we'll meet 'em both, Mike," someone answered. "Hands in the air all the time an' no shenanigan. We're not takin' chances."

Phil and Ann were let out and the door locked behind them.

"Don't try to run or any other funny business," they were warned by one of the besiegers.

Hands up, they moved forward to meet the guards. Both of them were taken to the nearest light for examination. The man in charge of the jail blockade did not intend to let any trick be played upon him. He had heard of prisoners escaping dressed as women.

When he recognized Ann he took his hat off. But he held her for a short examination.

"What you been doing there, ma'am?" he asked.

"I went to give myself up. This afternoon I heard Mr. Stone had been arrested for killing Tom McArdle. I shot him myself."

The man laughed, grimly. "That's a new play, hidin' behind a woman. I wouldn't hardly have expected that of Dave Stone."

"But that isn't true," Ann cried. "I did shoot him. Jasper Stark and that Gitner saw me riding away afterward. Ask them. They can't deny it."

"We can't ask them. They've lit out somewhere, an' that's funny too. Know anything about it?" he asked suspiciously.

"No. But it's true. Mr. Stone hadn't anything to do with shooting Tom McArdle. I did it. If someone has to pay the penalty let me."

Another of the group laughed harshly. "Funny Dave Stone claimed he did it if he didn't. I reckon you thought up yore story a li'l late in the day, Miss Gifford."

"I didn't think it up. It's true. I shot him because— because of what he did to my sister. I was coming home from one of our camps when I met him. He tried to make up to me, so he could come and see—come and visit at the house. We quarrelled—and I shot him. You don't believe me, and it's the truth before God," she cried desperately.

"No, ma'am, we don't believe you. We think you're tryin' to save Dave Stone," the leader said, not unkindly. "No man confesses to a killing he didn't do. That wouldn't be reasonable. We'll tell Dave you done yore best for him. If you'll take my advice you'll light right outa town. It's no place for you to-night."

He turned to Phil. "Who's up at the jail with Rand? Anybody else at all?"

"Four others."

"Who?"

Phil looked him hardily in the eye. "I've forgot their names."

"Meanin' you won't tell?"

"Meanin' just that."

There was a short silence. "How come you mixed in this, Stark?"

"If Dave killed McArdle it was in a fair fight an' he was justified. I know that. Dave never shot any one without givin' him a chance."

"He's just a kid, Phil is," someone spoke up. "You know how kids are about gunmen."

"I wouldn't call Dave a gunman exactly," Phil protested. "He's absolutely square—an' he's game."

Ann broke down and between her sobs begged

for the life of her friend. She kept repeating that Stone did not kill McArdle, that she had done it herself, that he was sacrificing himself because he was trying to protect her. The net result of her passionate entreaty was that in their minds she convicted herself only of being in love with the Texan.

Phil escorted her, still shaken with sobs, to the hotel. They passed groups of hurrying, excited men. The question they heard repeated several times was as to what had become of Jasper Stark and Gitner. Two men stopped Phil to ask him if he knew where his brother was. He knew, but he did not tell them. They glanced curiously at his companion, wondering no doubt what she was doing here. They had heard her name in con- nection with the McArdle murder before Stone confessed he did it.

Ann found the hotel a nucleus of activity for the few who opposed mob law. Julia was here, and Sam Sharp and Lyn McCann. But the leader was a lean grizzled brown man, a trifle bowlegged, with hard eyes and shaggy brows. Peter McCann had been enlisted by Julia to support his son Wilson.

This was his busy night. He had no time for aimless conversation. With sharp incisive questions he drew from Phil the situation at the jail.

"You say yore brother an' Gitner are there too?" he asked after the boy had told the facts.

"Yes, as prisoners," Phil answered a little

sulkily. He did not enjoy surrendering command to these McCanns, as he had been forced to do both at the jail and here. "Yore son got 'em there somehow."

"How do you mean got 'em there?"

"Arrested the two of 'em, one at a time."

"Walked into their crowd an' took them away?" asked Peter incredulously. "He couldn't do it. No single man could."

"All right. He didn't do it then," snapped the boy. "All I know is that Mike Rand says he did an' claims to have Jas an' Gitner locked up in cells for inciting riot."

Peter's eyes were shining. If this was true—if Wilson really had carried through this cutting out adventure and arrested the leaders of the mob—he certainly would be proud of his boy.

Ann had been talking to Julia, who now interrupted McCann by leading the owner of the sheep ranch to him.

"Do you know Miss Gifford, Mr. McCann?" she said by way of interruption. "She has something to tell you."

Again Ann told her story of the trouble with McArdle that had led to his death. McCann listened and believed. It was possible that Stone's story was true too. Perhaps she had missed the range rider and he had been killed later in a fight with the Texan. Or perhaps, which was just as likely, the little gunman had made up the story to protect her. In any event, it was clear to him that Tom McArdle had earned his doom and that he had not been murdered but shot down after due warning.

There were half a dozen men in the room in addition to Phil and the owner of the Flying V Y. To them Peter gave instructions.

"There's two ways of doing this job, boys. One is for us to get inside the jail an' stand off the mob. We can do it, but there might be bloodshed. The other way is for me to step in an' take the leadership in this job. That last is how it will be. You boys will sift in among the crowd an' talk me up as boss of this *rodeo*. They're millin' around out there and don't hardly know where they're at now Jas Stark an' Gitner have gone. So I'll take charge. When I make a play you back it strong."

"But—what are you going to do?" Julia asked.

Peter looked at her, flushed and bright-eyed and quivering with life. She was a lovely picture of youth, and at sight of it his eyes for a moment played tricks with him. The girl he saw was the one he had loved and lost twenty-odd years before.

"I'm figurin' on playing their game. But we'll change it some. We'll be vigilantes and not lynchers. That calls for a trial. Don't you worry, Jessie. It'll work out fine."

Julia understood now, when inadvertently he had called her by her mother's name, much that had puzzled her in Peter McCann's attitude. She knew, by that sixth sense of intuition which women have, that this hard man was not indifferent to her. In his eyes, while he had been staying at the Circle Cross, she had more than once seen an expression she could not fathom. But she knew now what it had meant. She was very like her mother, and when he looked at her the hatred for her family was no longer in his heart. The memory of Jessie Farwell made it impossible.

"Can you save him that way?" Ann asked.

"If you'll come through with yore story clean, if you'll tell what Tom McArdle did to ruin the lives of yore family."

Ann shrank back, white-faced and trembling. "I couldn't—before everybody."

"Just enough so they'd understand," he said gently.

Julia put her arms around the other girl. "I'll be with you, Ann," she whispered. And to McCann she said: "Leave it to me."

The old cattleman nodded. He judged her competent to handle that end of the situation.

CHAPTER XXXIII

The Vigilantes

MESA boasted a band of six pieces, called upon for music on all patriotic occasions such as ball games and Fourth of July celebrations. The man who played the big drum was Medford, clerk at Basford's Emporium. Him the owner of the Flying V Y pressed into service.

They repaired to the steps of the Court House.

"Let her go, son," McCann ordered. "Kinda slow an' steady."

With heavy measured strokes Medford beat the drum. The sound of it filled the night. It arrested the attention of every man and every group within hearing. All knew it was a call to gather for concerted action. Within three minutes the court house square was full.

The slow reverberation of the drum died down. Peter McCann began to speak. He had been a politician and more than once had stumped the county for office. The gift of winning an audience was native to him, perhaps inherited from the ancestors who had come across from the Emerald Isle. He never had trouble in getting hold of those who listened.

Except for Matthew Stark, he had been for twenty years the dominant figure in that section of the territory. By sheer force and capacity he had won his way to leadership. He was strong of will and body, sure of himself, and quite fearless. Men sensed in him that indefinable quality we call character. Some hated, many liked, all respected him. In no community is such a man without influence. But on the frontier, where strength and gameness are qualities most in demand, he cannot fail of preëminence.

Before McCann had been speaking three minutes he was not only one of the mob but its accepted leader. His assumption to begin with was that Stone must pay the penalty of his crime. But Mesa was, he claimed, a law-abiding community. It did not intend that killers should come in and shoot down its citizens. All it wanted was to make sure of the facts before it proceeded to summary justice. To that end a court must be organized and the accused man tried. If he was found guilty of dry-gulching Tom McArdle, of murdering him without giving the range rider a chance for his life, he ought to be executed promptly.

"What's the sense in wastin' time on a trial when he admits he did it?" a voice shouted. "We'll hang him first an' you can try him afterward."

"Come up here, Kelly Brown," the big voice of McCann boomed. "Don't hide back there, but come up and tell me that to my face."

The man was hustled forward, against his

desire. He was one of the hangers-on at Pedro's Place, and his reputation was not good.

Peter caught him by the arm and dragged him up to the top step. "Now tell us yore idea of what's the right thing to do," he ordered.

"Well, he's guilty, ain't he? What's the use oratin' about it?"

"I'm talkin' about a trial. You say hang him first an' try him afterward. Is that giving him a square deal?"

"Did he give poor Tom a square deal?" the man asked doggedly.

"That's what we're here to find out. How about the time you were arrested for blotting the Circle Lazy H brand? Would you have enjoyed being hung first an' tried afterward?"

A laugh went up at Brown's expense. He tried to slip down into the crowd, but McCann held firmly to his arm.

"Not yet, Kelly. Let's get this settled. How about Stone? Is he entitled to a trial? Or shall we hang him on suspicion?"

"Why, any way suits me," the man evaded.

"Would any way have suited you that time I arrested you in the Catalinas?"

"Better give him a trial, I reckon," Brown conceded sullenly, caught in a trap from which there was no escape.

When McCann appealed to the amused crowd a few moments later his suggestion was carried by a large vote. After all there would be more enter-tainment in trying the Texan before they hanged him.

"Ain't we got to get our bird before we cook him?" another voice shouted.

"True enough, Bill," the cattleman answered at once. "No use spilling any good blood in gettin' him either. My idea is to go up to the jail an' talk this over with Mike Rand. I expect I can persuade him to turn the prisoner over to us."

"If he don't we'll sure enough break in an' get him," a cowboy called.

A committee was appointed to guard the prisoner when he should be brought out, after which Peter McCann went to the jail alone waving a white handkerchief borrowed from Basford.

The deputy sheriff admitted him. McCann followed the officer to the room where Stone, Yerby, and Wilson were waiting. He explained the facts briefly.

Rand shook his head. "No, sir, I ain't givin' up my prisoner to be tried by any mob. If you want him you'll have to come an' take him."

"How about it?" asked the ranchman, appealing to Stone. "I named the committee that will guard you. Good men, all of 'em. They'll stand put. Question is, have you got a case good enough to stand a fair trial? But I'll tell you this straight: it's that or lynching, and you can take yore choice."

"I killed him because he needed killing. I'm willing to stand trial on it any time. Tha's why I gave myself up," the Texan said quietly.

"Seems to be up to you then, Mike," the older McCann said bluntly. "Will you bring him out for trial? Or shall we break in an' get him. If we have to do that I won't answer for the crowd. They're some excited."

The deputy surrendered. "All right. I'll bring him out, but I'll be beside him all the time."

A huge bonfire had been lit in the square and by the light of it Stone was tried. Fletcher, the only lawyer in the town, acted as judge after a formal protest against vigilante proceedings. A cattleman named Haskell prosecuted. Peter McCann called upon someone to offer himself as attorney for the defendant.

After a pause his son Wilson spoke. "I reckon I'm no lawyer, but if Dave will stand for me I'll do my best."

The Texan nodded imperturbably. "Suits me."

There were only five witnesses. Jasper Stark and Gitner, released from solitary confinement, told of finding the body and of Stone's suspicious actions. Wilson cross-examined them very briefly, asking the same questions of each.

"Did you mention yore suspicions to any one then or later?"

Both of the witnesses remembered one or two to whom they had spoken their doubts, but the persons named were hangers-on at Pedro's Place, loafers of no reputation in the community.

"If you thought Stone killed Tom why did you tell Sheriff Le Page about Miss Gifford?" young McCann asked Jasper.

"I figured she might be in it with him."

"Then you told Hank about Stone—I mean at the same time you went to him about Miss Gifford? Or did you?"

Jasper squirmed. His furtive eyes went travelling on a search for supporters. He felt that the tide had turned. The eloquence that two hours before had poured out of him was dried up.

"I hadn't a thing to go on but suspicions," he growled.

"Have you anything more to go on now?"

"He up an' confessed, didn't he?"

"We'll hear his story. I'm askin' you for yours now," Wilson cut back curtly.

"Well, he'd told us he was allowin' to bump off Tom on account of being jealous of him."

"When did he tell you that?"

"Several times."

"Who was present when he told it?"

"Carl Gitner."

"Anybody else?"

"Not far 's I recollect."

"What did he say he was jealous about?"

"About Tom's stand-in up at the sheep ranch."

Jasper's manner was sulky and unconvincing.

265

His vanity was outraged because his enemy had marched him to jail and was now firing at him questions he had to answer. A short time ago he had been leader of the mob. Now he was, as he bitterly phrased it, nothing but a two-spot.

"You haven't answered my question. Did you or didn't you tell the sheriff your suspicions about Stone."

"No, I didn't," snarled the badgered man. "Tell you I hadn't a thing to go on but suspicions."

"You didn't mention to the sheriff that Stone had threatened to kill McArdle?"

"I don't know as I did."

"Why not?"

"Well, Stone's a killer. I'd want to be mighty sure before I claimed he did it," Jasper said uneasily.

"You mean you are afraid of him?"

"I didn't say that."

"No trouble between him an' you now, is there?"

"No-o." Beads of perspiration stood on Jasper's forehead.

"How come you to wait nearly three months before you told the sheriff about meetin' Miss Gifford near the scene of the killing?"

"I hated to bring her name into it, she being a woman."

Wilson had talked with his father a few minutes while the jury was being chosen. Roughly he knew the facts as to Jasper's relations with the Gifford sisters.

"Ever have any trouble with Miss Gifford?" he demanded.

The witness hesitated. "Well, she didn't like it when I said I reckoned I'd have to tell what I knew."

"Did she order you off the place and tell you never to show up there again?"

Jasper rubbed his unshaven chin while his eyes again went on a sidelong search for help over the sea of faces lit by the flickering flames.

"She was some excited. I won't say she acted friendly."

Young McCann moved a step closer. He waited a moment, to give full effect to his question. "Did you tell the Gifford girls that unless Miss Ethel would marry you her sister would have to go to the penitentiary?"

"No, sir," blustered Stark. "I never said any such a thing. If they claim I did—"

"Never mind that." Again Wilson waited for absolute silence before he spoke. He was sending a shot in the dark, but he guessed shrewdly it would strike home. "Is there any reason why you an' Gitner want Stone outa the way, any reason why you're afraid of him, anything he knows you're scared he might tell?"

Jasper's jaw dropped. For a moment he stared at his questioner, struck dumb. He had to clear his throat before he could answer hoarsely, in a low voice that did not carry conviction. "Not a thing."

Apparently he felt the impression his near-collapse had made, for he tried to strengthen his denial by iteration. "Why no, w-what do you mean? I—I—we ain't scared of him tellin' a thing. If he claims he's got a thing on me he's a liar."

McCann's next question seemed to be far afield, but nothing he could have asked would have so startled the crowd with a sense of impending drama. The words of the sentence seemed almost to be spaced in their measured evenness.

"Were you and Gitner together between ten an' eleven o'clock on the morning when yore father was killed?"

Stark clutched at the railing of the porch to steady himself. He moistened his lips and the Adam's apple in his throat moved up and down spasmodically. "You got a nerve to ask me that, you damned murderer," he got out at last.

Not for an instant did Wilson release his fear-filled eyes.

"Were you with Gitner between ten o'clock an' eleven the morning yore father was shot?" he repeated steadily.

"I don't remember right now whether I was. Why?"

"Where were you at that time?"

Jasper, sweating blood, appealed to the judge. "Do I have to stand for his insults, Mr. Fletcher?"

"Not unless they have a bearing on this case. You'll have to show the connection, Wils."

The defending attorney smiled. He had got all the effect he wanted, all he could reasonably hope for. "I reckon I'll withdraw the question, Mr. Fletcher. Far as I'm concerned the witness may step down."

Limply Jasper descended. He felt himself the focus of a battery of eyes. As his glance dodged evasively from one to another, he knew they raked him with a newborn suspicion skilfully planted in their minds. Beneath the shock of it he quailed.

CHAPTER XXXIV

The Lawyer for the Defence

ANN GIFFORD was the third witness. Julia stood beside her while she testified. It was impossible for her to tell her story without emotion, especially that part of it which referred to her sister Nora.

Once Julia, her arms around the young woman, interrupted in a low voice. "Does she have to tell this here, Mr. Fletcher?"

The lawyer answered gently. "A life is at stake. I think she had better tell what she knows."

So Ann told the story, from the day when her sister first met Tom McArdle to the morning when she shot at him and left the man for dead. The impression of that story upon the tense crowd packing the square was remarkable. Wilson did not interrupt the young woman. He let her tell it in her own way, prompting her with a question only when necessary. She told the facts in the simplest possible way, but many of those listening were convicted of guilt. The tragedy that had filled the lives of these girls had been made possible because the men and women who lived near had ostracized them. She told how Stone had tried to be her friend and how in the bitterness of her despair she had pushed him from her with the others.

"Did you see Jasper Stark after Tom McArdle was shot?" Wilson asked.

"Yes. He came to the ranch. He had been there several times to see my sister Ethel, but I did not know it till one day I found him with her."

"Where?"

"In the grove of live oaks back of the house."

"Tell us about it."

"He was bullying her to marry him with the threat that if she didn't he would send me to the penitentiary for killing Tom McArdle."

"What did you tell him?"

"Told him I wouldn't buy his silence at the price of my little sister's unhappiness, and if he wanted to tell what he knew he could."

"What did he say?"

"He started toward her in his bullying way. I drew a revolver and drove him off the place."

There was a murmur of approval that passed through the crowd like a breeze.

"Had he offered to keep still about you if yore sister would marry him?"

"Yes."

From Jasper Stark, at the outskirt of the crowd, came a hoarse denial. "Tha's a lie."

Wilson whirled on him instantly. "Then why didn't you tell before? What made you wait three months before you went to the sheriff with what you knew?"

"I hated to get her into trouble," Jasper retorted. "An' this is the thanks I get for it."

"What thanks did you expect—that Miss Gifford would let you marry her sister for you keepin' quiet?"

Jasper growled, "None o' yore damn business," and retired from the field.

"I don't reckon I've got any more questions to ask you, Miss Gifford," Wilson said after low-voiced consultation with his client. "We're sure much obliged for all the trouble you took to come to town."

There was a little movement of those near the edge of the crowd. Presently it was seen that a girl was being brought forward as quickly as a way could be made for her. The girl was Ethel Gifford.

"I had to come," she told her sister piteously. "I couldn't stay at the ranch after I read your note. So I made Tony bring me."

Ann had not the heart to chide her. She had been moved by the same impulse herself.

"I'm going to use her as a witness now she's here," Wilson said, his eyes shining with the certainty that his most effective argument would be this shy-eyed girl.

"No," Stone objected. "This is no place for her."

"Yes," Ethel differed. "I want to tell what I know if it will help."

The girl was so young and sweet, her innocent

manner so engaging and childlike, that before she had given two sentences of her testimony she had won her way into the hearts of the hard rough men who crowded the courthouse yard. It was fortunate for Jasper Stark that he had vanished from the scene. Otherwise he might have been roughly handled.

When the three girls came down the steps to leave, a lane was made for them along which they passed among murmurs of approval.

The only remaining witness was Dave Stone himself. He looked round, quiet-eyed and fearless, waiting for the examination to begin.

The story he told was the same one he had narrated to the sheriff. Haskell questioned him briefly, then waved a hand to young McCann.

Wilson led him again through an account of the shooting.

"Did you fire in self-defense, to save yore own life?" he asked at last.

The Texan hesitated. "I did an' I didn't," he said. "He was reachin' for his gun when I started for mine. It was him or me one. Lookin' at it that way, I'd call it self-defense. But before that, if I hadn't told him what a lowdown orrery lobo wolf he was, I reckon there wouldn't of been any gunplay. I expect I called for a showdown when I served notice I'd kill him if he troubled the young women at the sheep ranch any more."

"When you fired was his gun out?"

"Yes, sir. In the clear."

"He reached for his first?"

"That was the way of it. I beat him to the draw."

Wilson passed to another point. "Did you tell Jasper Stark or Carl Gitner that you intended to get Tom McArdle?"

"No."

"Did you say anything like that a-tall, anything about having quarrelled with him?"

"No. I never had a word with him in my life till the time I shot him."

"Good friends, were you?"

"No, sir." The Texan's denial came cold and hard.

"Meanin' what?"

"Meanin' that I knew he was a cur an' suspected what he had done to that li'l girl at the sheep ranch. Till that day I let him strictly alone. He knew where he stood with me an' kept his distance."

"Is there any reason why Jas Stark or Carl Gitner might want you outa the way?"

"Yes."

"You know something about them. That it?"

"Yes."

"Something that might get them into trouble?"

"You're right it might."

"Trouble with the law?"

The Texan's answer was the dramatic sensation of the trial. "If I could prove what I suspect it might hang 'em both," he said evenly.

On that high note of suspense Wilson rested his case.

The jury reached its verdict of "Not guilty" in three minutes. A wild yell of approval filled the night. The men who had been clamouring for Dave Stone's blood nearly tore him to pieces trying to shake hands with him. In an hour he had become the most popular man in Mesa.

CHAPTER XXXV

Dunwig's Park

JASPER found Mesa no comfortable place of residence after the memorable night when he had tried to engineer the lynching of Dave Stone. Men with whom he had been hail-fellow now met him with a hard and stony stare. Children coming home from school one day threw stones at him and drove him cursing into Pedro's Place. Enough had been proved against him to wreck any reputation he might have had as a decent citizen, but it was the suspicion of a greater crime—one so evil that few even whispered it to each other— which made him a pariah among his kind.

At the Circle Cross he met the same chilly mistrust. Neither Julia nor Phil dared meet his eyes for fear of what they might read in them. The only one of the riders with whom he would have had a fellow feeling was Gitner, and the big Texan had been given his time and was now hanging around Mesa.

Except for vanity his hide was pachydermous, but he could not stand the universal condemnation in which he stood.

"Let's p'int for the hills, Carl," he suggested to his crony. "Even the greasers here treat me like I got yellow fever."

"Suits me fine," the other agreed. "We'll stake a claim an' make a bluff at mining. Whilst we're up there we'll sure find some way to turn over a rock."

Both of them took to their retreat in the mountains a venomous hatred of Wilson McCann.

"If ever I get another crack at him," Gitner raved, and broke off into a storm of curses. "An' I'll get it. I sure will. Next time there won't be any snivellin' women around to save him either."

"I'll shake hands on that," Jasper agreed bitterly. "Here's to the day, right soon too."

They drank to the death of the man they both hated.

They rode across the bare desert in the deceptive atmosphere which distorts form, colour, and distance. The mountains looked an hour's travel away, the outline of ridge clear cut, the light of barranca and gulch well defined. Foot-hills were definitely placed in relation to the rock wall behind. But a half day of riding brought them only to the upper foot-hills and showed a group-range rather than a single one. The pine-clad summit did not belong to the first spur at all, but was rooted farther back. This was as they had expected, for both were familiar with the illusions of the desert panorama, its erratic foreshortening and tele-scoped landscape.

"Where we headin' for?" asked Jasper in mid-afternoon.

Gitner slid a sidelong look at him. He knew the purpose of their choice of this locale better than his companion did. "Why, up here a ways. Back of that knob over to the left."

Evening brought them, by devious ways, to a well-concealed park back of a small cañon the entrance of which was camouflaged by a false-front rock face protecting from the eye a narrow gateway.

This was terrain foreign to Jasper.

"Looks like a fellow could lie holed up here long as he's a mind to if he was on the dodge," he commented.

The Texan grinned significantly. "I reckon he could."

In the wooded park they rode down to a log cabin on the slope. A man in blue overalls answered Gitner's hail. He brought to the door with him a rifle. There was a slight cast to his very light blue eyes that gave them a sinister appearance.

"'Lo, Mark!" the Texan greeted him. "Make you acquainted with Jas Stark."

The man in blue overalls nodded with no enthusiasm. Strangers coming to Dunwig's Park were not overwelcome. They had to come well recommended as bad citizens. The Starks were not that, in spite of the lawless streak in them.

"Don't worry about Jas," his companion said, hastening to reassure Dunwig. "He's all right."

The particular emphasis he gave the words meant that he was all wrong.

"Better fall off an' light," their host suggested.

They cared for their horses and entered the cabin. Jasper sniffed with the pleasure of a hungry man the odours of coffee and of meat frying in the pan.

Before he slept that night Jasper was committed to a new course of crime. He did not pledge himself to it of his own choice, for he felt it was dangerous. But Gitner knew too much about him. It was too late to draw back now. He had forfeited the option of being his own master.

For almost a year there had been systematic rustling in the hills. The cattlemen had at first been loath to believe it. Even after the evidence was too plain to deny they had been inclined to think the offender must be some Mexican nester. But of late the number of missing cattle pointed to organized robbery. Someone was running stock across the border and selling it.

It was a mark of Jasper Stark's declension that his reluctance to joining the rustlers was due to no moral scruples. Yet he had been brought up in a country where the crime ranked as a capital one. All the teaching of his youth reinforced this view. A rustler was a slinking coyote of the desert, to be shot down or hanged if caught red-handed. He had hotly argued this more than once. Now he had slid into that company of the furtive-eyed who must ride crooked trails and look upon all honest folk as potential enemies.

"We'll make a stake, settle our scores with Wils McCann an' maybe Dave Stone too, then light out for Sonora," Gitner predicted.

With a few drinks under his belt it was easy for Jasper to believe that this would come true. He would get away from this part of the country where he had been forced to get in so bad and he would make a fresh start in another land. He would have enough to buy a *hacienda*, maybe not a large place but a comfortable one, he would marry a soft-eyed señorita, and the years of his life would unroll as a pleasant vista of happiness. So he deluded himself, as so many of us do, with the hallucination that the joy of living comes from outward circumstances rather than from within.

The method used by the rustlers of Dunwig's Park was a simple one. They stole only cattle running in the hills within a day's drive of their holing place. Most of their work was done at night. No brands were altered till they reached the safety of the pasture ground at the end of the hidden cañon. Here the rustled stock was kept until a dark night made it comparatively safe to rush them over Horse Thief Pass and down across the border.

To avert suspicion Gitner and Jasper bought a few mining tools and some dynamite for blasting. But the attempt to draw a herring across their track was not serious enough to cause them to do any actual digging. Neither of them enjoyed manual labour. They preferred to sit around the house and play cards when not in the saddle.

Occasionally they rode down to Mesa and spent a day or two there. Both at Pedro's Place and at the Gilt Edge they heard stories of the rustling that was depleting the herds of the cattlemen.

"The Cattlemen's Association doing anything about it or just shootin' off its mouth?" Jasper asked when the subject was mentioned again at Basford's Emporium.

Simp Shell answered. "I understand they've put it in the hands of a committee to investigate."

"Likely the committee will report progress an' be discharged," Jasper jeered.

"Maybe so. An' maybe not. Wils McCann is at the head of the committee, an' he's some go-getter, that boy is." Simp's bland smile denied any specific personal meaning to this. "An' yore brother Phil is a member of it too. The talk is that they mean business."

"Since when has Phil been kow-towin' to Wils McCann?" Jasper demanded angrily.

"I don't know as he kow-tows to Wils any. Phil is the kind of a lad that stands on his own feet, I'd say. But when it comes to public service we'd ought all to pull together, don't you reckon?"

"If my father had been living Phil wouldn't be doing business with the McCanns. That's a cinch."

"You got the wrong angle to this thing, Jas," the fat man told him amiably. "The time for feuds in this part of the country is past. I've not heard that Phil an' Wils have shook hands, but if so they surely have done right. They're both mighty nice boys, an' there's no reason in the world why they shouldn't be friends."

"Except that Wils McCann killed Father," Stark retorted harshly.

Simp Shell's expressionless eyes rested on a dog scratching itself for fleas. He said nothing, but he managed to say it very significantly. Jasper's glance slid toward him, then moved away.

"You can claim that Father served notice he was aimin' to shoot McCann. I'm not denyin' that. But that don't make it right for Phil to have any dealings with the man who waylaid Father."

"No—if Wils did," Simp said evenly.

"He was caught right in his tracks. I don' know what more you'd want."

"I've been hearin' Dave Stone's story. It's right interesting. By his way of it Wils comes pretty near having an alibi."

"Why not?" Jasper asked truculently. "Ain't it up to one killer to stand by another? Didn't the McCanns save him after he killed Tom McArdle? You're certainly easy, Simp."

Jasper turned on his heel insolently and swaggered away.

CHAPTER XXXVI

Peter McCann Says Peace

PETER MCCANN stood before the open fireplace in his living room frowning at Joe Walters, one of his cowpunchers. He looked like a grim gray judge of the old school finished in brown leather.

"I won't have it, Joe," he said harshly. "While you're workin' for me you'll obey orders. Any time that don't suit you, why, you can ride down the road. I'll not have you pull yore picket pin. I'm boss on this ranch."

Walters looked down resentfully at his dusty hat. He was on the carpet, and his defence had been brushed aside. He felt this was not just, for it was a perfectly good one. But the old man was so bull-headed there was no use talking to him. Yet it had not been very long since Walters had been shot and wounded by some of the Circle Cross outfit and McCann had offered a thousand-dollar reward to find out who had done it. Now Walters was having the riot act read to him because he had knocked down one of the Stark *vaqueros*. Sure enough times had changed.

"I wasn't lookin' for trouble," he explained again. "Not none. That bird was full of forty rod an' ran on me aplenty. What's a fellow to do?"

"Weren't hogtied, were you? Nothing kept you

from walking out of the Gilt Edge when he started, was there?"

"Want me to stick my tail between my laigs an' run away every time some guy gets biggity with me?"

"You got my orders, Joe. If he belongs to the Circle Cross, duck trouble. I'm putting an end to this feud an' that is the only way to do it. I'd take the same medicine myself I ask you to swallow. If it don't suit you, get yore time. That's short an' sweet."

Walters grumbled but surrendered. He knew when he had a good job and he had no intention of giving it up.

Peter McCann wrote a note to Phil Stark and in it asked him to meet him at Garcia's water hole, a half-way point between the ranches. The answer came in a feminine hand. It was signed by Julia. She said that Phil was away on business connected with the Cattlemen's Association but she would keep the appointment in his place.

When the cattleman reached the water hole Julia was waiting for him. She was watching a mirage on the plain, a beautiful lake trembling and glowing in the heat waves. A little island appeared in it and vanished. Some cattle, with long legs like stilts, walked upside down suspended from the sky. Undulating tints of pink and violet made illusive magic of the scene. Then, at some change of atmospheric condition, the picture was not.

Lake, cattle, the envelope of wondrous colour, all were gone.

"It has been here ever since I came half an hour ago," the girl told McCann, the beauty of the marvel reflected in her deep eyes.

Peter, looking at her, spoke abruptly. "You're very like yore mother."

"I've been told so." She added, gently, "You knew her well?"

"At one time, yes." He offered no further explanation. His eyes were on the dry stark desert that had a minute before been a vignette snatched from fairyland. Perhaps he was thinking that there had been an hour in his arid life too when the glow and colour of a dream had irradiated it.

Julia, through clairvoyant eyes, did not see a hard and fierce enemy stamped with the brand of the desert in every line of the lean and leathery face; she saw a youth, a lover and a friend, good man and true, in that dim past when the pages of his future had not been dedicated to an enduring hate that had poisoned many lives.

"About that business yesterday at the Gilt Edge," he began, with no preface. "I laid out Joe Walters good this morning when I heard of it. I'll say for him that he had some excuse. Yore man was lit up and ran on him. But I brought Joe up with a short turn."

"I hadn't heard of it till I got your letter this morning," she said.

"Well, I want you to understand my men have strict orders not to get into any mix-up with yore riders. Far as we're concerned this feud is off. You ended it when you saved my boy's life."

"I'm glad. If only it had never started!"

He knew by the droop of her head that she was thinking of her father. "That would have been better," he admitted. Then, bluntly he asked: "Do you think Wils shot yore father?"

"No. Down in the bottom of my heart I never did think so—except just at first. I thought some of his friends did."

"Do you think that still?"

She looked straight at him, but her lips trembled. "I don't know. I don't want to know."

He knew what she meant, that she was afraid to learn the truth.

"Matt had other enemies besides us," he told her gently. "We hadn't a thing to do with it—not a thing. But I blame myself just the same. He an' I used to be partners. We played together when we were young colts, Matt an' I did. Always had to hook up with the same outfit. They called us David and Jonathan. Then trouble came between us. Both of us were hot-tempered an' bull-headed. We quarrelled. Our business interests conflicted. This damn desert wouldn't hardly feed all our cattle before we began to irrigate. Bad years we both lost a lot of stock from drought. So we drifted from bad to worse. But I'm clear on this—none of us McCanns had anything to do with the death of yore father. I thank God for that, because it might have been different the way things were shaping."

She believed him, with a heavy heart. For if this was true, it drove her back to a horrible dread that for a week had lain like lead.

He looked into her stricken face and pitied her. It came to him that he might clear himself with her at too great a cost. If Gitner had killed Matthew Stark there could be only one reason, to prevent him from making a will disinheriting Jasper. She did not yet believe it of her brother. She fought against the growing doubt that kept returning. For the certainty of his guilt would poison her life. But she could not trample down the fear that flooded her.

McCann spoke more cheerfully. "I've lived long enough to know that the things we're most afraid of never come to pass. They just ain't true. Any one might of shot yore father—some *vaquero* he kicked off the place or a cow thief he had sent to the pen. Matt was like me one way. He made enemies by pushing right through to what he wanted, regardless. I reckon he was kinda intolerant sometimes."

"Yes, he was high-handed," she admitted. "I'm that way too."

"Likely enough he'd trompled on some cur's feelings an' the fellow laid for him in the bushes. If I was you, Miss Julia, I wouldn't worry about who did it. This border country is full of bad *hombres* driftin' about."

"Yes."

He turned to another subject, one that had been on his mind a good deal of late. "It wouldn't be hardly reasonable to expect you to be friendly with us McCanns. Now that Matt has gone it's too late for me to fix things up. But I want to tell you how I feel. When I heard of what had happened to him it gave me a jolt. At first I was worried about Wils. But while I was sittin' there at the Circle Cross by his bedside, after he began to mend some, I couldn't get Matt outa my head. We were mighty close, like I told you, in those early days. I kep' seein' him as he was when we frolicked around together. An' there was you, lookin' the spittin' image of yore mother, first savin' my boy's life an' then lettin' me come to yore house an' stay with him. I'll say you made me feel like a plugged nickel, you an' yore young brother Phil. How could I go on hatin' you Starks after that? I reckon I'm a tough an' stubborn proposition, but I had to give in. No other way to it."

In her eyes swam little wells of tears. "I wish you had come to Dad while he was alive and asked him to make up. Why didn't you?"

"Because I'm a hardened old sinner hell-bent on gettin' my own way. I couldn't any more have come to Matt than he could of come to me. But with you it's different. First off, I can't ever pay what I owe you, not if I live to be a hundred an' lie awake nights figurin' out ways. Then too, whenever I look at you, I see yore mother shinin' outa yore eyes."

"You—loved her?" she asked, very softly.

Again he looked across the arid desert at the papier-mâché mountains. In the peculiar afternoon sunlight they looked like artificial stage settings.

"Yes." He spoke, it seemed, rather to himself than to her.

"Was it about her you and Dad quarrelled?"

"No. About some trifling thing to start with. We had kind friends to keep us stirred up. Pretty soon it had gone too far for us to get together on our differences."

"What a pity?"

"When he was for a thing I fought it. If I wanted it he was against it. The older we got the worse it grew. But I'm through now. I throw up my hands. I quit. If there can't be friendship between us, anyhow there will be peace."

"Yes," Julia agreed.

"We'll let it go at that."

"It's not that I hate you—any of you—any more. I see now there's nothing but loss in that. But I don't see how we can be friends. Dad stands between us and you. If he was alive I could go to him and tell him how I feel. But I can't do that now. I can't feel it would be loyal for us to be friends with his enemies." Her honest eyes appealed to him for understanding.

He nodded. "I reckoned you would feel thataway. Well, I'm glad we've cleared things up. The feud's off anyhow."

"Yes, it's off," she assented.

Peter did not offer to shake hands on it. He glanced at the descending sun. "I'll be hittin' the home trail," he said.

She turned, after she had ridden a little way, to watch him, a strong, straight-backed figure sitting his horse like a Centaur. A lump choked her throat. The sight of him carried her mind back irresistibly to her father. He too had been virile and purposeful and dominant, but beneath the gnarled surface she had known him tender and loving. What a waste that his last years should have been embittered by this implacable quarrel with the man who had been his closest friend! What a loss that he should have been cut off in his prime! Surely if he had lived the breach would have been healed.

CHAPTER XXXVII

A Hot Trail

PHIL was combing burrs out of his pony's mane when the cowpuncher, Red, rode into the yard at the Circle Cross and fell into the easy posture of the rider who intends to be comfortable while he stops and chats.

"How'll you swap that paint hoss for my buckskin?" Red drawled after greetings had been exchanged.

"I ain't swapping this peg pony for any other in Arizona," Phil announced proudly.

"You sure got some notion of yore broomtail, boy. I was allowin' you'd orta gimme about ten dollars to boot. Buck's no plug, I'd have you know. Mighty few broncs can travel alongside of him. Seventy miles he done yesterday in the hills an' never turned a hair."

"Where was it you an' Buck broke the world's record?"

"Up in the Mal País—taking a New York engineer over the divide to look at Basford's copper proposition. A man had orta have hooked horns on his haid to get up some of the trails we took."

"Didn't meet up with any rustlers whilst you were up there, did you?"

About to give a careless negative, Red stopped with his mouth open. "Why, dawggone my hide, maybe I did," he said at last. "I never thought of it till right damned now. We was 'way up above Guadaloup Cañon when we saw a coupla men driving eight or ten *vacas* into it. I hollered, but they was a long way off an' didn't answer. Maybe at that I'm lucky they didn't hear me."

"Headed south, were they?"

"Y'betcha! They went into this end of the gulch an' that's the last we seen of 'em. I thought it kinda funny they were up there, but the New York guy was anxious to reach Mesa before it got plumb dark. But honest, I never thought of waddies. If I had it wouldn't of made any difference for that matter. I hadn't lost any rustlers."

Phil spoke his thoughts, to himself rather than to Red. "Funny they were 'way up there. You're right. Who could they have been? Where were they goin'? Unless they were rustlers."

"You'll have to guess it, boy. I can't."

"Which way you headed, Red?"

"Well, I *was* goin' to Quinn's. Why?"

"Wish you'd ride to the Flying V Y an' tell Wils McCann what you've told me. It won't take you more than three-four miles outa yore way, an' Buck being the best traveller in the U. S. A. why—"

"Which I'm bettin' my boots he is."

"It'll hardly be any trouble a-tall. Tell Wils I'll

meet him at Jim Yerby's along about three o'clock."

The cowpuncher was still in sight when Julia came out to the porch.

"I'll have to leave, Sis," her brother said.

"Red tell you something?" she asked.

He repeated to her what the range rider had said. She nodded agreement. "Looks like you've struck a hot trail. What do you mean to do?"

"I'm going to put it up to McCann. My notion is for him an' me to drift up to Guadaloup and see what we see."

"Let me go too."

"Now looky here, Jule, you be reasonable," he protested. "This is no woman's job. You know that mighty well. We're out after bear meat."

"Then it would be foolish for you and Wils McCann to go up there alone. Probably if you found the rustlers you'd walk right into a trap."

"No such a thing," he denied hotly. "We're not kids. Besides, if we go it'll only be to find out what we can, not to arrest them."

"Then if it's not dangerous, why can't I go?"

"Because. It's no place for you. We're liable to be out three-four days. I never did see such a girl for wantin' to boss everything."

"I don't, either. I'm not trying to boss this. Far as that goes I've been up in the Mal País before. You remember when we went hunting with Dad and stayed a week."

"Well, you're not going."

"I don't want to go. How did I know you expected to be out several days? I'd think you'd take a pack horse?"

"Wils is bringing one. He'll load up at Mesa."

"I'll ride with you far as the sheep ranch. I can stop there to-night with the girls. I'll tell Ethel what a nice boy you are and how kind to your sister."

"I can tell her anything it's necessary for her to know," he said, flushing beneath the tan.

"You might omit something on account of being so modest."

He looked at her suspiciously, remembering something Jasper had once told him. "I reckon you're not going to meet Wils McCann, are you?"

His words struck out of her face the laughter, the gleam of sisterly malice that had sparked in her eyes. "What do you mean?" she asked tensely.

He was ashamed of himself, sorry he had spoken. "I didn't mean that, Jule."

"Of all the mean things you could have said—" She stopped, from sheer inadequacy, then turned and walked swiftly into the house.

Phil stood a moment, frowning at the ground, then slowly followed. He had not meant really to hurt her and he could not let it stand so. He knocked on her bedroom door, was told sharply to go away, and after a moment entered.

She turned on him angrily. "Well, have you something else horrid to tell me?"

"Sorry, Sis. I didn't go to say it. I reckon I was kinda peeved because you were joshin' me."

"If you think just because I was civil to him at Mesa, after he had worked his head off to save Dave Stone—"

"Shucks, I don't think a thing. Nothin' to it. I just shot off my mouth. Don't be sore about it. I'll slap saddles on the broncs an' we'll start."

"I'm not going."

It took him ten minutes of coaxing to get her to relent.

Harmony restored, Phil roped and saddled the horses.

Crossing Tincup Pass, they descended to the mesa above the Painted Desert. Vegetation close to the wagon tracks was covered thickly with gray dust, for the late winter rains had not yet begun. The horses' hoofs flung up clouds of fine dust in the fringe of desolation which lay between the mesa and the sheep camp.

"I was sure enough spittin' cotton," Phil told Ethel after he had drunk two glasses of the lemonade she made for them. "Down in the basin she's certainly dry as a cork laig this time of year."

Wilson McCann had not yet passed, Ann Gifford told them, so they sat on the porch and waited for him.

Ann's attitude toward her neighbours was much

changed. Her experience with them had broken the ice barrier that had dammed in her the flow of human fellowship. The manner with which she greeted the world was less hostile. Many of the kindly people who lived on the edge of the Painted Desert had come to her with warm eyes, a little awkwardly but manifestly in a friendly spirit, and had contrived to suggest that bygones be bygones.

Through Ann's new-born faith in her fellows ran a thread of distress. She knew that the testimony of Ethel and of herself had done much to save Dave Stone. A little flare of fierce and primitive joy rose in her when she thought of it. All her life she would be glad that she had done what she had. If she had been unwomanly in fighting so hard against those who had gathered to destroy her friend, she could not reproach herself for that. She had been forced to risk her reputation or let him die, and she had chosen the better part. The sting of shame in it was that she did not know what the Texan himself thought of it. He had come to her that night and thanked her formally. Since then she had not seen him. Beneath his cold and grave exterior, what was his real feeling about it? She tortured herself with doubts.

It was well past four when Wilson McCann rode across the mesa leading a pack horse. He had not been at home, he explained, when Phil's messenger arrived. Hence the delay.

Julia said a word to him before he left. They were for the moment standing alone. "You'll look after Phil, won't you? He's only a boy."

He was leaning negligently against the saddle, his body looking slender above the wide expanse of shining chaps. But it was impossible to look at him without sensing his virile competency.

"I'll do that li'l thing if I can," he answered, smiling into her eyes by way of reassurance.

"Is it safe to go up there—you two alone?" she asked.

"Maybe not just what you'd call safe. I don't reckon tiger hunting is safe, come to that, but there's few get killed at it."

"I wish you'd wait and take a posse."

He shook his head. "Can't do that. We'd be followin' a cold trail if we did. But I reckon it'll be all right. We're not allowin' to bring any rustlers back with us. Just now we're after information."

"Well, don't let Phil do anything foolish, please."

Again he promised to look after the boy.

He tightened a cinch before he made reference to another subject on his mind. "Father was tellin' me about his talk with you."

"Yes, we smoked a pipe of peace," she said.

"I'm sure glad. Far as I was concerned it wasn't necessary. I was through anyhow. You an' yore brother have done too much for me. I'd never lift a hand against you. But it's better to have an open treaty."

"If Dad had only lived," she murmured, more to herself than to him.

"Father can't get over that. I reckon they hated each other, but there was something between them deeper than hate. I expect Mr. Stark knows that now, if over there they know about things here. Likely their hate hurt them a lot more than they let on."

"That's what I think. Did your father tell you about how I feel?"

Her deep eyes met his and through him went a thrill that quickened his pulses. His drumming heart beat the tidings that he wanted this lovely girl, so quick and vibrant with life, so passionately desirous of the fine things it had to offer—wanted to take her for his mate and spend the years of his life beside her. Yet he knew it could not be. There was a chasm between him and her that could not be bridged.

"Yes. I understand that too. It's the only way you could feel. But . . . Remember that night we rode across the desert together an' talked about how it had got us, how it had made us tough an' ferocious an' harsh like that clump of cactus there; an' how you said it had another side too, for from that dry waste came lovely flowers an' outa the heat came hours when the air was all rose-coloured an' pink an' lilac? I've thought a heap about that, an' you sayin' it was thataway with our lives too. It's so. Take Miss Ann here. She showed only her dry harsh side to us, but when the time came she rode to Mesa to save Stone's life regardless of what it cost her. Take Stone himself for that matter, gamin' it out so cool an' easy while the mob howled to get at him, facin' the music steady an' cheerful, thinkin' of the girl who'd been given such a rotten deal an' how he could help her by takin' on the blame."

"Yes," she agreed, eyes shining, "and I don't know now whether Mr. Stone shot Tom McArdle or not."

"Nobody knows but him, an' I reckon he's told his story an' intends to stick to it. . . . What I'm gettin' at is this, that if the desert makes us gaunt and hardy, if it gives us endurance and fierceness, shows us how to survive when softer folks, untrained by it, would crumple up an' die, maybe these very qualities, brought into service an' subdued to use, are the ones we've got to have to win out on this thirsty frontier. We live where we're always seein' the flash of teeth. We've got to stand heat an' drought an' hardship or get off the map. All summer people have been tryin' to cut the ironweed outa their gardens, but it's still there, I reckon."

"Yes, it's tough, like the bisnaga and the cholla and the prickly pear," she agreed.

"Nature gives hooks an' barbs an' saw-edged teeth to those of her children that need 'em. A mule-deer learns to go a coupla weeks without water. Same way with prairie dogs an' coyotes. If they couldn't stand thirst they wouldn't last long. No different with us. We've got to meet the conditions. But there's something born in us that stays with us. Even when we get tough as leather we're all right inside maybe. On the dry desert things take a long time to rot. I've seen mighty tough citizens who had clean hearts when once you got to them." He laughed at himself. "I'm not gettin' anywhere, but you know what I mean."

"Yes, I do," she told him. "And it's true. They call Mr. Stone a killer, but I'd trust him anywhere. But I wouldn't trust that Gitner. I wish Jas would quit running around with him."

"No, you're right about Gitner. He belongs to the lobo family, I reckon. Well, I'll be movin' along."

"I don't think *you* belong to the lobo family, Mr. McCann," she told him impulsively. "I did once, but I've changed my mind."

Their level gazes met.

"Much obliged for that," he replied in the drawl of the Southland. "I don't reckon I'd better tell you what I think about you."

Into her dark eyes there flashed a momentary panic. She drew back, her pulses fluttering.

Phil called across to his companion. "Ready, Wils?"

The two horsemen disappeared round a bend in the road.

CHAPTER XXXVIII

The Neck of the Bottle

WILSON MCCANN and Phil Stark did not find Yerby at home. A Mexican boy herding sheep on the hillside near said he had seen him start townward in the morning.

The trail ascended steeply. The travellers left behind them the desert vegetation. The lean and haggard ocotillo, cruel of claw, no longer shared with the mesquite dominance of the landscape. Catclaw and cholla were still to be seen and occasionally a Spanish bayonet. Scrub oaks and juniper appeared, at first straggling and hesitant. The riders passed through a splendid grove of live oaks festooned with great clumps of mistletoe, and as they still climbed upward pines were silhouetted against the skyline.

They camped far up in the hills, choosing for the location a small park where grass grew in place of burro-weed. The very sky had changed its character. It had become more live, much nearer, a deeper blue. The tang of the pines was in the winy air.

Phil chopped fuel and built a fire while his companion undid the lass rope and removed the cross buck from the pack horse, picketed the animals, and brought water from the spring. After supper they smoked a pipe and chatted.

"We'd ought to reach Guadaloup by nine o'clock, wouldn't you say?" Phil murmured sleepily, his head pillowed on the most comfortable spot of his saddle.

"I reckon. If we get an early start."

They were up before daybreak. The sun was just peeping over the ridge when McCann threw the diamond hitch with the lass rope. It was possible, though not probable, that at any time they might jump up the rustlers driving stolen cattle. Wherefore they rode warily, following ridges where they could so that they could sweep with their eyes as much territory as was feasible.

Guadaloup Cañon opened before them after an hour or two of travel. Precipitous walls shut them into a defile, narrow and tortuous, up which they moved in single file. The soil was a red clay formation. Loose rocks strewed the floorway of the gorge, flung down ages ago from the heights above.

The trailers dismounted and studied the ground. Sure enough there had been cattle here and recently. Prints of horses' hoofs showed that they had been driven and had not strayed here by chance. This they already knew, by the testimony of the cowpuncher Red.

They followed the gulch for several miles. The walls opened out, so that the sun beat down upon the riders and baked them. There was no shade.

The only vegetation showing was the creosote clinging to the rocks. Even this was scarce and stunted.

A bend in the cañon brought them to a clump of small pines. A spring emerged from a fissure in the red stone strata.

Wilson stopped the other rider. "Hold on! Let's have a look before we mess up any tracks that may be here."

They swung down and grounded the reins of the horses. Through the red sand ran half a dozen tracks of sidewinders.

The men moved forward slowly to the damp soil surrounding the spring. What Wilson was looking for he found. His finger pointed out a heel mark. The boot was evidently much run over on the outside and the heel badly worn. The print of the same foot was stamped also in another moist spot below the spring. It had been made by a very large boot.

"Some folks are right careless," McCann said.

"Sure are. Fellow who stomped that track is a considerable sized guy. He had ought to be careful where he writes his signature."

"If he knows what's good for him he'll write it in Mexico *muy pronto.*"

"Looks like he's near the end of his trail here. Now we're on to him he'll not last long, I'd say. They must be holin' up near here."

"Not so far away." Wilson spoke apparently

without stress. "Gitner knows these mountains pretty well, I expect."

"You think it's Gitner." Phil was startled, though the words voiced a fear that had been in his own mind.

"Looks thataway. You know Gitner's big feet, an' how his boots are always run over at the heel."

The boy made no answer. A disturbing thought had found lodgment in his mind, one so full of ill omen that the muscles beneath his heart seemed to have given away. If Gitner was one of the rustlers—and he no longer doubted it for a moment, scant as was the evidence at hand—was Jasper also one of them? The thought of it shook his courage. There was nothing admirable in his brother, nothing that as a boy he could look up to as an example. But it was a long step from worthlessness to cattle-thieving. Almost the worst crime on the docket in the border land is rustling. It gave him a shock to face the possibility that his father's son might be guilty of it.

It was precisely because of this that Wilson had mentioned Gitner's name. If the boy had to meet such a facer it was better that he should have time to reflect upon it first.

"This isn't yore job, Phil," the older man said presently. "You ride home an' tell Jim Yerby an' Dave Stone to meet me at the mouth of the cañon in two days. I'll stick around an' do some scoutin' till they come."

Phil looked him straight in the eye. "It's my job much as it is yours. If you thought it was my job yesterday, what makes you say to-day it's not? Nothing has changed, far as I can see."

They were both thinking of the same thing, that one of the men whose trail they were following might be Jasper Stark. But Wilson could not refer to his fears any more than the boy could, except indirectly when they mentioned the name of the big Texan.

He evaded. "This is liable to be a bigger task than I had figured. If we meet up with Gitner he'll go to shootin' sure. I reckon we need more help."

"All right," agreed Phil calmly. "You go get it an' I'll scout around an' wait for you."

McCann's brown white-toothed smile flashed. He was not getting very far with the boy. "Feelin' real cock-a-doodle-do, ain't you? I'm not claimin' to be high, low, jack, and the game, but I'm some older than you. Seems to me it's my say-so."

"Afraid I won't keep my end up, so you want me to turn in my string of horses?" Phil asked, using the figure of speech of the puncher on the trail.

"No, sir, not a bit afraid of that. I've a notion you'd go through from hell to breakfast. But like I said, this Gitner's a lead pumper. He'll have four-five fellows with him, all of 'em tough nuts to crack. My notion is for you to go back an' pick up some of the boys—say Curt Quinn an' Stone an' Yerby an' my brother Lyn. You'll be back in two days if you're so hell-bent on bein' in this and we'll sure round up these birds an' tell 'em what-for."

"That wasn't yore notion when we started. This was to be a scoutin' party to cut the trail of these rustlers an' report what we found out."

"Sure enough. But we're hot on the trail of these gents. We're liable to catch 'em with the goods. If so, we had ought to make our gather right then. Otherwise they'll probably hive off to parts unknown. We're not enough to handle this job, you an' me. I was figurin' on runnin' down two-three Mexicans maybe. Gitner's another proposition, an *hombre* of quite a different colour. He packs his guns low an' comes a-foggin'."

"Someone has already mentioned that to me," the boy said quietly.

"Tell Miss Julia that we think Gitner is the man we're after."

Phil read his mind as though it had been a one-syllable primer. McCann believed that if he mentioned Gitner as the probable chief of the rustlers to Julia she would contrive some excuse to prevent her brother from returning with the posse.

"*You* can tell her that," Phil said. "I'm stayin' right here."

McCann rumpled his sunburnt hair and grinned. "You're some stubborn, if any one asks me. Boy, why don't you act like you had horse sense?"

The upshot of it was that they both stayed. They decided to find out if they could where the outlaws were camped. Circumstances would have to decide whether they would attempt an arrest or go for help to round up the thieves.

They took a diagonal trail up the mountain side after they came to the end of Guadaloup Cañon, for the hoof-prints, sharp-edged and clear-cut, led that way.

It came on to rain, a gentle mist that blurred the hills. They put on their slickers and followed the dim trail until it lost itself in the rubble of a stony precipitous shoulder hunched up above a deep gulch.

As the rain increased the pines and the scrub oaks began to shower them with baths of moisture when they pushed too close. The tracks of the cattle were blotted out.

"Our luck's not standing up," Wilson said. "I wonder which way they drove those brush-splitters from here."

Phil cast back into his memory. "When I was a kid Dad brought us up here hunting. We stayed a week, the four of us. Nick Rafferty an' Jule were the other two. Our camp was in a wooded park back of a gulch you'd never know was there unless you stumbled on it. Just for fun Jule called it Horse Thief Park, because it would be such a dandy place for rustlers to hole up. If I could find it. I recollect it's over to the southwest from this end of Guadaloup—six or seven miles maybe—or more, or less. They may not be camped there of course. But there was an old cabin some prospector had built, an' the grass was good. Plenty of water too."

"Looks like a good bet. Whichever way we go it's a gamble. Might as well try yore Horse Thief Park. If we could work around an' slip in the back way we could probably lie hid while we look around. How about that?"

The boy shook his head. "You can search me. We always went in by the gulch an' came out the same way. Point is, can I find the entrance to it?"

"Findin' our way in is one thing: gettin' out is another," Wilson cautioned. "I'd hate to find Gitner had shoved a cork in the neck of the bottle while we were inside. I'm not lookin' for a showdown with the odds against us."

"I'm not crazy about bumpin' into him myself," Phil admitted.

Through the drizzle they plodded, moving toward the southwest. It was a land of innumerable hills, gulches, draws, wooded slopes and mountain passes. To find in this maze the concealed entrances to one small cañon was no easy task. For Phil could recall no details of the country's contour, nor any landmarks that reminded him of the way they had approached.

They wandered rather aimlessly for hours, trying first one defile and then another, riding up draws that proved to be blind alleys, and circling hills patiently. The night fell still wet. With difficulty they lit a fire. The sodden wood sputtered and smoked. From the pines above the gusts of wind shook showers of gathered moisture upon them.

Beneath the tarp that bound together the pack they slept uncomfortably. The ground was wet and cold, their blankets damp.

Daybreak found rain still falling from a sky banked with clouds. Breakfast was a cheerless business. To make matters worse, the pack horse had pulled its picket pin and wandered away.

"I've sure got the feel of the rocks in my bones," Phil grumbled with a rueful grin. "Looked to me like they would work right through to my spine. Say, what do we do about that fool hawss—start after it before breakfast?"

"I'll look around while you are fixin' up somethin' to eat. It wouldn't get far from the others."

Wilson picked up his rifle and walked out of the draw. He could see where the picket pin had been dragged through the wet grass as the horse had grazed down the slope. The trail led him over a little rise and sharply to the left, skirting a clump of willows on the shoulder of the hill.

Abruptly Wilson stopped. The pack horse was not a hundred yards in front of him, grazing contentedly on the moist grass in which it stood to the fetlocks. But after the first glance he forgot the horse. For he was looking at a small gateway between two rock faces, one rising directly in front of the other. Even from where he stood he could see that the opening between led into some sort of gulch.

He walked down to the mouth of the ravine and verified his first impression. Back of the first rock face was the mouth of a hidden cañon up which ran a well-defined path. By some odd freak of luck the pack horse had led him to Julia's Horse Thief Park.

Wilson picked up one end of the picket rope and led the animal back to their camp. A smoky fire was struggling in a depressed fashion for its existence against the handicaps of sodden fuel and a steady rain.

"Better put out that fire, Phil, don't you reckon?" Wilson suggested. "Mr. Gitner or some of his friends might see it. That blamed lost gulch of yours is right round the corner."

Phil stared at him, saw he meant it, and began to throw dirt on the fire.

CHAPTER XXXIX

Horse Thief Park

PHIL recognized the mouth of the gorge as soon as he saw it.

"Same place," he said. "I recollect that twisted pine there."

They returned to camp and packed. Wilson felt an extreme reluctance at letting the boy go with him farther, for he knew that he might be going into a trap from which escape would be very difficult. His remonstrance was useless, as he knew it would be.

"I'm going through like I said I would," Phil told him stubbornly. "No use pow-wowing about it. What do you reckon I came along for anyhow?"

They rode up the cañon in single file, Wilson leading the way. Both of them carried their rifles across the saddle in front, for neither doubted that they were going straight to the stronghold of the outlaws. It was possible they might at any bend of the trail meet face to face the men they were seeking.

"Glad it's rainin'," Wilson said, twisting for a moment in the saddle to speak back. "Unless they've got important business to-day they're liable to stay indoors an' loaf. That'll suit me fine."

"Here too," agreed Phil. He had a curious sinking sensation about the muscles of his stomach, but he had no intention whatever of turning back. It was the natural dread that comes to all men when they are moving for the first time into an unknown danger.

Out of the defile they emerged into a valley of mist that had no outline then.

"Cabin's over to the left," Phil whispered. "We better get in this pine grove up here right away. Sun 'll be comin' out soon by the look of the clouds."

They deflected, climbing to the wooded slope to the right. From a break in the clouds the sun peeped out, at first timidly, then with more persistence. Slowly the mist settled, till the upper walls of the valley showed. The rock face opposite was painted yellow and green and ochre by the sunshine. It was half an hour before the fog was reduced to filmy shreds and a lake of mist nestling in a far corner of the valley.

From all directions sheer precipices rose. Technically the pasture ground inclosed was not a park but rather a depression driven down by some freakish trick of nature. It was as though some Titanic god in the morning of the world had stamped a gigantic foot on the soft plastic mountain mass and driven down with terrific force the crust of the earth.

The cabin lay across from them on the other

slope of the saucer-shaped valley inclosed by the cliffs. A man came out from it in his shirt sleeves and stretched arms in a wide gesture that was evidently a yawn. Wilson adjusted his glasses and looked. Presently he handed the binocular to his companion.

"Gitner," said Phil after a moment.

"What we've got to find out now is whether those cattle down there are rustled," Wilson said, pointing to a small herd grazing on the slope opposite. "I'm going to look into that and make sure if I can."

"How?"

"Going to circle the valley close to the walls, hide in that fringe of bushes over there, an' drop down about dusk to the cattle for a look-see. You'd better stay here with the horses."

"Hadn't you better let me go?"

"No sir, I hadn't. We've got to settle one point now, Phil. Whatever happens we can't afford for both of us to be trapped. If you're seen here, make a break on yore cavallo down the cañon an' keep goin' till you can get help an' come back with a posse. I'll stay hid an' look out for myself. If I'm the one that's seen an' you hear firin', light out just the same."

"I'd be liable to do that," Phil said hotly. "We're in this together, ain't we? I'd cut acrost the valley to you lickety-split—"

"Then you'd spoil my chance an' they'd get us

313

both sure. It's a cinch Gitner has four or five fellows with him, all gunmen. I hate to quit without knowin' what brands are on that bunch of *vacas*, but I'll have to give up the idea if you won't be reasonable. I'm kinda particular about who gets my hide to hang up an' dry."

"Looky here," protested Phil. "I'm no kid, an' I never was teacher's pet. I figure myself a full-grown white man if you want to know. You can get it right outa yore haid that I won't go through to a fare-you-well. We started on this job together an' it'll be even-steven with us. Why should I stick around here where I can make a getaway down the cañon while you go across there where you're liable to be bumped off?"

"Would there be any sense in both of us leavin' the horses and goin'?"

"Maybe not. Point is, I claim I'm the one had ought to go."

They had come to an impasse. Wilson was silent for a moment. A plan was filtering into his mind, one that would eliminate the boy from the risk of going down into the valley and yet would satisfy his pride.

"We'll draw lots for it," he suggested.

"Now you're shoutin'."

"First off, let's decide on one thing, Phil. Whoever goes has got to play a lone hand. If he's seen why he's outa luck. The other fellow has got to start for help right then. No fool boy business

314

of ridin' over and mixin' up in the trouble. That wouldn't get either of us anywhere."

"Could one of us hold out alone till the other got back with help?"

"If he could reach the brush. He might get a good place to stand 'em off."

"Don't look to me like he'd have a dead man's chance," Phil said.

"Would it be any better if the other fellow came ridin' across an' got shot down before he ever reached him?"

"I reckon not—if he didn't reach him."

"And he wouldn't. No, Phil, I'll not go into this unless it's understood that the one who stays with the horses will burn the wind to get help."

"All right. I'll stand pat on that. Far as that goes we're not figurin' on gettin' caught."

"No. But you never can tell."

McCann stooped and showed between thumb and finger a pebble. He held his hands behind him for a moment, then offered for choice two closed brown fists.

"The pebble is in one. The fellow that draws it stays here, the other one goes."

Phil chose the right hand. When Wilson opened it a pebble lay in the palm. He flicked it away.

"I stay," Phil said.

"I'll look my guns over while you fix me up some grub to take. Probably I won't get back till some time in the night," Wilson said.

Phil turned toward the pack horse.

From McCann's left hand another pebble dropped. It was the same size and shape as the first.

CHAPTER XL

Booming Guns

THROUGH the pines Wilson worked back to the foot of the cliff. In forgotten ages boulders had crumbled down from above and among them was a growth of soapweed, scrub oak, and manzanita. This offered cover while he circled the park to reach the opposite side of the valley. It was at least cover of a sort. There were open stretches to be passed where he stood out on the landscape, an obvious alien and intruder. He could only hope that no casual glance wandering over the park might become riveted on him and harden to cold and wary intentness.

It was easy for him now to doubt whether the plan he had chosen was the wisest. Would it not have been better to have slipped out of the park with Phil and returned for a posse, taking it for granted that this was the rendezvous of the rustlers and these cattle stolen ones driven here by them? Certainly it would have been far safer. For at any moment he might be seen or Phil's presence discovered. But he was thorough by nature. He wanted to carry back with him definite proof that he had located the outlaws and not merely a party of prospectors. Gitner and Jasper Stark had given it out that they were working a claim in the hills, location unknown. It was possible, though not probable, that their story might be true. Wilson did not propose to risk being laughed at the rest of his life for crying "Wolf!" when there was no lobo in sight.

While he moved forward through the brush his worried thoughts went back to the young fellow he had left with the horses. He wished now that he had flatly refused to come with Phil on this scouting expedition. If anything happened to the boy he could not forgive himself. This brother was all that Julia had left. If she should lose him, as she had lost her father—Jasper being far worse than dead—her life would be clouded with tragedy.

She had put Phil in his charge, and he had pledged himself to look after the lad. Was he doing it now, leaving him alone there among the pines across from the cabin, where at any moment the barking of a dog might betray him? He could say of course with truth that he had himself chosen to take the greater risk, since Phil if discovered had a way of escape open while he would have none. But there was always the possibility that Phil might be killed and that he might survive. In that case, how could he ever look into Julia's accusing eyes? He was nothing to her of course. He never would be. But she was the centre of all his cherished dreams.

He tried to find comfort in the reflection that if

Phil were discovered and captured Jasper would never let his companions do the boy any harm. That Jasper was a scoundrel he knew, that he was a villain he suspected. It was Wilson's conviction that he had incited Gitner to kill his own father to protect himself from being cut out of Matthew Stark's will. But vile though he was the man would never stand by and let his young brother be murdered if he could help it.

All his senses were alert as he crept forward, keeping close to the sheer rock walls that shut in the sunken valley. He made use of every bush, every depression, every hillock, that might serve as a screen. But his underlying thoughts clung to the perplexity which somehow had come to involve his life. A few months ago he had been free. Now he was fettered fast by inhibitions. For instance, if he should meet Jasper now face to face! What would he do? What could he do? He was Julia's brother.

The man was an insolvable problem to him. More than once he had seen cowboys "go bad," as the phrase of the country was. He had known killers, men of the Gitner type, with cold cruel eyes that held no mercy and into which one would look in vain for any faith or loyalty. But Jasper was different. He had come of good stock, had been given advantages which he had deliberately thrown away. His type was that which is both weak and vicious, which chooses by some perverted instinct the bad instead of the good. Led astray by greed and vanity, he could plot some horribly evil thing and afterward probably be tortured by the memory of it. It took strength to be bad in the thoroughgoing fashion of Gitner. The devil that lurked in Jasper's heart was an erratic and impulsive one, a shivering cowardly demon afraid of its shadow. How could such a man possibly be the son of game grim Matt Stark, the brother of so decent a boy as Phil, of so sweet and gallant a desert flower as Julia?

The afternoon was half spent before he reached a clump of manzanita back of the grazing cattle. Here he lay quietly, with the patience bred in him by the desert, waiting until dusk should fall over the valley and lessen the risk of being seen when he moved out into the open pasture.

His mind was not easy. He could not get Phil out of his thoughts. Was the boy still concealed in the pines safe from observation? He had heard no shots, but his anxiety was keen. If it would have done any good he would have given up his purpose and hurried back to his companion. But to do so might be increasing the risk, since he would run a chance of being seen himself.

"Soon now," he told himself as the sun dropped back of the cliff behind him. "Half an hour an' I'll be moving."

The shadows crept up the face of the wall opposite, leaving only the upper half a canvas of yellows and ochres and copper greens. The ribbon of sunshine narrowed, at last disappeared.

Through the long grass Wilson crept, pushing his rifle in front of him. The nearest cattle were grazing head on toward him, so that he did not get a chance to see the brands well. All afternoon they had been out of sight behind a clump of alders, making it impossible for him to use the field glasses on them.

He circled round to see the brands, taking a wide detour. Presently, with the glasses, he was able to make out the markings of the cattle. He read the Flying V Y brand and the Circle Cross. That was all he wanted to know. Cautiously he began to retreat toward the cliff.

The sound of a galloping horse stopped him. Someone was swinging round the cattle to drive them to the other end of the valley, probably to take the stock to water.

Wilson crouched low, but he knew he would be seen. For he was in the path of the approaching rider. His heart dropped into his stomach.

Not twenty yards from him the horseman pulled up with a startled oath. The man was Jasper Stark. He looked down, with fear-filled eyes, at his enemy. McCann was kneeling on one knee, rifle ready for action.

It could not have been more than a fraction of a second that Jasper stared at this unexpected and menacing intruder. Before the other could speak he gave a yell of terror, swung his horse in its tracks, and drove home the spurs.

Mechanically Wilson raised his weapon and covered the flying man. He drew a dead bead on him—then lowered the weapon. Swiftly his thoughts canvassed the situation. Deliberately he pointed the barrel of the rifle into the air and fired four shots.

This done, he ran back quickly to the cover of the manzanita, passed rapidly through it, and headed for a mass of rugged boulders at the upper end of the park. Here he could make a stand with some chance of success.

Several times his anxious eyes travelled toward the grove of pines where Phil was waiting. Already the mist of darkness was falling like a cloak from the darkening sky. He could barely make out the pines and he knew it would be impossible to detect any sign of life among them. Had Phil reached the entrance to the cañon? The rustlers would of course promptly close it, but if he had moved instantly at the signal he ought to have got there first, for they would wait to hear from Jasper the cause of the shots. No doubt they would be greatly disturbed at what he had to tell them. They would hurriedly debate the situation, would decide that McCann could not be alone, and might perhaps in their dread be driven to flight.

Wilson's fears were all for Phil. Later he might

himself have to face the outlaws, but his immediate concern was for the boy. Had he escaped? Was he now galloping down the cañon, at every stride of the horse increasing the distance between him and danger?

As McCann reached the boulder field there came to him the faint far-away explosion of a gun. Another almost merged in the first, and a few seconds later came a third sound like the popping of a distant firecracker.

That was all. Carried on the evening breeze to one not keyed by apprehension, they might have seemed friendly greetings of the night. But to Wilson there was something in those sounds that shook his soul. They seemed to him sinister signals of tragedy. For he did not doubt that Phil had been challenged while escaping and that in the flash of guns which instantly followed somebody had been hurt.

He listened, nerves taut, heart drenched with dread, but no other shots came to break the stillness. The boy had either broken through or they had got him. Which?

He had intended to lie hidden in the boulder field till he was discovered and make there a stand against the rustlers. But he found it impossible to wait there quietly while in doubt about Phil's fate. Julia had put her brother in his care. Perhaps the youngster lay wounded somewhere on the trail. He must find out.

Only a few stars were yet out. In the darkness he strode across the park through the grass, headed for the pine hill where he had left Phil and the horses. He wanted to make sure that Phil had at least started for home.

In the hollow back of the pine-clad slope Wilson found the pack horse and his own mount Jim-Dandy. The latter was saddled and tied by a slip knot to a young tree.

He swung to his seat and rode down the hill. The entrance to the gulch was perhaps a hundred and fifty yards from the house. He was still some distance from it when a rider emerged, galloping hard, and made straight for the cabin.

Wilson pulled up. The man had come from the cañon bringing news with him. What was the important message that drove him so fast to his confederates? He would very much like to know. It might greatly simplify the problem before him.

"I reckon we'll not go right now, Jim-Dandy— not till I've had a look at that cabin anyhow. There's just a chance they've got Phil there."

He left the cowpony in a draw and moved with a long even stride toward the house. His rifle he left beside the horse. It would only hamper him at close quarters. If it came to a gunplay his .45 would be better.

No dog came barking to sound warning of his approach. He came by the rear, to a curtained window of a lighted room.

Inside were four men—Gitner, Jasper Stark, Mark Dunwig, and Kelly Brown. All were on their feet, intent, and one at least frightened. From the edge of the curtain Wilson could see two thirds of the room. To sweep with his gaze the rest of it he had to move to the other side of the window.

Brown stood just inside the doorway telling a story.

"An' when he wouldn't stop I let him have it." He made his narrative dramatic by an instinctive crouched gesture of throwing a gun on someone. "He blazed away at me as he went by. Before he turned the bend in the trail I fired again."

"Hit him?" demanded Gitner with an oath.

"Don't know. He sure kept travellin'. I followed a li'l ways, then lit out up here to tell you boys."

"Know him?" asked Dunwig.

Brown pointed to Stark. "His kid brother."

Jasper's high voice betrayed his fear. "They've got us trapped," he whined. "I told you I didn't want to throw in with you in this rotten game, Carl. By God, we've got a rope round our necks right now."

The Texan looked at him scornfully, his legs wide apart, cruel eyes narrowed. "You're one hell of a pardner, Jas. No guts."

Dunwig spoke, his light blue eyes taking in Jasper with swift furtive appraisal. He was convinced that Stark would betray them to save his own hide if the chance came. "Don't look to me like we're trapped. Not by a jugful. What's yore brother breakin' his neck to get away for if they've got us? I'd say it's the other way round. Likely two or three of 'em butted in here lookin' for us. This McCann wanted to make sure about whose cattle were here. He must of left the others an' the horses up in the pines. When yore brother heard the shootin' he figured the game was up an' lit out *pronto*. I'll bet he was alone up there. Anyhow, I'm goin' up to find out. We'll know then where we're at. With Manuel posted at the Narrows this McCann can't get out down the gulch. My notion is we've got that guy where we want him."

Gitner shook a huge fist savagely. "I speak for him. Lemme have him an' I'll sure riddle him aplenty," he cried with a fierce oath.

Again the terror that was riding Jasper Stark cried out. "Tell you we're trapped. If ever I get outa here alive—"

He did not finish the sentence. But as it stood the meaning was clear enough, a threat to abandon those with whom he was allied, perhaps to betray them. The eyes of Gitner and Dunwig met, and a message passed between them. In that long look he was condemned. For they knew their lives were at the mercy of this weakling who would turn evidence against them whenever pressure was brought to bear. Neither of them doubted that Jasper Stark would save himself at their expense if he could. Every word he had spoken since he burst into the room a half hour ago convinced them that this was true.

"First off, we'll all go up to the pines an' see if any one is still camped there," Dunwig proposed. "That suit you, Carl? If we bump into this McCann an' his friends we'll fog it out with him."

Gitner straddled to the wall and took a rifle down from the deer's horns on which it rested. "Suits me fine," he boasted. "I always did want another crack at that Wils McCann. I 'most sent him to Kingdom Come oncet."

"I'm sick, boys. Reckon I'll stay here," Jasper said.

"Reckon you won't," Gitner told him with a brutal laugh. "How about it, Mark?"

For a fraction of a second Dunwig's sidling eyes met those of the Texan. "Why no, I 'low he'd better go along, Carl."

The man crouched outside the window knew that it was time for him to be gone. He retreated carefully a few steps, then broke into a run. After he reached his horse and had reclaimed the rifle lying near he hesitated.

"Where do we go from here, Jim-Dandy?" he drawled aloud. "Blamed if I know. The gulch is closed. It would be suicide if we tried to make a break down thataway. It's back to the big rocks for me, I expect."

Already the outlaws were pouring out of the

house. From where he stood he could have shot them down in comparative safety, but he could not harden his heart to do that though he knew they would murder him without scruple if they got the chance. Hurriedly he mounted and rode back into the pines.

"Have to leave you here, J. D.," he told his horse. "I'm playin' for time, old fellow, an' you're too big to hide. So I can't take you along."

He left Jim-Dandy with the pack horse and retreated to the foot of the rock wall. The voices of the outlaws came to him, though he could not make out their words. They had evidently found the two animals and were deciding what to do.

The sound of their voices died away. Probably they had decided to wait till morning. Then they would thoroughly search the valley and find him.

Wilson made his way back to the upper end of the park. The big rocks offered the best cover he had seen for a last stand.

CHAPTER XLI

The Old Maid Sheepherder

JULIA stayed at the sheep ranch the night after her brother and his companion started for Guadaloup Cañon. It was long before she could get to sleep. The enterprise upon which the two men were embarked was a dangerous one, even though they had gone only to spy out the land. She wished she had insisted more strongly that they take a larger posse, for if they should meet the rustlers and there should be a battle they would probably be worsted. Thinking of it now, in the darkness of the night, their undertaking seemed foolhardy.

She was glad of the darkness and the freedom it brought from the need to talk. Her thoughts were of Wilson McCann. What had he meant when he said he would not tell her his opinion of her? She tried to vision again the look that had accompanied the words, and her pulses throbbed with joy and apprehension. He was no friend. The lines in which their lives had been cast made that impossible. But he was the man she loved. No longer did she deny that to herself. It gave her a stinging delight to admit it. They could be nothing to each other. Never! Never! None the less he was everything to her.

It was long past midnight before her eyes

closed. They opened only when the tinkling of knives and forks told her that Ethel was setting the table for breakfast.

"What time is it?" she asked drowsily.

"We've been up hours," Ethel told her. "Ann said to let you sleep. She's had her breakfast and started for one of the camps. You don't have to go home to-day, do you?"

"Think I'd better. Phil's away, you know."

"Mr. Rafferty will look after things. He's been doing it a good many years, hasn't he?"

During the day Julia continued to argue that she must be getting home, but she made no move to go. The fact was that she was very reluctant to put that half dozen extra miles between her and the men who had gone to Guadaloup. She was not easy in her mind and she knew that whatever news came would reach the sheep ranch before it did the Circle Cross.

Ethel and she washed their hair and let it dry in the sun. The contrast they offered to each other was striking, the one with soft fluffy ripples like molten gold, the other with long abundant tresses black as coal. There had sprung up between them a swift impulsive friendship, an intimacy made possible by their differing temperaments. One was soft and tender and clinging; the other strong and generous and warm-hearted.

When Julia talked of Phil the younger girl's blushes came, but when the conversation veered to Wilson McCann Julia gave no sign of peculiar interest.

Toward evening Ann returned and vetoed Julia's halfhearted suggestion that she must be going. Wherefore the guest stayed another night and was awakened next morning to the odour of frying bacon.

They had not finished eating when a man's voice outside hailed the house. The man was Dave Stone. He had come, he said, to say good-bye before leaving for Texas.

It was Julia, not Ann, who asked him questions.

"Texas! I didn't know you were even thinking of going. How long are you going to stay there?"

"I'm figurin' on joinin' the rangers there."

"Staying for good? Not coming back?" she protested.

"Yes, Miss Julia."

"But why? Don't you like it here? I thought you were settled with us."

"I'm a kinda rollin' stone," he explained.

"You haven't had any trouble with Dominick or any body?"

He smiled. "No, ma'am. Nothing like that."

"I wish you wouldn't go. Why can't you stay at the Circle Cross?"

"Every once in a while I get sorta hungry for Texas."

Julia was not one to give up easily, but she did not find it possible to move him from his purpose.

"You talk to him, Ann, while Ethel and I do the dishes," she said at last.

But Ann had nothing to say. She sat mute and still while the Texan maintained as best he could a flow of small talk. Presently she rose.

"I've got to look at the feed troughs," she said.

He walked beside her to the corrals. The girl put her forearms on the top bar of the fence and looked across at the distant Sierras.

"Am I driving you away?" she asked at last.

For a moment the surprise of her direct question caught him with his mask off. But almost instantly he divested his eyes and poker face of all expression.

"Why no, ma'am. I'm just restless."

"I ought not to say anything about it," she went on, with a flare of her old bitterness. "It's not womanly, I suppose. But you're either my friend or you're not. I want to know which."

"I'm yore friend," he said in a low voice.

"All you did was to try to save me from prison and to protect my good name when folks were talking about me. Nothing to speak of, just almost give your life for me. Now you come and say, 'I'm going away,' without telling me why. Is that fair?"

She spoke with such passionate resentment that he knew he could not stand by the reason he had given for leaving.

"Maybe not," he said quietly. "Fact is, Miss Ann, I *am* leavin' on yore account. It's not fair to you for me to stay. I've worked it all out in my mind. Folks have got a fool notion that—that—"

"—that I'm in love with you," she finished for him.

"No, ma'am, but that I'm right fond of you."

"And since it isn't true you're going away to stop their talk?"

"Yes, Miss Ann, I'm going away to stop their talk, but not for that reason. I'm Dave Stone, Texas killer. It won't do any young lady's name any good to be associated with mine. When I go the talk will die right down."

"I see, and you'll not be troubled by it or by me any more."

"Did I say I was troubled by you?" he asked gently.

"No, you haven't said anything. I never see you."

"I thought it best not to come."

"Best for you or for me?" she demanded.

"For you."

She laughed, shortly. "Good of you to be so thoughtful. Why didn't you just send word you were going away?"

"I wanted to see you."

"Well, you've seen me now." She held out her hand. "Good-bye."

He shook his head. "I don't want to part thataway. We're friends."

"Only it's better—for me—that we don't see each

other. Friends at a distance. Shall we exchange Christmas cards?"

Stone reflected, smiling a little at her tart suggestion. Women were not reasonable. She ought to see that it was right for him to go, that he could not stay and let people talk as though there were or had been something between them. If he walked out of her life the gossips would have nothing to whisper about. Yet it was not a matter he could discuss freely with her.

"If I was like Wils McCann, say, an upstanding young fellow with a good reputation, why it wouldn't be important if folks did talk about us. But I'm different. I'm a bad man, as the sayin' is. My friends suffer from knowin' me. I don't want anything but good to come to you. So I'll just pull my freight kinda casual."

"Who says you're a bad man?" she demanded.

"Why, everybody. That's understood."

"Do *you* think you are?"

"I expect that's not a fair question," he answered, and again a smile blotted out the impassive coldness of his poker face. "Probably Carl Gitner justifies himself to himself. But the fact remains that I killed Tom McArdle and have killed others."

"No, I killed him," she said, looking straight at him.

"I'm tellin' the truth, Miss Ann. I shot him."

"Maybe so. I don't know about that. But whether you did or not it was I that killed him. It was my thought, my impulse, and it's my sin." She stopped a moment, shivering at the memory. "I'll have to pay for it all my life."

"If you'd only spoken to me about it," he said.

"Is that very generous of you—to want to be my friend but not to want me to be yours? All the giving is to come from you. I'm just to sit and receive. You haven't a very high opinion of me, have you?" Her little smile was wistful.

"It's because I think so much of you that I don't want you to be tainted in folks' minds by their associatin' me with you."

She rejected that with an impulsive gesture.

"That's ridiculous. Even if it were true I wouldn't let it influence me. But it's not. People think differently of you now. They know you're not like that Gitner or Jasper Stark."

"No, but I'm still Dave Stone."

"And I'm Ann Gifford, an old maid sheep-herder." She looked down with a wry little grimace at her dusty khaki shirt, her coffee-brown hands, and her cactus-torn boots.

"That's not quite how I think of you," he differed.

She looked directly at him, a faint colour beating beneath the deep tan on the thin face. "How do you think of me?"

Stone measured his words in order not to say too much. "I think you're a mighty fine an' handsome young woman, one I'll be grateful to as long as I live."

"But that's all?"

"Why, I don't reckon I know what you mean, Miss Ann."

The girl pushed on breathlessly, afraid her courage might fail. "You kissed me once. Why did you do that? Because you were grateful?"

A muscle twitched in his immobile face. "If I did wrong that time—"

She brushed that aside impatiently. "Who's talking about right or wrong? Do you—care for me, Dave Stone, or don't you?"

"You know I do."

"You're not—just grateful?"

"What's the use of going into that?"

"The use? I'm a grown woman, hard and tough like the desert. I know what I want. Don't treat me like a china doll." There was in the manner with which she faced him something of the lean ferocity of the desert she had mentioned. She had cast aside all feminine coquetry, all the allurement of her sex. For she knew that unless she broke through his reserves now he would go away with the word she hoped for unspoken. The situation was beyond finesse.

"Am I treatin' you like a doll?" he asked. "I certainly don't aim to do that."

"Do you claim that you're frank with me—or fair?"

"Fair? Yes, ma'am."

"Not in the least fair. Haven't I any right to help

decide about my own life? You want to shield me from what people might say, even at the expense of shutting me off from living." She flung toward him a little appealing and rueful smile. "Why are you making it so hard for me, Dave Stone? I don't want to go all the way. . . . Or don't you really care?"

He felt her beating against and wearing away the hard rock of his resolution not to compromise her by involving her fate with his.

"Say I care for you. Would that make it right for me to speak? I'm Dave Stone. We can't get away from that."

"I don't want to get away from it," she answered, her eyes meeting his bravely. "It's Dave Stone I want. I'm tired of fighting. I want to rest. It is only your stiff pride that stands between us— that is, if you do care."

Her work-hardened hands moved ever so slightly toward him. In her look were gifts of more than friendship.

In that long meeting of the eyes the barrier between them was burned away. He knew, by the clairvoyance of love, that nothing else mattered. If he had been a "bad man" he was now one no longer. That belonged to yesterday's seven thousand years. He was at the sunrise of a new day. He had sloughed his past as a forest creature does its horns.

So he took her in his arms and told her, as lovers

have since time began, how wonderful she was and how amazing this experience that had come to him. As she looked at him she wondered how she could ever have thought that face impassive and those eyes hard.

An hour later they remembered that this is a world made up of more than two. Slowly they moved toward the house. A cry startled them. Julia was standing on the porch with Ethel. Her hand pointed up the trail.

A horse and rider were coming down it in a very strange way. The man in the saddle sagged forward in the seat like a drunkard. He lurched unsteadily from side to side.

Julia ran to meet him. She stopped the horse and helped the rider dismount.

"Phil," she cried.

He was pale and haggard and piteously spent. His breath came with difficulty. On his shirt below the shoulder was a wide deep stain of blood.

Ethel looked up white-faced at her sister and murmured, "He's dying."

"No," the boy reassured. He closed his eyes, then with an effort opened them. It was to Stone he spoke. "Wils is up there—in Horse Thief Park. They've got him cornered—Gitner an' his crowd."

Stone carried the boy into the house and looked to his hurt. "Clean wound in the shoulder. Ought to be all right. He's lost a lot of blood of course, but he'll make that up fast."

"Fellow got me—while I was comin' down the cañon," Phil whispered. "We fixed it, Wils an' I did—that I was to come for help if he got caught. He was at the other end of the park lookin' up brands when I heard the shootin'. I lit out. Get help to him quick."

The message given, Phil fainted.

CHAPTER XLII

A Rescue Party

BY THE bedside of the wounded boy they held a hurried council. Doctor Sanders had to be brought and a posse to be raised. But it was essential that help be got to Wilson McCann without delay. Many valuable hours would be lost before Dominick Rafferty could be reached to guide an armed party into the hills.

"If I only knew the way," Stone lamented. "But I'd never find the place."

Instantly Julia caught his meaning. "You'd go alone—if you could?" she cried. "Then I'll take you. I've been there."

She had flashed from despair to sparkling life. Her tortured soul craved the chance to do something for the man she loved beleaguered in the hills.

"Do you reckon you could find it again?" the Texan asked.

"I'm sure I could."

"You wouldn't be afraid to go with me?"

"No."

"Then we'll start right now."

To make sure, Stone questioned Phil as to the exact location of the hidden valley in relation to Guadaloup Cañon. For there was a chance that

Julia's memory might fail at the critical moment.

Ann started for the Circle Cross and Doctor Sanders at the same time Julia and Stone took the trail in the opposite direction. It had been Phil's own request that Ethel stay with him as nurse until the doctor came.

The parting between Ann and her Texan was not dramatic.

"You'll be careful, won't you?" she asked.

His brown hand met hers in a strong grip. "I sure will."

"I'll look after him," Julia promised.

"And we'll take care of Phil," Ann said. "Good luck."

Driven by her fears, Julia would have set too fast a pace if Stone had not moderated it.

"We got a long way to go on these *caballos* over a mighty rough country an' we can't push on the reins too hard," he explained. "I know how you feel. I'd certainly like to hop right along, but we mustn't run the broncs off their feet."

"What do you think? Will we get there in time?" she asked.

"That's a question I can't answer, Miss Julia. I'll say this: Wils McCann is a sure enough fightin' buckaroo. If they didn't get him at the first jump he's liable to stand 'em off quite a while. You never can tell."

"If he only hadn't gone—if he'd waited and taken a posse," she cried.

"I'll say 'Amen!' to that," he agreed. "But don't you worry. We're liable to find him kickin' real lively. Wils is six-foot of wild cat an' he'll take a lot of killing. If he's had half a chance for a getaway I'll put my money on him. He's a better man than Carl Gitner any day of the week."

It was two hours past noon when they reached Guadaloup Cañon.

"Not far now," the Texan told Julia cheerfully, glancing at the sun. "We'd ought to be there before dark."

"What's your plan?" she asked.

"Haven't any. We'll have to go up the gulch. If we get in we'll see what develops."

"Maybe it's guarded. Maybe they won't let us in."

"Tha's how it's liable to be."

"I was thinking that maybe I could ride on and ask to see Mr. Gitner. If he knew a posse was on the way he wouldn't dare to do anything." With a question she voiced another thought in her mind, quaveringly: "Do you think Jas is with him?"

"Now don't you worry about that either. We don't know a thing about it. Like as not he isn't."

"I thought if I could get to talk with Jas—"

"We'll see how that works out. I don't reckon you'll get a chance. This is mighty serious business. It wouldn't surprise me if the rustlers had lit out for Mexico. Now they've been located they won't stick around long, for they know they'd be smoked out soon as a posse can get to 'em."

The directions given by Phil, together with Julia's recollection of the country, guided them straight to the gulch up which the trail to Dunwig's ranch led. They fell into single file. Julia thought she ought to go first because she was a woman and would not be attacked, but the Texan absolutely refused to consider such an arrangement.

"You're goin' up into the park only because I'm scared to leave you alone down here," he told her with a smile. "Do you reckon I can hide behind you an' hold my haid up afterward?"

They travelled the whole length of the gulch unchallenged, passed through the narrow exit, and entered the grassy valley beyond.

"Looks like the birds have flown," Stone suggested after a long look around.

Even as he spoke there came the sound of a shot, and after it a rattling volley of them.

Julia, much excited, pointed to a small puff of smoke in the upper end of the park. "Look! Look!" she cried.

"You wait here," Stone ordered as he gave his horse the spur and galloped forward.

After a moment of indecision the girl followed.

CHAPTER XLIII

Trapped

WILSON MCCANN knew that with the coming of dawn the storm would break upon him. The escape of Phil would drive the rustlers across the border. But there was no immediate haste. They would have thirty-six hours probably before a posse could arrive, and meanwhile they would take pains to destroy the man who had spoiled their plans.

In the darkness he picked his way among the big rocks, selecting a spot from which he could make the best stand. He had to get his back to the cliff; otherwise they would reach him from the rear. Also, he would need protection in front.

It was not possible to find an ideal location for defense, but he chose a sand pit surrounded by boulders. Without a fire the night was chill. There were piñon knots near he could have lit, but he did not intend to start a smoke signal for his enemies.

The hours wore away slowly. He catnapped a little, but he dared not let himself get sound asleep for fear they might creep on him in the darkness.

Gray light sifted into the sky. A meadow lark piped up its gay chirrupy challenge. The jig-saw top of a white range showed above the opposite cliff. An agitated patch of greasewood brought him to a focussed attention until a coyote trotted out from its cover and ambled away on a search for breakfast.

Dawn was at hand. He ate a sandwich and drank from the canteen he had replenished at a spring.

"Soon now," he told himself.

He saw signs of life about the house. Smoke rose from the chimney. A man came out and went to the spring for water. Through his field glasses he presently saw others emerge. All carried rifles. They trooped to the corral, saddled horses, and rode cautiously into the pine grove. Evidently they wanted to make sure he was not hidden there. After a consultation they rode down the hillside and disappeared into a dip of the valley floor. Wilson knew they were coming to get him. Presently he would see their heads rising out of the meadow, almost within range.

They came out of the shadowy dawn like wraiths of evil, not boldly riding grouped together but slinking, coyote fashion, through the mesquite that fringed the park walls. He counted them— one, two, three, four. No doubt they had left the Mexican to prevent him from escaping down the cañon in case he should slip past them.

He watched them dismount and take their horses back of a clump of small pines. One by one they came out and disappeared into the chaparral. They had guessed he was in the boulder field and

345

were creeping forward on a still hunt to find exactly where.

The net was tightening. Wilson knew the enemy was drawing closer. Once or twice he observed a slight rustling of greasewood or manzanita. But those stalking him kept well hidden.

Cool though he was, his pulses pounded. Inured to danger from early youth, he knew he had never been in as tight a place as this. The meadow lark flung out again its gay love song. He wondered if he would be alive tomorrow to hear that rising lilt and cadence.

The ping of a bullet whistled past. He ducked instinctively. From a clump of bushes three hundred yards away a puff of smoke thinned into the clear air. He watched that brush screen, but not steadily, since his glance had to sweep the whole field of vision in front and discover any suspicious object or any slightest unusual motion of vegetation.

Those surrounding him were all oldtimers except Jasper Stark, and he had been brought up on the frontier. Wilson understood what that implied. They would take no unnecessary chances, would make use of their knowledge of the terrain to get him at a disadvantage if possible. The business of exterminating him might take many hours, but they were prepared to attend to it efficiently without undue loss. He held a strong defensive position in the sand pit flanked by boulders. That there would be no attempt to rush him out of it by a frontal attack in the open he was convinced.

The development of the day's campaign proved his conclusion a correct one. After the first shot there was no other for at least an hour. It was quite likely that the man who had located his position was communicating with the rest.

Waiting was a nerve-racking strain. The silence was ominous, yet every little rustling of twigs suggested that a foe might be lurking in the bushes there. His alert gaze continuously swept the landscape. Every bush of greasewood, every clump of mesquite fell under his keen observation.

A spurt of sand flew up beside him. He caught sight for a moment of a face peering over the edge of a rock and flung back instantly a bullet in answer to the one intended for him. The face was withdrawn.

From the right a shot sounded, and another from the left. They were fired from invisible rifles by invisible foes. Wilson shifted his position a few yards to get out of sight behind two flat-faced boulders.

The sun climbed higher. By noon the attackers had worked Wilson out of the sand pit and driven him from rock to rock. He had fired perhaps eight or nine times, usually without actually seeing the persons at whom he shot. So far as he knew none of his bullets had scored a hit. His enemies were not taking chances. Their intention evidently was to force him from the cover of the rocks and pick him off as he dodged for the chaparral. The plan was one very likely to succeed, McCann judged.

By mid-afternoon it came on to rain mistily. He had reached the edge of the boulder field and within a few minutes must have been dislodged from his last stand in it. The rain gave him a respite.

He slipped deeper into the rock field, moving warily so as not to be caught unprepared. What the outlaws would do under the circumstances was uncertain, but he guessed they would follow him to the open expecting him to make a run for his life across the valley.

Not fifty feet from him, on the other side of a ledge of rock, a revolver boomed. He crouched, every sense keyed up, nerves taut.

A moan came to him, followed by a cruel laugh.

"You've got yores, Jas Stark," he heard a remembered voice say. "Thought you'd fix it for yoreself by givin' us away, didn't you? I'll learn you to try to play traitor with Carl Gitner."

Swiftly Wilson clambered up the rock ledge and looked over. The big Texan was standing straddled over the man he had just shot down and was sneering at him.

"You always was a white-livered coyote, Jas, an' you got what was comin' to you. When they find yore body, if they ever do, they'll think Wils

McCann bumped you off. I'm figurin' on gettin' him too *muy pronto*."

From his place on the shelf above Wilson spoke in a low hard voice. "Then get busy, you murderer, an' come a-shootin'."

Gitner looked up, snarling. The eyes of the two met in deadly combat for a fraction of a second before the revolvers began to roar.

Of the number of shots fired Wilson lost count. In the smoke he saw the face of the Texan, distorted with rage and pain, sinking down to the ground. He kept on throwing bullets at the man till his revolver was empty, for the outlaw had not stopped firing.

Wilson reached for the rifle he had laid beside him. But there was no need to use it. Gitner had fallen across the body of the man he had shot. He lay, limp and lax, arms outstretched, no sign of life in him. Cautiously McCann descended, never lifting his eyes from the prone body after one swift glance round to make sure none of the other rustlers were in sight.

Gitner was dead. Not a flicker of life remained in him, not a muscle still twitched. Wilson dragged the body from where it lay on that of Jasper Stark.

The eyes of the wounded man fastened on those of McCann.

"He shot me from behind while I wasn't expectin' it," he explained feebly. "I'm dyin' fast."

Wilson lifted his head and offered him a drink

from the canteen, but Jasper rejected the water with a weak gesture of the hand.

"No use. I'm done for," he said. "Listen. I've been a bad lot. Seems like I never got a square deal. Anyhow, I went bad. But tell Jule I'm no rustler. Gitner brought me here an' I couldn't get away somehow. The cards was stacked so I had to take a hand."

"I'll tell her."

"Tell her . . . Gitner shot Dad an' you that day. . . . Nobody knew it, but the old man fired Carl that mornin' . . . claimed he'd been a bad influence over me. I was with Carl when he shot Dad, but I was scared to tell . . . an' Dad hadn't treated me white."

A shout at the edge of the boulder field brought Wilson to attention. He answered the call, for he recognized the voice of Stone. Presently the Texan stood beside them looking down at the dying man.

"You shoot him?" he asked.

"No. Gitner did it, from behind."

Jasper confirmed this.

The sound of light footsteps brought Wilson round, gun in hand. Cautiously he circled a big boulder, and stood face to face with Julia.

"Thank God," she cried at sight of him, and her voice broke in a wail of gladness. "I was afraid. I thought maybe—"

Her hands went out to him in a little gesture of weak reaction from the strain, and somehow they were in each other's arms.

CHAPTER XLIV

Homeward Bound

FOR a moment Julia rested in his arms, trying to control her sobs. After the long strain she felt a touch of hysteria. She had been afraid, desperately afraid, that she would find him stark and lifeless; and behold! He was warm and strong, ready to love and to be loved.

Her grip tightened round him convulsively. "I saw them, as I came across the valley—three of 'em—riding hard for the cañon. I thought they had—I thought—"

He understood the shudder that went through her slender body. A swift leap of joy throbbed his pulses. This dear girl cared for him. Down through all the ages her sweet brave soul had come to meet and mate with his. That was his first instinctive reaction; the next was that she must be prepared for the tragedy awaiting her.

Gravely he looked into her eyes. "I have bad news. You must have courage."

Her mind flashed to the truth. "Jasper!"

"Yes. He's been badly hurt."

"Not you." It broke from her in a cry of horror.

"Thank God, no. Gitner shot him treacherously."

"Where is he?"

351

"Come," he said, and he led her to the spot where her brother lay.

She went down on her knees, with a wailing sob, beside him. He was sinking fast, but he recognized her.

"Jule," he said faintly. "Gitner . . . got me . . . from behind . . . I . . . had it comin'."

The girl looked up quickly at Stone. "Can't you do anything for him?" she begged.

The Texan shook his head, but it was Jasper who spoke.

"No use . . . I'm goin'—fast. . . . He shot Dad too, Gitner did."

The girl's arm pillowed his head tenderly. She forgot he was a ne'er-do-well and worse, that he had been discredited and disgraced. All she remembered was that he was her brother, the little boy with whom she had played and quarrelled and made up, one around whom a hundred dear memories twined.

"I've been a . . . bad lot," he murmured. "If you'd—pray for me, Sis."

She did, brokenly, with a heart from which welled love and tears.

Within the hour, peacefully, he passed away.

The two men were grateful to him. He had not told the whole truth. If he had been guilty of complicity in his father's death Julia would never know it now. She could not wear her heart out in bitter shame, since both of those who knew the facts were lying here dead. Her grief could be clean sorrow.

They carried the body of Jasper to the cabin and laid it on one of the bunks.

Hours later, in the middle of the night, while Julia lay sound asleep, worn out by her exertions and her sorrow, Dominick Rafferty and his posse reached Horse Thief Park. Not till morning did she know that they had come.

While she was asleep their plans had been made. They would bury Gitner on the edge of the rock field and bring Jasper's body back to the Circle Cross. Meanwhile Stone and McCann would ride with her to the sheep ranch.

To her anxious enquiries Dominick reported Phil doing well.

After breakfast the three started homeward.

In Julia's grief there was an element of relief that at moments distressed her. For months she had been oppressed by fears and doubt and shame. These were gone. The end had come, and it was not so bad as she had dreaded. Wilson McCann had explained to her that her brother was not a rustler but had been brought there by Gitner and killed because he knew too much. She was anxious to believe this, to believe that he had been weak and not wicked. The conviction that he would have gone from bad to worse she pushed from her and refused to consider, but it was this feeling that made the loss of Jasper bearable. In the hour of his death at any rate he had come near to her and clung to the comfort she had to offer.

They rode through the golden dawn, for the most part in silence, below them lilac lakes of light in the shadowy hollows of the hills. Julia, riding knee to knee beside her lover, felt him very close to her. Words were not necessary to tell her with what a tender care his sympathy enfolded her. She knew that the barriers built between them had been swept away as though they had never existed.

Out of the fierce and ruthless desert he had come to her, bringing its strength and endurance, the deep-hidden tenderness and the imagination that transforms it from a devouring and rapacious Sahara to a fairyland of magic light and shadow.

She knew he would not speak to her yet while her grief was green. To-day was to be for her dead brother. All the years to come were to be for him and her. Not even the eyes that met hers would tell the story that filled his heart, not until he felt the time had come.

Julia loved him for it, for the strength that held repressed the emotion of this straight-backed brown-faced rider of the plains.

Once only she yielded to the feeling that surged up in her. It was when they came to an opening in the hills and looked down on the Painted Desert set in its rose and golden envelope of air.

"The morning of the world," she whispered.

He looked at his Eve, for one vivid moment the mask off. Their eyes fastened, plunged to the bottom of each other's heart.

"Of our world," she added, and in her dusky eyes was reflected the glow of the newborn day, warm, vital, sparkling with hope.

Wilson McCann drew a deep breath of joy. Never in all his hard years had he known a soul so radiant, so noble in its generous gift of living, as hers. She was to be his mate. She would bring to him all the warmth and colour of her shining glory. The beauty of life flooded his being to the point of ecstatic pain.

His brown hand went out to hers in a strong grip.

"Yes, of our world," he murmured.

William MacLeod Raine, hailed in his later years by reviewers and contemporaries alike to be the "greatest living practitioner" of the genre and the "dean of Westerns," was born in London, England, in 1871. Upon the death of his mother, Raine emigrated with his father to Arkansas in the United States where he was raised. He attended Sarcey College in Arkansas and received his Bachelor's degree from Oberlin College in 1894. After graduation, Raine traveled throughout the American West, taking odd jobs on ranches. He was troubled in his early years by a lung ailment that was eventually diagnosed as tuberculosis. He moved to Denver, Colorado, in hopes that his health would improve, and worked as a reporter and editorial writer for a number of newspapers. He began writing Western short stories for the magazine market. His first Western novel was *Wyoming* (Dillingham, 1908), that proved so popular with readers that it was serialized in the first issues of *Street & Smith's Western Story Magazine* when that publication was launched in 1919. During World War I, Raine's Western fiction was so popular among British readers that 500,000 copies of his books were distributed among British troops. By his own admission, Raine concentrated on character in his Westerns.

"I'm not very strong on plot. Some of my writing friends say you have to have the plot all laid out before you start. I don't see it that way. If you have it all laid out, your characters can't develop naturally as the story unfolds. Sometimes there's someone you start out as a minor character. By the time you're through, he's the major character of the book. I like to preside over it all, but to let the book do its own growing." It would appear that because of this focus on character Raine's stories have stood the test of time better than those of some of his contemporaries. It was his intimate knowledge of the American West that provides verisimilitude to all of his stories, whether in a large sense such as the booming industries of the West or the cruelties of nature—a flood in *Ironheart* (1923), blizzards in *Ridgway of Montana* (1909) and *The Yukon Trail* (1917), a fire in *Gunsight Pass* (1921). It is perhaps Raine's love of the West of his youth, the place and the people where there existed the "fine free feeling of man as an individual," glimmering in the pages of his books that will warrant the attention of readers always.

Center Point Large Print
600 Brooks Road / PO Box 1
Thorndike ME 04986-0001 USA

(207) 568-3717

US & Canada:
1 800 929-9108
www.centerpointlargeprint.com